THE
MUSIC STOPS
AND THE
WALTZ
CONTINUES

THE
MUSIC STOPS
AND THE
WALTZ
CONTINUES

a novel by

David G. Smith

CHATTO & WINDUS
THE HOGARTH PRESS
LONDON

Published in 1983 by
Chatto & Windus · The Hogarth Press
40 William IV St, London WC2N 4DF

Smith, David G., *1949–*
    The music stops and the waltz continues.
    I. Title
    823'.914 [F]   PR6069.M/

    ISBN 0 7011 2721 X
    ISBN 0-7011-2722-8 Pbk

Lines from 'Bagpipe Music' by Louis MacNeice
from *The Collected Poems of Louis MacNeice*
courtesy of Faber & Faber Ltd.

Printed in Great Britain by
Richard Clay (The Chaucer Press) Ltd,
Bungay, Suffolk

THE
MUSIC STOPS
AND THE
WALTZ
CONTINUES

The Waltz

AT FIRST SIGHT I didn't find her attractive in the least. Ugly would have been nearer the mark, in my opinion.

Then one day I woke up to the beauty of her, and the indifferent man became the unreachable shadow he remains today. Perhaps the metamorphosis that occurred in me through sharing my life with her was so explosive that the half-finished sculpture still puzzles over a previous existence as a heap of clay.

To her I owe, if you want to call it a debt, my knowledge and understanding of such stuff as literature, philosophy, nothingness: for I was a true barbarian whose pleasures and pains were calculated in quarts and gills, punches and stitches, alien bedrooms.

It is written that he who disowns the past has no present to speak of. I was a solitary, living in complete ignorance of real life.

One read books on trains, and I had developed a taste for Dostoevsky's thrillers in preference to the extravaganzas of the more popular Harold Robbins; and like everybody under twenty I reeled off the odd page of doggerel. What's more, I knew exactly who El Greco was. But above all stood my ability to hold forth, timorously it is true, on the works of George Bernard Shaw, to which I had been introduced by a whore called Cindy: Cindy couldn't respect a man who knew nothing of her favourite authors.

These things notwithstanding, the great life of the mind was a notion as alien to my life as Chartreuse jaune. What Jesus did to the calendar was done to me by the heroine of this elegy.

Suzanne Winchester was twenty-six when she met me. She was happily married and had a daughter of eight months. I was nineteen and had nothing worth mentioning.

I shared a large flat with my friend Josh. We sat up every night writing songs, and in the daytime we tried to sell them. Punctually at dusk I would sit down at the piano, Josh on the couch with his notebook, the tape machine whirring, a city scene. Then Josh fell in love with a girl hundreds of miles away and I became a weekend lyricist specialising in haunting laments.

One such weekend there were strange noises in the kitchen. Investigating, I was bushwhacked and quietly mauled by the landlady's twelve-year-old dog, who had long since mastered the mechanics of door handles. Cupboards and refrigerators were his chosen field.

"Canis!" a blues voice, "Canis, where are you?"

I encouraged Canis to follow me back to the room where I'd been playing. He sat down promptly by the fire and I at the piano. Suzanne knocked and the lonely man rearranged his notebooks, ran fingers through hair, willed Canis to sit still, reached for tobacco, responded as though accustomed to visitors:

"Yes?"

"Oh hello. I'm sorry about Canis. He thinks Mummy still has the run of the whole house."

"He's very welcome."

"He's very bad."

"You're welcome too. I was just about to make some coffee."

Smiles and cheerful lies issued forth automatically while our eyes held and I registered a string of impressions, photographic stills: the child in her arms, its sleeping head on her breast (*Women's hips are for resting babies on*), the free hand flicking wanton hair from dark cheek, frisky eyes that narrowed when she talked and widened when she listened (*I speak posh Cockney really*).

I had seen her before, taking tea in the garden when she came visiting her parents, but we had never met; and what did not happen at first sight happened at first word: I was soon out to get her. This in spite of her general appearance, which I found fairly repulsive (*My sluttish ways*), what with her dirty bare feet, dirty nails, stained leotard and arsewarming sailor's jersey. Did she walk out of doors in this apparel? Perhaps she owned a long trench coat or a cloak.

[4]

The baby roused and gurgled.

"This," she said making the child comfortable, "is Laura."

"All eyes and mouth," I said, intending a compliment worthy of a born father. "Is she yours?"

"Yes."

The word was a soft laugh rather than speech. Suzanne looked at the baby, rocked her and she fell asleep again. We both looked at the baby. Preliminary conversation was running thin. Again I brought up the subject of coffee, exhumed it and suggested they sit down on the sofa.

"If you're sure I'm not stopping you from playing the piano."

"Lack of talent is what stops me."

"My mum," she assured me, "is always talking about her musicians."

"An exaggeration."

I saw immediately that my mordant wit was more tolerated than appreciated, and this might have deterred me had I not been raised on the dictum that a woman's mind is to be found nestling between her thighs. I retreated to the kitchen and spied on her through a crack in the architrave.

"Did Mummy tell you your kitchen is haunted?"

"Sorry?"

Her voice, cool but modulating, as if she spoke nothing but the truth, gave such pleasure that I was often to employ this first-night trick of feigning deafness.

". . . kitchen is *haunted*?"

"Yes, after we'd paid a month's rent in advance."

"What?"

"To tell you the truth, Josh and I have heard strange noises."

"I've never seen the ghost myself," she called above the noise I was making; and I grew unusually pensive about the self of Suzanne Winchester.

"The lid," I said, recalling an interesting night, "flew off the dustbin once. But that can be explained scientifically. I mean it's a plastic dustbin . . ."

"That kitchen used to be a bedroom, you know. Before the

[5]

Second World War. Extraordinary things happened to people who slept there. Nothing *ghoulish,* but quite remarkable."

"Your mother told me the ghost used to get into bed with people."

"With men actually. All they feel or see is the indentation in the pillow—I mean *felt* or *saw.* I hope I'm not terrifying you. Anyway she hasn't manifested herself lately unless she's sleeping in your dustbin."

"It's a woman?"

"Yes," she said, as though disbelieving the whole story.

"How could they tell?"

"They just knew. Isn't it *macabre?*"

I brought the coffee in. The baby lay asleep in a corner of the sofa. Suzanne was flapping through the heaps of records, tapes, sheet music.

"Doesn't it frighten you a little? A ghost in your kitchen. No milk," she mouthed, shaking the long hair which seemed to hang in fistfuls.

"No. But sometimes I can't sleep for the noises, and the corridors are a bit creepy. Even in the daytime. But in a house this size there's a lot of timber to expand and contract."

"My brother," she said eagerly, "used to hide in that little black alcove by the bathroom and jump on me when I came out of the loo. Actually I'm still on the lookout for him, or something worse, when I spend the night here."

"My grandfather said you can always get rid of a ghost by asking it to lend you money. He was a sailor," I added proudly in an attempt to rescue the anecdote. She didn't look bored, but certainly I was not taking her by storm.

"How do you get on with my parents?" Her tone acknowledged that they were an unusual brace.

"Quite well. Your dad often asks who I am and what I'm doing in his house, but he's okay once I remind him."

"Daddy's rather odd. He'd like to be a retired colonel."

Her easy conversation, the hint of intelligence lurking, was something new for me. No room for my normal flattery routines and mating habits; and compliments on her dress were out of the question. What should I say?

"Can you tell me why your dad calls your mother *Snuff* ?"

"Yes. It's because she nearly died once, you know, snuffed it. Daddy made a great joke of it. He used to keep bees (he liked to let them crawl up his nose and suchlike) until we found out that Mummy was fatally allergic to their sting. She got so badly stung one day he had to give her a tracheawhatnot, you know, where they cut the windpipe so you can breathe. Her throat swelled up so quickly he had to do it right away. In this house."

Suzanne's eyes glazed over in recollection and she let her head fall back on a cushion.

"*Snuff!*" I said, and she looked up and smiled.

"I suppose it *is* a bizarre nickname," she almost whispered.

"I never knew your father was a doctor."

"Oh, he isn't. But he knows about such things. My husband's a doctor though," she added after a pause. There was another, quite separate pause. I listened to the baby breathing. Suzanne stood up. She must put Laura to bed and then join her parents for dinner.

"Come back later," I suggested. "I enjoy talking to you," this intended to mitigate the shock I felt at my straightforwardness.

"It will be very late by then," she said quietly as she scooped the child into her arms without waking it.

"I never go to bed before three so come if you feel like it. But I won't expect you."

This was already too presumptuous for words.

I walked them to the door and we parted politely, like merchants of old China striving to outdo one another in demonstrations of goodwill.

And I was abroad till four thirty, strumming the guitar and occasionally dropping hard objects on bare floorboards, opening and closing doors, just in case anyone was listening to find me awake.

I had never known any serious women. Alone in the aftermath I marvelled at her existence, her flesh and blood and voice, the raw inspiration for countless well-trained, handsomely decorated impostors. Intermittently I conjured up her face in its former ugliness. Was it good or bad for me, this sudden interest in a woman whose looks went beyond the jurisdiction of personal aesthetics? Slowly a new life began to dawn.

It was not what I might have expected, this new life, involving as it did the instant repudiation of half my repertoire of beliefs and utterances and both halves of what I called my wit. For how could I continue to embarrass Suzanne Winchester with stupid remarks like that one about the ghost and the advance rent? She was tolerant because she saw the good in me, bless her sharp black eyes. Women had been irreparably demystified to me; in the resultant disorientation I waited up for Suzanne, wanting less to kiss her than to shake her by the hand.

Still, she stayed away that night.

Josh and I were running a night club in those days. The plan had been to use it as a vehicle of publicity for our songs. Open only two nights a week, it was a slow starter, so to swell the attendance we offered free admission to those willing to perform a few numbers, with the fascinating but unprofitable result that nine tenths of the audience arrived equipped with guitars, mandolins, clarinets, tambourines, poetry in dirty typescripts (to be recited deadpan in front of a recondite assortment of occult instruments), gimbris, nose flutes, gongs, wreathèd horns, Jew's harps, tortelleli, ocarinas, and one night a complete set of timpani which were to be played as back-up to improvisations on the harmonica.

So it was not much of a cash in hand enterprise. On the contrary, we had to fork out extra from our own pockets to pay the rent on the premises. And brawling was a regular feature against which we, as management, were expected to take preventive measures. The fighting usually broke out between rival groups of musicians, the traditional versus the contemporary, trained versus untrained, loud versus inaudible. At the end of a night we were invariably short of cash and rather badly shaken.

Coming home from the club on the second day of Suzanne Winchester I met her on the stairs and offered her, of all things to all people, a cup of tea. Nothing was mentioned of the previous evening. I didn't let a thing slip about prowling the corridors, she in no way suggested that she'd been lying awake wondering. Our talk concerned subjects of greater import, more burning pertinence than the involuntary palpitations of strong hearts.

She began at once about a book she was reading, had I by any chance read it myself? It was called *Sculpted Being,* she would lend it to me, it was such an important work. And the author— she'd been lucky enough to meet him last week at a seminar— was a terribly intense person, very vibrant.

I tried to think of anyone I knew who was vibrant. Then I struck farther out of my depth by asking what the book was about.

Names I vaguely recognised but had never heard spoken before fell on my ears like so much mumbo jumbo, coloured hail. Now and again I stuck my neck out to taste one while Suzanne, cross-legged on the sofa, moved her hands through the stations of the cross in explication. To me these names, evidently household words to the intelligentsia, were fairytale characters come to take their places in real life, as if Tom Thumb or Tinker Bell were to turn up on your pillow in the morning. My receptive blankness was jolted by the mention, in an unusual pronunciation, of Dostoevsky, but all I contributed was a delighted cry of recognition—*The Possessed!*—before drying up in shame.

"What do you do for a living?" she asked me after a quiet spell. "Do you work?"

"No. Well, Josh and I write songs and we've got this club . . . I sometimes get engagements in pubs and folksy places. But it's not really work. Or wages."

"Will you sing me a song?" I had only to lean over and take the guitar from its open case. This was a fine opportunity for me to prove my worth.

But I made a complete mess of an unusual song Josh had written about two parents who run away from home because their son is a tyrant. Suzanne, however, appeared not to notice the mistakes.

"Did you write that?" she asked, breaking a longish silence which I failed for once to punctuate with coughs and devastating epigrams.

"No, Josh wrote it. I think maybe I wrote one of the verses. We often forget who wrote what."

"It's a very sad poem."

"I think Josh meant it to be funny."

She smiled and shook her head. Poem . . . I wondered what Josh would do to someone who called him a poet—the word still reeked of teachers' pets and schoolboys who never wore jeans. "The world," she said, apparently to herself, "is a ghastly place to have to live."

"What!" I said, astounded to hear such a thing at a time when my vision of the world had never been better. "No it isn't," I added gently to soften my vulgar outburst, "Suzanne." It was the first time I'd called her by name to her face.

"Do you know *The Bell Jar*?"

"Is it a pub? Oh no—it's something you use in science isn't it?"

"No, it's a book. But it doesn't matter."

This time I didn't make the mistake of asking to be enlightened, but that didn't prevent my uncomfortableness growing with each new topic of discussion, each fresh insight into the blind ignorance in which I had been living for so many years. That Suzanne Winchester would soon lose interest in an oaf had already become my deepest conviction, my first principle. Had I perhaps read all those Dostoevsky books without understanding them properly? It was true that I thought nothing of skipping a chapter or inventing meanings for the long words. What had I to say about a book? I like it, I don't like it, I can't remember the story.

During times of poverty or inactivity I had tried miserably to better myself in some nebulous way through the study of acknowledged masterpieces, most of which had failed to induce me to read farther than the translator's introduction; but I had thus gained a working knowledge of the names of several great authors and in my usual social milieu I was considered fairly learned. In spite of this Suzanne confounded me effortlessly and unintentionally, almost every time she opened her mouth, by alluding to notable people in various fields of knowledge—whose unpronounceable names I later jotted down phonetically—as if they were as well known to the English-speaking world as Sinbad the Sailor.

I was wholly impressed, utterly inferior. Unable to articulate beyond the occasional monosyllable, I lay back and tried to understand, feeling honoured at being spoken to in this way. Clearly she had confidence in my ability to follow her lines of thought. Here and there, hypnotised as I was, I grunted, nodded vigorously, laughed and kept quiet. For me it was the rarest of conversations, but its effect rather than content remains.

I remember the names, each one of which has a life of its own in my past: Georg Andrzeyevski, Egon Schiele, Krishnamurti, Ronald Laing, Eugene Ionesco, Arthur Koestler, Günter Grass, Gustav Klimt. . . . That I came one day to lose interest, not to say faith in most of them, matters not a damn: their names still form what I must call the cultural background to the meeting that made an unusual character of me.

I began to regard myself with a strange respect.

"Do you know the feeling of nothing being real?" she said, holding me with her eyes as she always did after a question: "When everything seems to be shapeless and pointless."

"I don't know. I think so. Maybe not . . ."

"It's how I've been feeling quite a lot. Recently. I don't know why really because Laura and I have been having such lovely times. If it weren't for Laura," she paused and smiled at the thought of Laura, "I suppose I'd just let myself go under. I mean just get sucked into the unreality and become blank and catatonic."

"Is Laura sleeping now?"

I wanted to ask her straight out what catatonic was but doubted my ability to repeat the word accurately.

"Yes. Mummy's looking after her. *Am I boring you?* You must tell me."

"No. I'm not bored."

"I don't think I'll ever become catatonic," she laughed.

I laughed.

She was wearing a dress that night. Really it was a man's shirt, an old one at that, but it still looked grand. She had dyed it using the batik method and with it she wore a black scarf as a belt, and black panties, and that was it. When she sat down the slits in the sides of the shirt opened up and showed off her thighs, which were slim and brown; and when she crossed or uncrossed her legs her panties were clearly visible to me. When we laughed with faces close as we sat together pouring out cups of tea she smelled strongly of garlic. Her bare feet were as dirty as before.

She expounded so much pretentious nonsense at such great length it is a miracle that even a man of my disadvantages was impressed by it; but the greater miracle is that every earnest word she spoke, every baffling cross-reference she pulled out of the hat, transported me to fresh bright horizons far in advance of my experience. In introducing me to such elevated topics Suzanne was encouraging a man of hod-carrier mentality to view himself as no ordinary individual but as one within whose hands lay limitless powers, the ability to understand everything, resolve contradictions, exorcise the ghosts of misconception. *Amor Vincit Omnia* was shown to be a classic example of Roman understatement.

"I like it here," she said, rolling a cigarette from my tobacco.

"It's the best room in the flat."

The gas fire hissed, the night was cooling. Reflected in the slate-blue of the window the fire's glow suggested a tree-lantern hanging in the dark outside.

"I wasn't talking about the room."

Ineluctably my eyes tracked her as she rose from the sofa— flash of black—dropped her cigarette in an ashtray and sat down on the arm of my chair. Then from the chair to the floor, an accidental touch of hand on arm became a breathless embrace, plunge of mouth savage on mouth, shivering between astonishment and lust, half-discovering that the first kiss of love subdues the embers, does not inflame.

It took no longer than a minute to envisage the trouble I might end up in.

"Do you . . . love your husband?"

"Very much."

"Ah." It wasn't a question, but she explained:

"He and I are both free to do as we like."

I had read of such things in magazines.

"Do you mean that you'll tell him about me?"

"Of course!"

She was smiling as at a fool.

"Why of course?"

"Because I love you." I looked away.

"But you love *him* . . ." I looked again and she smiled.

"And I love you."

It was five in the morning when I told her I had to leave. I was expected in the afternoon at a city some four hundred miles away where my blood brother Marcel MacMarshall planned to get wed. I was to officiate as best man.

One hitchhiked everywhere then, except to funerals. In my bag I carried a borrowed suit and tie, a clean shirt which my mother would iron, tobacco and wine for the road, and in my breast pocket a note from Suzanne with her telephone number and a secret message.

On the road I made plethoric conversational reference to my woman in London—the drivers were uniformly sympathetic—and I crossed the Scottish border for the many hundredth time but for the first time with the love of an Englishwoman.

And the wedding was an unqualified success handled competently by the charming best man who singlehandedly outwitted four attempts by the bride's mother to sabotage the ceremony and prevent the marriage of her youngest daughter to the reprehensible MacMarshall on the questionable grounds that he was making a hobo's wife out of a state registered nurse.

In my speech I celebrated their love in a nuptial limerick, I danced with assorted old aunts, persuaded the reluctant mother-in-law to bury the hatchet and come and take a glass of something (*Poison,* MacMarshall had yelled in his elation). I even came near to seducing the fiancée of an up-and-coming television personality, but I let slip the name of Suzanne Winchester. That the whole marriage, mortgage and all, culminated two years later in vengeful divorce does not detract a crumb from the capital picture I retain of MacMarshall's wedding.

Immediately upon my return to London town—that's what she called it—I learned that Josh had been forced to leave the country for a short while, bad circumstances, so I had to find a smaller place I could afford by myself. I took up residence near the school at Harrow sharing a house with some jazz musicians and a heroin addict who had a small son. There were parties most nights and an extended one at weekends.

I joined the public library and disciplined myself to read a whole book every day. Whenever I remembered the name of an author mentioned by Suzanne I noted it down and borrowed, sometimes bought, his books. A dictionary was essential. Often by accident I came across words she had used—*semiotics, ambivalent, ontological*—and it was a genuine education to discover that complex notions could be expressed so briefly.

Suzanne, to whom I had failed to post countless letters, had become the meaning of my life. Three weeks had passed since our meeting. In my uncultured state I was ashamed to contact her lest she should see me for what I was and lose faith in me, cease to love me, if she did love me.

The discovery that there existed such things as anthologies, encyclopaediae, compact histories of philosophy and literature, made me jump up and down in enthusiasm: enlightenment progressed at speed. The recurrence in my reading of phrases in Latin, French, German, impelled me to disinter what I had been taught at school and get down to achieving fluency. The demand for books escalated until it became necessary to persuade the other members of the household to apply for library cards and hand them over. The librarian was adamant that I borrow no more than six volumes at one time so I was forced to steal from his stock indispensable items like bilingual dictionaries and grammars.

What I did to earn money was to set aside one day a week for street singing. In the underground station at Leicester Square or the subway complex at Marble Arch I would strike a pitch in the morning, say nine o'clock, to catch the early rush hour, then continue throughout the day moving from station to station with guitar and sagging pocketsful of loose change.

It was an excellent way of making acquaintances: by lunchtime I would usually be in a pub with some out of the ordinary person, often a girl at the outset of her musical career. After lunch I returned to work drunk enough to see me through till six or seven; then, having earned enough for a week's board and lodging, I allowed myself an evening free of studies.

I studied to a strict schedule, setting the alarm for six thirty and forcing myself to learn something new before breakfast. I observed that knowledge, like fucking, was something that gave only ephemeral satisfaction, that grew increasingly unaccountable and had a way of continually stepping up your desire for more of the same. Every sine qua non led to another and my wall-chart filled out into a dangerous-looking incantation: Greek, Mineralogy, Relativity, The Third World, The Dalai Lama, The Absurd, Hermes Trismegistus—they all stood there shoulder to shoulder, terrifying me every morning.

Of course I made mistakes. I cheerfully read the complete works of Belloc and didn't find out for a long time t'.at she'd said Bellow, but it was all useful knowledge to have, and as long as I was leading the life of the mind my greater purpose was being fulfilled.

The time came when I felt that I was ready to telephone Suzanne and casually arrange a meeting, but on each of several occasions I pretended to have been connected to a wrong number. None of the voices was hers. Finally, three months after our first meeting, I spoke to her. On the line (said the wall-chart poem) her voice voluptuous.

A row of derelict terraced houses all the same colours with peeling window sashes and unmatching curtains. I thought it peculiar that a doctor and his family should want to live here, sharing their house with the odd artist and Zen layabout. Suzanne's husband was always being pestered by his fellow communards on the subject of drugs and they used to phone him at work for advice on dealing with overdoses.

Conrad Winchester, his existence everywhere in evidence around the house, remained a name and a notion for a long time, partly, maybe wholly, because I was afraid of meeting him and partly because his medical training, now coming to a close, obliged him to live in at one of the big London hospitals where by all reports he cut a memorable figure in his jumble-sale suits, batik shirts, size twelve workman's boots with string or rope laces, his oddly matched socks (*I've an identical pair at home*) and his secondhand ties that identified him as a member of a Masonic order or a former Polish wartime pilot; and his doctor's quarters were a Hippocratic outrage, the walls spray-painted in fluorescent colours and hung with the artistic efforts of his wife and friends—and vibrating more often than not to the sounds of Conrad's outlandish tastes in loudly played music (this *is* Cecil Taylor, that *was* Albert Ayler) from his staggering collection of tape recordings or from the tarnished saxophone that he kept under the bed . . . and all the while he kept his doctor's bleeper hooked onto the collar of his shirt so that he'd be sure to hear it if he were called to deal with an emergency; and when they bleeped him he'd stroll over to the phone, looking puzzled (he was notoriously contemptuous of his reputation as a brilliant young doctor) and he would say, after a good pause, *er . . . yeah?* . . . and if the tape recorder was playing he'd turn the volume down: perhaps these idiosyncracies were not altogether uncultivated, but Conrad's truly personal effects, those that were visceral expressions of his inner life, were of a far higher order of the remarkable, for Conrad, so far as I could see, appeared to have no jealous heart beating in his ribs: maybe, I cursed on occasion, he had a doctor's bleeper or a saxophone, or maybe he was one of those rare Minds I had come across in the books—which had nothing to do with his wife falling for a beast of burden like myself, but it's always wise to keep these things in mind in case they should later prove to bear on facts—anyway, Conrad struck me right away as being Great Mind incarnate, though it goes without saying that there is more to Conrad than that—and how!—but the main thing to note is that from the start I viewed us as diametric opposites back to back, two-faced Janus, always looking away so that when our eyes met the inner eye ranged elsewhere—yet well I know that Conrad, whose refuge was the pursuit of the truth, could no more than I stomach the horrors we shared and perpetrated, I whose refuge was pained laughter. Ach, Conrad, appear before me now and supply mnemonics: what were we doing in those days? You were trying to wake us all up. It began with that Gestalt stuff in which we tried to assume the identities of inanimate objects; then came the violence therapy—punching our blues away, pulverising cushions and shredding telephone directories. And then you discovered the marvellous book—what was it called?—that fired you with that brilliant enthusiasm which in itself was enough to ensure you a place in my heart for ever. Does it matter that the book meant nothing to me, that I pretended in order to save face? Would you understand how little my lies mattered to me then? Conrad . . . tramping down the High Street on your way home from the supermarket, knapsack of provisions on your back, wearing those tubular jeans that you refused to discard—inches too short as though by express design, patched and repatched with old curtain material—and reading as you walked, unable to stop reading the great fat book that had changed your life and the lives of those who knew you, that had *tied in* with everything you considered worthy of thought or action and had superseded what you called your many previous convictions. But within the year a certain obscure linguistic theory (followed surprisingly by your discovery of Yaqui knowledge) tied in with your existentialist and Zen Buddhist adolescence to form the springboard for your next move: the journey through madness had long been in the cards, as you said yourself, and maybe you dealt the cards too, believing them to be unbeatable, for you spoke afterwards as one who had finally, gratefully, touched zero and was now preparing for the climb of a lifetime. And that was the moment I began wholeheartedly to believe in you. . . .

But I am speaking of a time when Conrad, the husband and lover of my lover, could be an enigmatic threat to every corner of my life without having seen as much as a photograph of me. A photograph of him lay on Suzanne's bedside table. He was tall, good looking, with broad shoulders.

She opened the door of their house and stood for an instant, legs and lips slightly parted, before stretching out an arm to welcome me, no words. It was hot summer and her teeth were like white shells, her face tanned, small teeth and small lark's tongue in her wide mouth. We walked into the room she shared with Conrad, their only room, and I noticed that they had black silk sheets on the bed. A wedding present, I learnt later.

There were no chairs, only the bed, so we lay down and I told a rehearsed string of lies concerning my silence during the three months since we'd last seen each other. For all the disarming honesty we were to maintain in love she never found me out about that, my weeks as an autodidact. Perhaps I had to retain a slice of deception just to keep my head above water.

She's a phony, a put-on. It was Josh who said that, not me: he had strong objections to her accent for one thing. But I took the trouble to put Josh right on these points—she was merely different, not what we were accustomed to. Josh had also insinuated that in view of her affluent parents she could in no sense be regarded as a person stuck for drinking money; he hoped that this consideration was far from my thoughts.

And it certainly was, particularly here in their austere room. It even crossed my mind whether the baby was getting enough to eat, until I saw that breastfeeding had come back into fashion: Suzanne in midconversation undid her blouse and guided the sleepy mouth towards its food. I was surprised later to realise that I'd been staring not at her fresh white breasts but at the baby's eyes and its cheeks moving like a bellows. This and other alterations in my behaviour were to preoccupy me in the early days of knowing Suzanne.

Laura had been asleep in her Moses basket only minutes when her mother and I, naked amidst strewn clothes, came together in love for the second time. She'd not had time to button her blouse. For me the great revolution was that she kept looking at me and said such things as I'd never heard before. Evidently a novice, I was accordingly taciturn.

"You do love me," she said in the quiet.

"Is that a question?"

"No."

"Yes."

"I can tell," she said.

Summer, in London town as elsewhere, and it was a bright afternoon with hours of daylight ahead, all the night to sleep through. We made love again, talked a little and made love again. Outside, the sounds of a derelict neighbourhood, the screaming children laughing, whooping, the old and young wives, the many voices of English, Indian, African accents. Suzanne was a great favourite in the street even with the old ladies who ruled it; children gathered around her street-level bedroom window to chatter at her or borrow dressing-up clothes and rudimentary musical instruments with which to make an excellent nuisance of themselves. She'd been a schoolteacher before she had Laura, carried it on right up to the eighth month.

I woke up feeling the sheet slipping from my shoulders, down over my body. She laid her head on my thigh and kissed.

"I love you."

"I love you."

"What are we going to do?"

The question, in common with all fatuous remarks in this old sonata, was voiced by no other than myself. Suzanne, lithe, slinky, a giant pet weasel I thought, straddled me and smiled in my face.

The afternoon was moving on.

"Shall we take my little daughter to the park? Your boots," she laughed naked, "are under the table."

"Battersea Park?"

"Yes! Battersea Park!"

She made it sound like the Cannibal Isles.

"Oh well . . . here I come. Have you seen my panties anywhere? Never mind. Shall I tart myself up?"

"Of course."

Tarted up she undulated back and forth through the cathedral of a prehistoric velvet dress, grey, a type of dress which later became fashionable, perhaps as a direct result of her influence. I watched her: miniature white knickers, brown skin, brown hair then the dress. And like many a struggling man of letters I watched pen in hand

> (*never stop remembering*
> *hair trickling over*
> *her spine*
> *sheathing shoulder*
> *on and off breasts*
> *and grazing their mouths*)

letting the last erotoleptic tremor take the form of handwriting. A few days later of course, after a conversation in which Suzanne told me of a man she knew who could write up to half a dozen poems a day, I was determined to have everything.

I pushed the little pram as we made the transition from the back streets to the park where Laura was set free to investigate daisies while Suzanne told me about people who were transformed by love. Her favourite piece of music told the story of a girl who became pregnant by a man other than her true love. All seemed lost, but when she told her lover what had happened their love transfigured the night and they were able to go on together to even greater heights and depths. Was Suzanne telling this story to draw my attention to something? I tried not to worry.

Already we had reached that point of raptness in our own world at which we couldn't keep our hands off each other for very long. Laura, who could crawl, snuggled up between us on the grass and all three of us smiled, perhaps not for different reasons. I suffered fears about the effects on Laura of my involvement with her mother, but Suzanne was confident in her belief that babies don't really mind one way or the other so long as they don't get left out of anything. She had a wonderful talent for setting my mind at rest.

An old lady passed by, stopped and turned round slowly, smiled at us for a while before making her approach. Respectfully we disentangled ourselves. She spoke first to Laura then to Suzanne, and she swore, as many old ladies were later to do, that Laura, bless her, was the spit and image of her dad: which provoked precisely those embarrassed nods and smiles that would have come from a real dad.

The summer weeks passed swiftly. We were together every night except when Conrad came home for the weekend. I continued to educate myself while working as a street singer, reading everything that sounded abstruse and modern, writing poetry and blatantly learned critiques. Pathetically I kept it all secret. If I put forward a borrowed opinion I made sure to translate it into gutter language so that I would appear to be what the books called an untutored genius. Suzanne lent me books by the bagful and I devoured them gratefully, knowing that I was coming that much closer to being her equal, for there was nothing in which she was not my superior. Except music: Suzanne played no instrument; she liked Schoenberg, Snooks Eaglin and mariachi bands, and after those the world of music blended, in her ears, into a not unpleasant unknown. I talked constantly about music.

One morning when I had spent the weekend away from her a sudden guilt caught me from behind. I was accustomed to the guilt and to my impotent attempts to dispel it, but this partic-ular morning brought such a heavy dose that I felt compelled to act, to do what was right and have done with it. I had involved myself in a fateful relationship—novels abounded with such relationships—that was doomed to calamity, suicide; unbearable pain and torment at the very least. And now Conrad Winchester wanted to meet me. It seemed a reasonable idea but I knew it would mark the beginning of troubles. I must call an immedi-ate halt.

About my own life I couldn't have cared less, or more, in my normal state which was one of physical intoxication, spiritual delight. But this state of grace rested entirely upon the woman I loved loving me in return. And she, understand, loved and was loved by Conrad, and they loved their baby, Laura, first child to become my friend, who trusted me implicitly and would, in the absence of her mother, crawl instinctively towards the man she saw oftener than she saw her own father. The incipient catastro-phe centred on me. I had to get out, there was simply no argument. I must never see Suzanne again, not to say goodbye, fatal, not even to remain acquainted. I would let her know at once.

Her phone was engaged.

I sat down to a letter but my pen ran out.

Clearly the best, noblest way was to tell her face to face. I would do that, I would, although the thought of it was petrifying.

Then, on that same perplexing day of coincidences, a rap on my basement window told me Suzanne had come to visit. She liked to climb the garden wall and sneak up on me.

"I'm sorry," she said, dumping her shoulder bag, "but I had to come and talk to you."

"What is it? Has something happened?" (Had Conrad died?) "Where's Laura?"

"Laura's with Conrad. It's nothing terrible," she smiled at me who knew it was, "there's just something . . . but let me kiss you first."

One or two hours later I woke up with Suzanne making love to me again. Her face at such moments lost all of its intellectual compactness and grew loose, as if to accommodate a different gamut of expressions or set of features. She would curse lovingly and mouth gibberish up against my ear. I wanted to be able to do the same.

The something she had come to tell me was that I'd have to forgo spending the coming weekend with her.

"I'm seeing Conrad. He complained, quite rightly I think, about not seeing much of me and Laura since I've been seeing you."

"That seems fair enough to me," I said, proud of myself.

"Well, I suppose I *have* spent nearly every day with you. And he's incarcerated in that *abysmal* hospital."

"Not every day, we haven't been together every day," I defended, forgetting she'd said *nearly*.

"Conrad's quite justified I think. Do you feel all right about that, lover?"

"Of course, Suze."

"It's so bloody difficult. Every *day* I have to decide . . ."

"There's no deciding to be done," I said enigmatically.

We stood up, naked, and kissed warmly.

"I was looking forward to you this weekend you know. Conrad was supposed to be seeing Sylvia . . ."

"Who is Sylvia?" I asked thickly, and she laughed at me.

"Conrad's girlfriend. Well, she's Sam's wife as well, as well as being Sylvia. You remember Sam? You met him at my house."

"Not bad," I said, outraged that Conrad should have a girlfriend: did that explain why . . .

"Sam was going away this weekend, so Sylvia and Conrad . . ."

"Doesn't anybody object?"

What had I been drawn into? A clandestine network of ritual prurience and libertinage?

"I suppose Curly objects."

"*Curly?* Where does he fit in?"

"She. Sam's girlfriend in Oxford. But Sam has to stay in London because his mother's arriving from Tennessee. He got the letter today . . ."

"So Sylvia can't see Conrad and you can't see me."

"Oh come on! It's not as bad as that."

"Did I say bad?"

A phrase from a book ran through my head: *he evinced a thorough lack of grounding in psychology and rhetoric.* I'd had to look up two words to understand the whole sentence but it had been worth it now.

"Listen lover," she said, running her foot over mine. "It isn't just a quick change routine. And it *is* true that I haven't spent two consecutive days with Conrad for ages. I want to see him. And it isn't fair on Laura. I'm sorry."

"No, you're right, I agree. Don't be sorry. In actual fact I agree completely with everything you're saying. I'm totally in the wrong. *I'm* sorry. It's ridiculous me being angry. In actual fact I'm not angry, I'm pretty happy. Let's get dressed. I'll buy you a whisky and walk you to the station."

"I do love you," she said happily. "Very very much."

We kissed at the station as the automatic doors closed between us. I went home to write a letter. She may be, I said aloud to the night on Harrow Hill, the only woman for me. What then? Share half a life with her and spend the rest in constant sorrow, or give her up altogether and prepare myself to regret it? How to move, how to stand still.

If I were to give her up I'd be certain of support from my friends, many of whom were emphatically against Suzanne. They believed she was using me to rekindle a marriage which had cooled off as a result of too much freedom nonsense. This was a shallow-minded inference which illustrated how little my friends knew of the true nature of love, a failing I understood perfectly since it was only through knowing Suzanne that I had overcome it in myself: love was amoral, merciless, and didn't think twice about passing by the ones most in need of it.

Reluctant to go home, afraid of my room and the cowardly letter I expected to write, I lay down on a lonely bench. From certain angles the light atop the church spire was a star in the sky. Suzanne would be nearing home by now, Conrad would be there with Laura. Would Suzanne have a bath before going to bed or would Conrad and I conjoin within her? And what if she were to conceive? I'd asked and she'd replied that both she and Conrad felt all right about it. I'd said hastily that I felt all right too.

I wondered if Conrad loved the same Suzanne that I loved, who brought such intensity of meaning to everything we did together. I, born in the country and raised a bumpkin, knew nothing about trees, flowers, the beauty of objects as insignificant as a wet leaf, a dirty pebble, a broken twig, until I walked through a London park with Suzanne. Literature, plays, films were real things in her life, they were alive and they spoke to her, and through her they began to speak to me. A brilliant idea might make her sit up all night, a tragic play make her cry. Really cry too, no maudlin sobbing, as we walked, my raincoat over our shoulders, around Soho or Mayfair after seeing some foreign film, black and white with subtitles, of which I had understood not a frame. I often wondered whether Suzanne

[25]

read more into these films than the director had intended, if indeed he had intended anything at all. But she was always able to explain them to me if I asked.

Her most acclaimed characteristic was an ability to converse, uncompromisingly at her own level, with all manner of individuals. She'd talk with Charlotte, the heroin addict who lived in my house, about children and the best ways of looking after them. Charlotte's son was four, a frightened child who never spoke more than a dozen words a day—except when Suzanne came to visit: then he would become almost playful. Charlotte gradually stopped referring to Suzanne as "your bourgeois bitch" and took up reading the works of A.S. Neill.

Suzanne was out walking one day, Laura asleep in the push-chair, when a man came up behind and tapped her on the shoulder. Hello, she said, doubtless in her ingenuous way: *Who are you?* Suzanne was forever being outrageously propositioned by men and boys: they seemed to sense that they could get away with it. The man asked her at once to come home with him. She told him not to be silly. He said that the baby was no problem, he liked children, she could sleep in his spare room while they "talked." The man put an arm round her and she told him to fuck off, which he did.

Turning a corner five minutes later she saw him again, in a doorway, staring, beckoning frantically with one hand while masturbating his exposed prick in the other. Laura was waking up. Suzanne crossed the street to the safety of a department store.

She had just paid for some small purchase when the man tapped her shoulder. He said he was sorry, he hoped he hadn't offended her. She said angrily that he might have frightened her daughter. The man glanced at Laura, suddenly squeezed Suzanne's breasts and dashed into the street. She telephoned me to come and meet her.

Why had that episode, which Conrad appeared to find amusing, impressed itself upon me? It seemed to tell me something about Suzanne, about why I loved her. Or was it that I identified myself with the man who followed her?

In her final weeks as a schoolteacher the children used to line up every day to touch her stomach and feel the baby kicking. She'd used her pregnancy to teach them where babies come from and the response had been enthusiastic. The exception was little Arthur who said he wanted to punch the baby. Arthur had a reputation for assaulting the other children, smashing up their clay models, destroying their fingerpaintings.

Suzanne had a dream about him in which he threw a clock at her face. She woke up mysteriously inspired to make a present of a clock to Arthur. Arthur spent a day in silence dismantling his clock, arranging the pieces on a table, and the rest of the term trying to reassemble it. In the mornings he gathered with the other children to feel the baby kicking.

I rose from the bench and walked down the hill, trying to summon my former but evanescent nobility of sentiment. I must write that letter, against the grain if necessary. After all, if she really loved me would she want to see Conrad *at all*?

Suzanne,

I think you have the mind of a scientist and the instincts of a whore. How else could you live the way you do? I mean me and Conrad. There's no sense in seeing each other again and I advise you not to be involved with two men because it's no good for anybody. I still love you but it doesn't make a difference anymore. Good luck.

I stole the first sentence from a novel and I left a blank space where my signature should have been, but I did complete my letter. Failure to post it seemed of secondary importance. I slept that night like a martyr.

But on the Sunday of the weekend that we were to have spent together I got a phone call from Suzanne inviting me to visit her at Guy's Hospital. *Conrad* wanted to meet me. I agreed, why not, it would be easy to meet him now that I had decided to extricate myself.

At the hospital reception desk a deaf pensioner instructed me peremptorily to wait while he consulted a file. Directions to Conrad's quarters were supplied with solemnity, apparently in strictest confidence. Before I could hesitate prior to knocking, the door was opened by Suzanne, my Suzanne, who had once been compared to a whore and a scientist by a plagiarising young autodidact. An embarrassing kiss from her to me, then Conrad and I met.

"Hello," I managed.

"Well . . . er . . . *yeah*! Hello . . ."

Not for anything was I going to admit that I'd heard so much about him. I pretended to survey the premises.

"Suzy," he said and I winced at the familiarity, "has just been talking about you. I was beginning to think that her Young Man didn't exist."

How far would I get if I simply ran out of the hospital? I felt like a criminal guilty of heinous offences against nature. Conrad was on top, a better man than I by such a long and brightly coloured chalk.

"Well . . . er . . . I don't know," Conrad began smiling, "but I feel we've been avoiding one another."

"Oh I don't think that," I lied, piling crime upon crime, ashamed to see him smiling affably at me.

I asked if it was difficult having to live in the hospital. Laura lay asleep in Conrad's minuscule bed. I knew that he and Suzanne had made love, you could taste it in the air. Minuscule was a word I'd picked up from Suzanne. Conrad used the word twice in our conversation, intoning it just like Suzanne. Had they made love on that rug? I stopped scrutinising when I realised Suzanne was responding to the question I'd asked Conrad.

"Well this final year was something we knew was coming, and I suppose *knowing* was tantamount to experiencing."

"Hmm."

"Hey listen," Conrad said, perhaps to change the subject out of embarrassment about Suzanne's halfbaked epistemology. "Listen, Suzy said you like Robert Johnson—do you want to listen to something? I've got this extraordinary tape."

"Yes, yes," I nodded appreciatively, glad to avoid further conversation.

While Conrad fiddled with the tape machine I told spurious anecdotes about Robert Johnson. Did you know he was first attracted to the guitar because the six strings recalled the cell bars in the penitentiary? He used to say the first guitar was designed by a lonely man who carved the shape of his woman's body in wood. I realised at once that I was talking too much. Conrad wondered who first decided to put a hole in it; then he sang along with the peculiar

You can squeeze my lemons
Till the juice runs down my leg (2X)

and I looked away towards the crazy designs on the walls, the photographs of Suzanne and Laura naked together, of Laura feeding at the breast. There was no easy escape.

"How long have you two known each other?" I asked between the tracks.

"What? Oh it must be about fifteen years. Suzy?"

"Yes. We were at school together."

"When did you get married?"

"Seven years last October," Suzanne said.

It was hard at that moment, as it always is with theories of the Old Wive's Tale school, not to consider the veracity of the Itch hypothesis. Maybe that's all there was to it for Suzanne, the simple itch for a new body to hold, a fresh accent of speech at night. Meanwhile there was I, feeling easier with Conrad and already burying the problems of the immediate past, concocting plans for a future where Suzanne and I would wake up like the song Josh had written in his sleep one night:

That evening, to my immense joy, she and I left the hospital together. Conrad, enigmatic as ever but through no fault of his own, went on duty at eight saying how good it was that we had met up at last. Suzanne had left us alone while she took a shower and we'd stumbled along in conversation, Conrad saying the unsayable and I trying to ignore it, both of us aware of our nervousness but unable to dispel it.

For my part I refused to believe in his friendly advances, having assumed that he'd arranged our meeting to get to know the opposition. I did not know that my sullen demeanour with Conrad was the prelude to a mental state which would facilitate refuting his existence whenever it suited me; all I felt was strong reluctance to befriend a potential betrayer.

But it was difficult to dislike him. His detached manner, unattainable to the likes of myself, was something I held in esteem, considering it the greatest single lack in my own life: internal turmoil had always sabotaged my aspirations to the objective approach. Conrad though, while I sat knotting my guts in unconscious insecurity, could discuss sharing his wife and show no sign of jealousy within. For God's sake, she wasn't even *my* wife, which word had assumed a life of its own. I no longer saw husbands and wives as mere men and women.

Suzanne and I rolled home along the Embankment, I in a delirium of relief, pleased as Punch to be alone with her. We stopped beside Cleopatra's Needle and watched the lights on the river.

"I want you," she said in a strange voice. "Now."

There were only the sounds of the traffic and the river as we made love on the concrete floor of the metropolis, desperate characters in the dark. Afterwards I burst into tears, didn't know why, couldn't help it. I couldn't remember ever having cried before. She put my head on her lap and I cried more because she hadn't marched off in disgust. She didn't speak except to say my grip was hurting her. I felt her hand burning my scalp, the wet of tears and saliva on her dress.

"Were you sad about something in particular?"

"No. I was happy. I don't understand . . ."

"I'm the same, I cry all the time. So does Conrad."

The comparison made me determined never to cry again. We walked hand in hand up the steps of the Simpleton's Arms, a music pub we often visited. A traditional folksinging ensemble was on the stage.

> *We'll kill Paddy Doyle for his boots me-boys,*
> *Aye we'll kill Paddy Doyle for his boots.*

Suzanne went to the bar and bought us some rum. We were well liked in this establishment where we had a lovers' reputation. Now and then I would take to the stage and sing a song myself.

Carmina morte carent, I had read in a bilingual text in the communal library at Suzanne's. Ovid, I could see, was not a man to call a pick a mattock. Songs never die, true, but the singer loses his fine voice. I watch Suzanne watching me as I sing. The force in me that goes out to her is invincible.

But Conrad exists, has become true, and his forms may now comprise my vision.

Odi et amo. Catullus was another who knew the score, he and Ovid both. But the hate and love were symbiotic, gluttonously feeding off each other and growing ripe, almost overripe, and neither would fall.

A newly formed band took the stage at the Simpleton's. They were reputable performers who had come together in protest about the amount of serious music being played. Eastern instruments droned out snake-charming sounds while an ecstatically writhing dancer sang in gravest tone, and everybody found it quite hilarious, even Suzanne who had no sense of humour to speak of.

On the way home we fucked each other senseless on Clapham Common and sang our way down the back streets, but in bed that night I had never been quieter. Sylvia, Conrad's other woman, had collected Laura from Conrad at the hospital and Laura was sleeping with Sylvia and Sam tonight, so there weren't the usual reassuring sounds of her breathing. I lay rigid, silent. Even when Suzanne from deep sleep moved closer to me and whispered her husband's name in my ear I hardly flinched. Instead, I decided to murder Conrad. Or should I do away with Suzanne? No, there was Laura. Maybe a merciful God would see to it that Conrad met an untimely death while crossing the road at Camberwell Green. Would I then lead an exemplary life?

The sad truth was that I liked Conrad. After a second meeting I began to look forward to the days when we would be together, which grew numerous as my involvement deepened with Suzanne and I cast my fate up in the air.

Conrad avoided casual chatter, neither tolerating it with secret disdain nor complying with it in superficial social interaction. He impolitely rejected out of hand any comments on the weather, facetious jabber, gossip, and grew quickly impatient with anyone wishing to force these things upon him. If you told him something at which you expected him to laugh, he never would; he'd immediately change the subject to one of consequence, a move that always devastated me.

Conversely, if he himself made a joke, and you were the kind who automatically reciprocates laughter, Conrad's expressive mug would turn at once into a mask of profound weltschmerz. He eschewed the shared prop, be it jest, chat, getting drunk, mocking other people. Though gregarious he seemed to be a lonely man with no close friends of his own; they were all Suzanne's friends, and rather obviously so.

Conrad spoke each phrase as if his future depended upon getting it just right, made elaborate digressions (which bored you in the telling, satisfied in the conclusion) to ensure that nothing be misconstrued. He demanded to know your inmost thoughts on subjects both elevated and sordid, sticking his neck out in human relations and giving, if I may quote him, not a tinker's fart about what anybody thought of him. In his own house he was respected and perhaps feared for his manifest intellectual powers, and in the outside world his status as a doctor commanded a similar deference. Conrad spat on all such deference. "I am a Martian," he once said to me; "I mean—if I am living with ten people and nine of them see me as a Martian, then I am a Martian, effectively. Obviously I don't think in terms of Martians myself, but they do, and it's supposed to be a democracy."

Was Conrad's fearless behaviour, I wondered, based on ignorance of the effect he had on others? Josh's young wife for example, who turned up around this time, refused to treat Conrad as anything other than a Martian. He destroyed her illusions about handsome young doctors the moment they met. Walking from room to room blowing his sax, Conrad saw her and stopped, not to be introduced but to say, smiling, "You're rather gorgeous, aren't you," and then go on to explain in detail the mental processes which had led up to his making the remark. *Madman!* she muttered aside to me later. Josh himself, who was becoming mystical, saw Conrad as a kind of mattoid in possession of the key to a door that he was yet to find; and even Suzanne would talk, with his wholehearted approbation, of Conrad's essentially schizophrenic nature.

But Conrad as he appeared to me was basically a cheerful man, unmoody, energetic, multitalented. Music was one of his chief enjoyments and he played well on sax and flute, adequately on piano, dreadfully on the guitar for which last I was thankful. Sometimes he and I would have a session together, and one night Suzanne, grand mover, danced a few steps as Conrad and I blew a tuneful improvisation, and she danced on, rolling and

[33]

stretching, as the music grew weird and gutsy, her eyes rolling behind closed lids, leaping across the floor like a lovesick animal while we hammered and blasted, piano and sax, both of us fixing her with our eyes and watching each other watch her.

Deftly, the reality of one part of our lives crept in to impair the reality of another. We grew discordant, unattuned. The woman, or our attitudes towards her, came between us and put a ceiling on flight. The dance (her dance, mine or his?) dissolved and we laid the instruments aside, congratulating one another. Soon it would be time to go to bed.

At Suzanne's suggestion and with the approval of everybody concerned, I had moved into a room in their house and immersed myself in the roundabout of sexual interrelationship that was making the place notorious. Suzanne lived with Conrad and I was her lover; Conrad's lover Sylvia lived with Sam whose lover, Curly, was also sapphically involved with Sylvia so they were often a threesome. Upstairs lived William and his wife Paula who had been known, in William's absence, to have encounters with me, not to mention my friend Caspar and two other rank outsiders.

Paula, a sensible Northerner, was by far the most promiscuous and said she preferred *fooking* above all other activities. Farther up the stairs lived Percy and Ingeborg whose marriage was complemented, and no doubt complicated, by Ingeborg's lover Hugo who lived in the attic.

Curly took a liking to me and to my friend Caspar, who started visiting regularly, and it was she who told me that both Percy and Sam, who had failed in an attempt at homosexuality, were interested in *getting closer,* as the phrase went, to Suzanne. Only my heartfelt shame about being a roughneck with a temper among so many people of high sophistication prevented me from becoming a mass slaughterer.

Under interrogation Suzanne admitted to having slept with Percy and Sam, separately, but that had been before my time: she was presently fighting them off. She frowned when I told her that I wouldn't want Paula if I could have . . . The undercurrents were fast if not furious, and they were invisible to the untrained eye.

Dinner guests did their utmost to appear broad-minded when someone would yawn, look at the clock and say "Ahem . . . er . . . who's slee . . . what are the *sleeping arrangements* to-night?" Or maybe it would be a great bathroom-door type of incident, for the bathroom, which also contained the lavatory, was subject to unwritten law, viz., that it be kept unlocked at all times. Many visitors committed the solecism of transgressing that law, notably William's mother who arrived unannounced and full of bladder to find her son in the bath making love to someone's wife, myself half-naked having a shave, Sylvia on the loo as if waiting for a bus, and an unknown girl trying to get her diaphragm into place. At the first of many shrieks from William's mother the bustle ceased and dispersed forthwith. Some moments later Conrad came up from the basement knowing nothing of what had passed and could be heard thumping on the bathroom door: "Who's locked the fucking bog? I'm dying for a shit!"

Our life was viewed by those unable to participate in it as a sprint macabre along the road to perdition, and for the wrong reasons they were probably right. But I who lay awake while my lover loved somebody else in the adjoining room, worse still in the room above, who was forced to turn up the volume to prevent my going insane or committing crimes, I thought I was going through a temporary hell on the road to something better.

The first morning, before it became a regular occurrence, I was shocked when Conrad came tiptoeing into the bedroom carrying a large tray.

"Good morning," he said in a quiet pleasant voice. "Is anybody awake? I brought you some breakfast."

I lay doggo in the half-light, observing him through tight lashes.

"Oooh," Suzanne moaned, waking up. "Good morning, darling. O, breakfast! How luxurious. Is Laura still sleeping?"

[35]

"Yes she is."

They kissed noisily, then Conrad poured out some tea, asked Suzanne if he should pour one for me.

"I think he's fast asleep," she said, ruffling my hair.

"I started writing that magazine article this morning," Conrad was saying, ignoring the attention she was paying me; "there's something I'm not quite clear about and I'd like you to read it and tell me what you think, but otherwise it's coming along marvellously."

"Oh that's really good, darling. Do I see toast and marmalade on this tray? I'm very lucky," she said, giving him another kiss. "Are you managing to get it all down the way you wanted?"

"Yeah!" Conrad always said yeah as if someone had asked him if he wanted to inherit a fortune. "Yeah," he repeated, "everybody who deserves it has been demolished."

She laughed and drank some tea almost simultaneously. Conrad was sitting on the bed now and I was feeling like a child eavesdropping on its parents. What did he mean by strolling in here at this time? Anything might have been going on. Was Conrad bisexual? I heard her running a hand over his unshaven face—it sounded like the distant croaking of frogs. The familiar knots formed in my stomach, I became conscious of clenching my teeth, I found fault with everything Conrad said. Suzanne was telling him about the lovely time we'd had at the Italian restaurant the night before—was she going to mention . . . did she tell him *everything*? What exactly did he know about me? Did he delight in taunting me like this? I hadn't the courage to wait until they started discussing me, I woke up and presented myself. My hand was still on Suzanne's belly.

"What's the matter, lover?" she asked on entering my bedroom and finding me still in bed at four in the afternoon.

"I can't be bothered getting up."

"Why is that?"

She sat down beside me and put her hand on my chest, under the blankets, laughing softly in her way that told me she knew something was wrong but would ignore it if I wanted her to. I wanted to tell her right away that I'd already been up and about, at dawn in fact, with the vague intention of killing myself. I had a knife under my pillow. But the certain knowledge that she would worry about me—or the fear that she might not?—made me withhold what was on the tip of my tongue and sink deeper into my torpor of obfuscation.

"Do you want to come to the cinema with me and Conrad tonight? *The Blue Angel.*"

"No." Where would I be expected to sit?

"I wish you'd tell me what's wrong," she said evenly.

What was wrong! Maybe I should have told Suzanne exactly what was wrong with me—that I was an outcast the moment she left my side in this house where everybody had an honours degree, a bank balance, a wife and a lover. That Conrad was scheming to make my life untenable, that I prayed daily for a horrible death to befall him. That I was an impostor who had taken advantage of her open warmth and love by posing as an intelligent man worthy of her friendship. Instead:

"I wish you'd go away and leave me alone, Suze."

"Oh don't . . . Please . . . Can't you talk to me, tell me what's going on? Are you angry with me? Because if you are you should say, and we can talk about it—don't turn away like that. Whatever it is, I know we can get through it. Whatever it is."

I pulled the blankets over my head. This was insupportable, trying to resist her demand that I give her everything, jeopardise my cover and come out and show myself. Ramming a childishly uncontrollable fist into the pillow I felt the knife hard against my knuckles.

"Don't hide away, lover," voice always calm, drawing the bedclothes from me.

I sat up and slapped her hard in the face. It was the first time I'd ever done such a thing to a woman. Perplexed, she looked at me, stroked her cheek and I looked away, finally sure that I'd overstepped the limit. Then she backhanded me across the mouth and we stared sadly at each other, both knowing that a line had been crossed. Abjectly I let the blood dribble over my lip.

"I'm sorry I hit you, Suze . . . I just hate you so much."

"But *why?*"

One thoughtless remark, however spontaneous, was more than enough to silence me.

"What do you mean," she asked, "when you say you hate me?" her voice breaking in her throat. When I didn't answer she went on: "Hating doesn't do anything for anybody if it's kept locked away . . . except make life pretty miserable. If you hate me," she paused for me to vindicate or deny: I did neither, "if you hate me it's because . . . well . . . because you love me, I mean, because you love me and I'm making you unhappy, so you hate me. Isn't that what happens?"

I concentrated on keeping my lips between my teeth. Only with silence could I resist that voice whose colours conveyed to my ears every subtlety of love and understanding inexpressible through words.

"Are you going to leave me? I wouldn't blame you. It isn't what *I* want to happen . . . but I know that I ask a lot of you . . . and I just wouldn't ask it if I wasn't so much in love with you. I know it must be hard, terribly hard—it's hard enough for me, not knowing if I'm doing right or wrong, not wanting to hurt you, not wanting to hurt Conrad . . ." She began to cry, her voice grew huskier, I turned farther away from her. "Oh I know that we must hurt each other sometimes. But I *am* in love with both of you . . . I can't, I won't, choose one or the other. You know that. Do you believe that I love you? I want to say it over and over, that I've loved you from the minute I . . ."

"Suzanne," I looked at her and she threw her arms round me. "It's all wrong," I said in a dead voice.

The day came for Conrad and me to have a basic talk. What exactly did I want? What he wanted was my instant removal, although he put it better than that. All his common sense and detachment vanished as he accused me of monstrous selfishness and unfairness, giving as an example of decent behaviour an episode from his own life in which he had harnessed his desire for a woman who loved him; she was a married woman and there would have been no sense in his messing up her life with her husband. . . . Intimidated I sat in silence. Maybe he was right, but how dare he suggest *that* as a parallel to my love for Suzanne! As if I'd had any choice. This was a new side of Conrad, not the man ready to risk all in the name of new frontiers. And for the first time I felt that much of his talk was sheer casuistry based on premises of panic. His eyes were empty, able to look at me but not at himself, and his mouth fought downwards against the unavoidable smiles. We were in the same hell and Conrad was coming to resemble me at my despicable worst.

I began to feel uncomfortably terrified in my room at nights, in this world where locked doors aroused both suspicion and contempt. I kept my old gully to hand.

One serendipitous winter night after a splendid dinner with plenty of rough red wine, when the sleeping arrangements had fallen in my favour and no indissoluble questions barked in my lately fecundated head, I fell prey to a brilliant notion: *Carry her off!*

"Suze," I whispered excitedly.

"I love you," she said in her sleep, "I love you. . . . Come into me again," and her eyes opened.

I woke her up again at dawn, lovers' hour, and kissed her face.

"Suze."

I touched her.

"Suze," louder this time.

"Hello . . ."

"Get up. Fetch Laura. We're going away."

"Where are we going? I'm still asleep I think."

"We're going away to live by ourselves. Come on, before anybody else wakes up."

"I think I'd better wake up. What is it?"

"I don't want to share you anymore. I want you all to myself, I can't bear it here, I'll kill somebody. I want us to live together on our own."

"I'd like to live with you . . ."

"Well, get Laura and we'll leave now."

"But . . . I can't just leave here. Where would we go?"

"Caspar can get us quite a large flat, not expensive. And I can make money to look after everybody."

"Oh . . . I'd like to . . . I mean we've never had that sort of . . . you and I . . . But I can't, I couldn't just leave this house. It's my home, I mean my whole life is in this house, and Conrad . . . And all the others, they're my friends."

It came to me that since living in this house I had drifted apart from nearly all of my own friends.

"That's true, I should have kept my mouth shut."

"No, no. I'm glad you told me. Maybe we could go away somewhere together for a while; but I don't think, I mean I'm sure about it, I couldn't move away from here."

"It's all right Suze, I just . . ."

"Are you tired of me? Are you sick and fed up with me altogether?"

"Don't be daft. Would I ask you to come away if I didn't love you? You should forget what I said. In actual fact I want to stay here with you. What difference does it make where we are? Maybe I was feeling a bit jealous or something."

"Will you give me a kiss?"

From that night Suzanne and I were together at every opportunity. Whenever we were alone we fucked and loved with despondent passion—in bedrooms, kitchen, garden, bathroom, on trains, even in a bus.

Any inhibition still untouched by the general atmosphere of sexual freedom fell to the sword and we became like healthy animals in rut, gleeful, crazed, drooling lust from the pores. It was like the days one reads of when soldiers are about to leave for the front. I saw Suzanne grow as depraved, enslaved as myself, her eyes seeming to swim in honeydew and saliva. We were continually surprised in flagrante delicto, our naked bodies became local monuments, the subject of humourous table talk in between mouthfuls of food, and even Conrad made mild reference to the prolonged satyriasis which was causing Suzanne to fall prematurely asleep by his side at night.

The last friendly conversation Conrad and I had was when we, as the only practical-minded members of the household, were renewing the electrical wiring on the ground floor. Suzanne and Conrad had spent the past three nights together and I, playing the substitute rule, had invited Cindy the whore, now a stripper and aspiring film actress, to come for a brief holiday. Cindy had enormous breasts and wore expensive fashionable clothes and was thus very conspicuous about the house. Conrad was desperately interested in Cindy and this was the subject of our friendly talk as we worked.

It was a job requiring that we pull up floorboards and prise off the skirting; I found myself armed with a large axe which I'd been using in lieu of a hammer and bolster. Conrad was kneeling with his back to me, rummaging under the floorboards for a length of cable. I decided at once to kill him.

Raising the axe above my head, casually in case he should look round, I tried to envisage the result of splitting his skull, cleaving him from nape to navel. Death and jail. I returned the axe to my side and stared at the back of his head. An involuntary movement brought the axe back into the air, I took a step forward. And returned the axe to my side and got on with the work in hand.

Some nights later I was sleeping with Suzanne. She turned to me in the dark and said that Conrad was scared that I was going to kill him. Suzanne found this queerly amusing, as if nothing could have been more preposterous.

Conrad by now was doing very little to conceal his dislike of me. He demanded of Suzanne that she ask me to leave the house once and for all.

"What do you want me to do?" I asked her.

"*I* don't want you to go."

"I'll go if you want me to," I said dejected. "We can still meet."

What I wanted was for her suddenly to realise that she'd had enough of Conrad.

"Don't go. We'll have to talk this out, all of us. You can't just leave! It's all my fault, I know, but I really can't help it. Conrad's very upset."

"Well what about this, Suze: I'll go and find a flat and you can live half with me and half with him, that way we——"

"Yes but . . . well the thing is . . . the thing is that Conrad wants me to spend a lot more time with him . . . now that he's finished at the hospital . . ."

"Oh."

She was holding my hands in hers. Somehow we managed to end up, me literally ripping her clothes off her body, mindlessly passionate, as if we had just been reunited after a long absence.

"You feel you want to, Suze?"

"What, be more with Conrad?"

"Yes."

"Well it *has* been more than a year, you know, since we were really together. And we'd always planned, you know, to . . ."

"I'm going now."

"Where? Where are you going?"

"Leaving."

I gathered my odd possessions, omitting those that had connections with Suzanne. She rose from the bed and her skirt fell back into place. She picked up her ruined panties and tried to raise a smile from me before dropping them in the wastepaper basket.

"Are you coming back?"

"No."

"Where are you going? We'll see each other soon, won't we?"

I had to hurry. I put the guitar in its case, threw the bag over my shoulder. She followed me out of the room and down the stairs, rushing to keep pace with me. Catching my arm as I opened the door she kissed me and I manhandled her body in a way I hoped was pornographic. I had to hurry.

Blindly down the street now with nothing more to lose, jostling people too slow to get out of my way, vaguely aware of the wind on my streaming cheeks.

At Victoria station I sat down and scanned my book of telephone numbers. *Caspar!* He knew the whole story, I could go to him and he would understand. But really it was a woman I wanted. I decided to turn up unannounced, thus obviating a refusal, at the home of two student nurses whom I'd known since the days before Suzanne.

I bought some wine and turned up in time for dinner. We all got drunk and flirtatious, I slapped their bottoms, they told me what a terrible man I was. The noise we made, however, was too much for the landlord, a fat Maltese who received a blow to the paunch for his trouble. I had to leave before the police arrived.

Midnight came and went as I tramped along a deserted thoroughfare in a part of town that was strange to me. If I hadn't hit the landlord I would certainly have slept with Josie tonight, maybe with both of them, Josie and Breda, tasty seventeen-year-olds without a scrap of learning, a change from that old bitch . . . . Christ, I thought, it's my birthday the day after tomorrow: twenty, and less than ever to show for it. I began to miss Suzanne.

I walked past two telephone kiosks before the idea struck me to call Cindy—she'd just be getting home from the strip club around this time. After spending a couple of days as my guest Cindy had advised me strongly to get out. I ought to forget about all their freedom nonsense, they were just old children compensating for a boring adolescence.

"Cindy?"

"You! Jesus Christ."

"What is it?"

"Oh I was just talking about you to somebody."

"Somebody?" Had Suzanne contacted her?

"I showed him that thing you wrote," she gave a peculiar laugh. "He said you're in great danger."

"Not bad . . . Listen Cindy, can I come and stay the night? I'm not in very good shape but . . ."

"I'm sorry love, not tonight."

"Have you got a man there?"

"Well . . ."

"He's listening on the extension? Hello mister! But listen Cindy, all I want is a place to sleep. I left Suzanne . . ."

"Good."

". . . so I'm on the street tonight. Anyway, I've got a sleeping bag, the kitchen floor would be perfect. You won't even have to talk to me, think of that!"

"Sorry love, no way. Ring me tomorrow."

"For fuck's sake Cindy, who have you got there? *Fellini?*"

"Not quite," and she whispered the name of a well-known actor.

"What if I offered you some cash?"

"Listen love, I must *go*."

"But couldn't I just sleep? I'm stuck out here in a place called Haringey."

"Sorry love."

"Cindy!"

"*Sluts!*" I screamed into the dark as she hung up the phone. "*Sluts!*" she and Suzanne both, opposite sides of the same false coinage.

I spent the night in a shop doorway. Trying to get to sleep I wondered was Suzanne also alone tonight, lying awake in my old bed, or had she gone downstairs to sleep with Conrad?

Marcel MacMarshall

❧

IT WAS A DARK NIGHT, quiet, and there was no moon. The old people said that nights like this were *black as the Earl o' Hell's waistcoat,* and we derived courage against the dark from our uncharacteristically fond repetition of the phrase.

The Lane was an eerie place to go but it attracted a fair amount of pedestrian traffic, mainly because it provided a short-cut between our village and the main road, reducing a walk of fifteen minutes to one of five, but also because it was the most convenient wenching spot for local couples with nowhere better to go. We came often to the Lane at night and had heard, if not seen, a great deal concerning the complexities that underlie the deceptive simplicity of village life.

There was nobody about tonight, but it was early yet. The owl was up there in the dead white oak as usual, and in the distance we could hear Nettie Beattie's pet goose Giblet making a fearful racket. Maybe Nettie had decided to put Giblet in the pot and was trying to wring his fat neck. When a sheep coughs it sounds just like a man. The bull from Maltman's farm escaped and ran through the Lane one night and Haddow the bookie's runner was trampled. Shouldn't have been down here with Mugs Mendelson's wife . . .

We'd been sitting around for half an hour before the clacking sound of a girl walking in high-heeled shoes along the main road brought us abruptly to attention. We got into position as she approached the top end of the Lane, where you could see, in the weird light of a streetlamp obscured by trees, the silhouette of the disused Nissen hut where they found the dead tramp. There was another streetlamp at the bottom end of the Lane but it too gave no light until you were almost directly beneath it. Between these two sources of light the Lane ran in a vague *S*-shape; on both sides the bushes and hedges stood taller than a man and the trees leant into each other to form high and gloomy archways.

The girl stopped at the mouth of the Lane. She was alone. We had never known a girl to run the ordeal of the Lane alone at night—in fact there were few girls who would venture down here with a man to whom they were not engaged to be married. She was twenty or thirty yards from us but we clearly heard her mutter the peculiar phrase, "F—— *you Douglas!*" In the silence her voice—who was she?—came and went and was immediately superseded by the scraping of her high heels on the rough pathway as she started down the Lane.

Thinking perhaps that she would soon be home again, our victim sang a few quiet bars of a song whose lyric contained those very words, but she stopped when she heard something that sounded like a cough or burst of choked laughter. Silence. Speeding up her step she began to sing again until suddenly she stopped on one leg and dropped her handbag to the ground as her whole body jerked up and back in a violent seizure. *"Jesus God!"* she breathed in a loud whisper: she was staring at a dark shape, a heap, lying on the path before her. She was sure she had seen it move. No. She stared and took a quick glance into the darkness behind her. Just nerves. She picked up her handbag and took two long paces forwards . . .

"I am a log," said Marcel MacMarshall.

The girl screamed as the talking log rolled briskly towards her feet.

"We are logs," I called out in a deep voice, emerging from my hiding place in the bushes shuffling my feet and waving my walking stick. In my long heavy overcoat, muffler and cloth cap I was sweating copiously. MacMarshall struggled to his feet with the aid of his cromach and adjusted his tweed bonnet. We must have looked identical as we hobbled after the demented girl, chasing her back to the top of the Lane. Beneath the streetlamp she paused and looked round and we limped towards her with redoubled speed and malevolence, brandishing our sticks and grunting imprecations against the young.

"Wait a minute," MacMarshall whispered incredulously, "it's Porridge Oates!" This observation, which I realised at once to be perfectly true, provoked irrepressible laughter from both of us.

"Porridge!" I yelled after her, "Por-ridge! *We are logs!*"

She stopped dead and alive, turned round deliberately and marched down on us. We shook our sticks, gnashed our teeth and danced with rage but she kept coming. We should have guessed who she was the moment she said *"F—— you Douglas!"* but we never thought of Douglas by his proper name. Sponey Jameson, who'd recently had his hands on Porridge and his mind on discussing it later with his mates, had mentioned to us that she was having boyfriend trouble. Maybe that's why she was walking home at night on her own. MacMarshall fished two cigarettes from the lining of his cap and handed one to me.

"Have you got a light please, Fiona?" I asked as she approached, pointedly avoiding the use of her unfortunate nickname. Sponey Jameson said that she signed her letters *Fiona McCluskey Oates (14)*, even though it was common knowledge that she was only thirteen and a bit and that her real name was Porridge.

"Wee buggers!" she spat at us, "I'll half-kill the pair of you."

"What about a feel, Fiona," MacMarshall piped up. She already had a considerable reputation in the village.

"Dirty wee bugger Marcel MacMarshall. If your mother gets to hear about this . . . And what's all this *log* rubbish? Terrifying folk at nights."

"Take a joke, Fiona. It's my birthday," he explained.

"Well grow up. What age are you then? Pest."

"Nine. I *have* grown up," he said shaking his cromach.

"Many happy returns."

"Thank you, Fiona."

It was always an occasion, MacMarshall's birthday, because from that day forth we would be the same age for a number of months: this increased and rendered palpable, in our own minds and in the minds of others, the great affinities we enjoyed. Porridge's anger subsided as she surveyed our grandfather outfits beneath the streetlamp, she even laughed when we tried to raise her skirt with our walking sticks, and the three of us started back down the Lane. In the darkness we grabbed at her and felt, or hoped we had felt, her spongy breasts, and she accepted a few drags at our cigarettes, turnabout. "Gi'e's several sooks o' yon fag," MacMarshall said in faithful mimicry of Sponey Jameson, but it elicited no response. "What about a feel, Fiona," he said furtively when at a prearranged signal we turned on her, prodding her with our sticks and slavering like old men. She wasn't altogether laughing.

"Ha! You've had enough already, Marcel MacMarshall. Paws off."

"Just one," he said in his BBC voice.

"Dirty wee bugger. Nine!"

I mooched ahead, acting the fool.

"Sponey Jameson," MacMarshall began, "had his hand——"

I wheeled at the smack of her hand across his ear, expecting him to start crying.

"——up-your-skirt."

"I'm warning you, Marcel MacMarshall."

"Jenny Culpin," he resumed brightly after perfunctory heeding of the threat, "did something to your boyfriend. Wee Dougie."

"His name's Douglas."

"We call him Wee Dougie," I said informatively.

"Anyway," MacMarshall coughed.

"What about Jenny Culpin anyway?" Porridge's nose was testing the climate.

"You want me to say?" MacMarshall limbered up for it. "You want me to tell you, Fiona?"

"Shut your puss," I told him.

"You'd better bloody tell me son, if you don't want your dad to hear about this."

"Okay Fiona." Then triumphant: "But give me a feel up your skirt first."

"Filthy wee bugger!"

She slapped him again, he laughed, I gave Porridge a boot in the arse.

"You'll tell me what you know about Douglas and Jenny Culpin."

"Certainly, Fiona." MacMarshall made to lift her skirt.

"I said paws off."

She pushed him away and his cap fell to the ground.

"I'm telling nothing," he said, adjusting his cap, "unless you let me . . ."

"Oh all right, all right. But not here."

"Where then?"

"Johnnie the Pole's hut," I suggested, referring to a garden shed belonging to Porridge Oates' next-door neighbour who was a Hungarian refugee. She shrugged irritably and assented.

"Do you promise?"

"Yes."

"Inside your knickers," MacMarshall specified.

"Yes, all right, now shut up and tell me what . . ."

"Jenny Culpin kissed Wee Dougie's cock," we said simultaneously.

It had been the talk of the neighbourhood for days. Fiona didn't speak, even when we coughed chestily and menaced her with the walking sticks. We were well out of the Lane by now.

To get to Johnnie the Pole's hut you had to get on your hands and knees and crawl past the Porridge family's window, then jump a hedge into the garden next door. MacMarshall and I went first, one after the other, then waited to help Porridge across the hedge. But when it came to her turn she walked directly to the window and rapped on the glass. Her mother parted the curtains immediately and MacMarshall and I fell flat in the long grass.

"Night night, boys," she murmured victorious. Her mother opened the door berating her for staying out late.

Here is my earliest memory of the quintessential Marcel Mac-Marshall: we took a kitchen knife and cut the wrists of our right hands, tied our wrists together with a rag, difficult, so that the blood mingled. Then we cut the rag with the knife and lapped up the mixed blood from our arms. This made us blood brothers according to a tradition cited in a picture book for boys.

We were five and had been close friends for upwards of three years.

It came to us one morning that it was high time we ran away from home. We were enjoying one of the notorious interminable summers of childhood where you rose with the sun and blue-and-white skies, where the grass was alive, the hills breathing. Today, when seized by such wheatfield-with-crows visions of objects natural and otherwise, I touch the pulse of melancholy and am precipitated back to the Scottish Lowlands, Marcel MacMarshall and some hallucinated afternoon in the nineteen fifties when we took all such things for granted.

There was a barn we had explored once on one of our evening strolls. Standing half a mile from the farmhouse to which it belonged the barn was an ideal place for hanging about out of harm's way, there being little reason for anyone, farmer or passerby, visiting it at this time of the year: it therefore made first and final choice in our search for a new home.

MacMarshall told his mother that he'd be spending the night at my house, I told mine I'd be at his. This hackneyed ruse would allow us plenty of time to get well out of the way without arousing suspicion.

The billiard hall where we'd arranged to rendezvous at six o'clock was empty when we arrived, the caretaker asleep in his cubicle, wooden leg stuck up on the table in a Nazi salute. We helped ourselves to cues and balls and set up a game of snooker, one playing while the other kept an eye on the cubicle, ready to escape without paying and, due to the man's inagility, without much difficulty the moment he should awake. Halfway through the second angle a local hardman swaggered in and roused the caretaker, tapping with a cue on his wooden leg. We set off for the barn.

"Which way'll we go?"

"Rowan's Dyke."

Rowan's Dyke runs or ran the length of a rough pathway, two or three miles, after which the barn was within spitting distance. With woodland to one side and the Dyke—a seven-foot drystone wall—protecting the Duke of Buccleuch's extensive property on the other, the pathway at night, unlit and narrow, was a grisly ramble even to the old men of the Lane; who, incidentally, had taken stringent but tacit care to prepare a schedule that ensured reaching the barn well before sundown.

On the village outskirts we stopped at the local petrol station whose proprietor, an African colossus—conversation piece of the district, the only black man for miles (excluding Bob Cunningham who was a mulatto anyway and had a pure Scottish accent to boot), former university lecturer—the remarkable Dr. Ranghapohl had an understanding with us to supply cigarettes in smaller than normal quantities and at a fair price. We bought two each and lent an ear to the doctor's fabulistic notions.

"Gentlemen of Westhouses, good day to you! Four nonfilter cigarettes and would you also like a packet for them?"

"Please, doctor."

We enjoyed being on friendly terms with Ranghapohl and set ourselves far apart from the popular village attitude of contemptuous reference to him as Abullah Bullah the Witchdoctor and fatuous jokes about Zulu warriors running petrol stations. In our estimation the doctor was a great man of affairs and of the world. He kept us informed in detail of all his plans. It was still in the early stages, he told us, but the petrol station was shortly to become the nucleus of an exciting enterprise.

"You see there?" he pointed. "Yes! Right where you are standing: that will be the café." Ranghapohl paused to allow registration in our minds of the implications of his astonishing statement—*a café in our village*—before conducting us through

[53]

the workshop to the enclosed showroom space beyond. "This," he stamped his foot, "will be the ballroom, the dancing hall, with the stage in a half circle over there where the breakdown truck is standing; and the bar will be here and here and here, all the length of the space! Now," he raised a finger, "tell no one of this, you gentlemen of Westhouses."

MacMarshall and I shook our heads. We were trustworthy.

"And upstairs," the doctor's voice grew louder, "in my property upstairs I shall make a motel—do you know what a motel is? Yes? Good. Good, you young gentlemen of Westhouses!" and Ranghapohl tossed back his head to release one of his much parodied belly laughs.

"Are you lying?" MacMarshall asked sharply.

"Ha! Gentlemen! Let me give you information. The swimming pool: in the field which I shall buy from Mr. Maltman. A gymnasium for the sports—this I shall construct later for I have not enough money. But in one year all the villages will come here to visit the gentlemen. When your school is over you shall come and work for me."

"Doing what?" our disbelief dwindling appreciably.

"Ah, we shall see. Many things! What age are the gentlemen?"

"Eleven."

"And what shall you study to be?"

"We're singers," MacMarshall told him, annoyed that it wasn't perfectly obvious.

"Then you shall sing in my dancing hall."

"Really?"

"Oh yes. You are very talented, very skilful."

The Rowan's Dyke pathway had its normal quota of couples, stray cats, old men with pipes and spaniels. You said Aye to the old men and avoided looking at the lovers until you were well past them, even those who in ordinary village life might stop to say hello or ask you to run an errand. The path was hallowed soil upon which even the most venal soul underwent transmogrification and ceased to respond, or be expected to respond, to quotidian stimuli. In this pious state Teapot Price and Invisible Isabel sailed by on the arms of their scruffy suitors, fat Teapot Price and her shadow, the emaciated daughter of the village policeman.

"She's a big tall cunt," MacMarshall observed as they moved out of earshot.

"You always say that. Every time we see her."

"Well look at her."

It was true: Invisible Isabel stood six foot three, and were there a gladiolus of corresponding height she might have hidden behind it. Fortunately her boyfriend was even taller, a compensation perhaps for his being many years her junior and having a face peppered with enormous boils. Teapot Price weighed in at around thirteen stone and was knee-high to a man standing on a chair but her boyfriend looked extraordinarily normal. Their silhouette at dusk turned out to be indelible.

"Big tall cunt," MacMarshall enunciated, perhaps remembering the ignominy of last Christmas Eve when she, as Sunday school teacher, had refused us entry to the midnight service. We had to stand singing in the snow. But more than likely MacMarshall was about to embark upon philosophical speculation, inspired by contact with evidence of nature's caprices. *It stands to reason,* he might say, or, *It's all part of our psychophysical makeup,* phrases picked up from his father who was our adviser on intellectual matters.

When he did speak again it was to point out that there was nothing so strange as human beings. Then he said, *Such is Life,* repeated it in questionable German, and Invisible Isabel's extremes of height and thinness were fully accounted for in his world view. Remained her horsey voice: MacMarshall sang out in cruel falsetto,

> *Follow J-e-s-u-s*
> *And J-o-y will follow!*

which song was Isabel's favourite.

The barn was waist-high in old straw, windowless and dark.

We dived in and rolled in the straw, threw our shoes at a plump rat, got bored and went out into the twilight. Behind the barn there was a seven-acre turnip field and we were beginning to get hungry. Unaware that the turnips were grown to feed the beasts of the field but not of the kitchen we helped ourselves to a couple, lopping off the shaws with a sheath knife and tucking the plunder underarm in the style of decapitated ghosts.

"Talking about turnips, Davy . . . *How's your head?*"

"Go and boil yours."

"Game rugby?" MacMarshall was running forward, head down sleekly, turnip clutched to his breast. *"Out! Out!"* he bleated in the voice of our effeminate sports instructor, and I ran veering off to his right. When the positioning was strategically correct he lobbed his turnip back at me but I failed to hold the catch. Both turnips went down and the game was abandoned for supper.

The accepted method of preparing and eating raw a thirty-inch-diameter silage turnip, also called a neep, is as follows: cut off the top as you would a green pepper for stuffing and hollow out the flesh as you would a pumpkin for lantern-making. When the neep has been hollowed—in our case hewn—to a depth of four inches, sit down with the neep between your knees and scrape the inside with a stout knife. As the grated turnip falls in on itself, scoop it out in handfuls and eat it.

We passed a quiet half hour, speaking only to comment on the tasty food. Stars began to appear and grow brighter, and soon there were lights switched on in solitary cottages and farmhouses along the horizon. We lit up our cigarettes and sat smoking, the silence of the night taking a firm yet imperceptible hold on us.

"Why are we whispering?"

"I don't know."

"I feel more like singing."

We lit the last two cigarettes and retired to the barn. The rats were out in force so we comforted each other with rat stories: if you corner one it will go for your throat; they gnaw out the eyes of sleeping babies; Gall's brother Pud saw one down the pit—a rat almost three foot long—but knowing Pud Gallagher it was as likely to have been a famished badger; in France they eat rat stew, Cassoulet à Grande Souris; you can also bake them in clay on an open fire and when you break the clay the skin and fur come clean off and the baked rat is ready to eat; Uncle Dod caught a pregnant rat and threw it into a drum of stagnant water, a twenty gallon drum three or four feet deep, but next morning the rat plus five newborn rats were swimming round and round and trying to run up the sides.

"We should've brought some sandwiches and a flask of coffee."

"I wish we had Becky in here. Or even Porridge Oates."

"It's really warm when you get down in the straw."

"It is. But what about the rats?"

"Ach, they can't be that bad."

"No."

"Dod catches them with his bare hands."

"Does he get bitten?"

"Scratched sometimes."

We had recently outgrown the fetish for comparing penises and making hamfisted attempts at sodomy: our nocturnal discussions now turned solely on girls and fame, the union wages of celebrated singers. Chief among the girls was Becky Sinclair who was ten and wanted to be a chorus girl. She taught us a game, in the form of an improvisational playlet, called *The Sailors and the Nurse:* Becky Sinclair took the part of a nurse who had been forced through straitened circumstances to work as a waitress during her hours off duty. MacMarshall and I, the sailors, come into the bar where she works, order whisky and start making merry. The waitress-nurse brings more drinks which she accidentally spills all over the sailors, who are then obliged to remove her pants and smack her bottom.

When you kissed Becky Sinclair she had a smell all of her own. We persuaded her to bring a friend one day, but the friend ran outside and vomited at first sight of MacMarshall's cock. She returned for a tentative encounter with him but in the end had to be blackmailed out of squealing on us: rumours of unbridled lubricity would be linked with her name and circulated via Porridge Oates to the grandparents with whom the girl lived.

A fortnight ago the sailors and the nurse had been caught redhanded, the nurse's pants conspicuous on the floor of Johnnie the Pole's hut. I got a deliberated crack on the jaw, Mac-Marshall emerging unscathed by blaming the whole thing on me, which was fair enough; my punishment was a thing of the distant past by the time MacMarshall's father got home from work. Remonstrance was always a fatherly thing and meant a torturous wait if you happened to misbehave in the mornings.

As we eased farther into the straw MacMarshall postulated the unquestionable existence of God. There was simply no argument: take the case of McCombie the history teacher, renowned for gratuitous brutality, who smacked you in the face with his stiff tawse if you coughed during his mediocre lessons. He'd even hammered Hector Chalmers who had the build of a baby and the mind of a goose.

McCombie overshot the limits of hoodlum ethics when he made Hector Chalmers *crawl* back to his desk following a public flogging. Not that anybody liked Hector very much—he stank—but few absented themselves the day McCombie's car was wonderfully vandalised, tires slashed, wing mirrors wrenched off, windshield shattered, upholstery shredded and a pound and a half of Tate & Lyle's fine granulated poured into the tank. Lipsticked on the window: *McCombie is a sheepfucker.*

Retribution was not slow in coming. Every boy in class was called upon to stand with bare arm outstretched while McCombie, former commando, took twelve calculated swings with his strap. Girls were given detention for a week.

Less than a week later the headmaster materialised in our midst with the message that Mr. McCombie would not be taking classes today, nor indeed for some time. He had been mysteriously hospitalised. This news was felicitously received, but the joy it brought was as nothing when compared with the piquant schadenfreude throughout the school upon McCombie's return a number of weeks after the mass flogging episode: for his right arm had been amputated at the shoulder. He looked rather miserable and seemed to have difficulty keeping his balance.

"Do you remember that song?" MacMarshall broke the affirmative silence following his proof. "The one we had at school,

> *I stood beside a brooklet*
> *That wandered on its way."*

"The Trout song."
"Yeah,

> *And saw beneath the wavelets*
> *A tiny trout at play.*
> *And here and there he darted . . .*

how does it go after that?"
"I'll try to remember."
"It's been in my head all day."
"I can't think. I'm pretty tired. Try it again from the beginning, that sometimes works."
"Yeah. Do you mind," he said rustling in the straw, "if I put my head on your arm?"
"No."
"I stood beside a brooklet . . ."
I wanted to be already asleep. It was scary, the dark and the silence, the scurry of rats in the barn and other small animals outside. Now and then I'd stiffen, red alert, feeling Mac-Marshall do the same, when a sound passed unidentified. His head on my arm helped dispel the fears without too much ceremony.

> *"Across the crystal water*
> *And hid the fish from sight. . ."*

he sang under his breath, trying to recall the lost lyric.

That moment in the barn marks my first awareness of Marcel MacMarshall as someone other than just my friend. Already I was seeing his life as a series of spectacular tableaux vivants: Big Leonard pins me down and holds a penknife to my throat . . . MacMarshall boots him so hard in the ear that it bleeds for days; MacMarshall for a bet jumps from a tree fifteen feet up, lands badly, breaks a leg, wins a tortoise that dies during its first hibernation.

> *"But skilful was the angler . . .*

Pretty stupid words anyway," he said.

"Good tune."

"It is that."

The moon was rising, illuminating the yard and the open doorway of the barn.

"Got it:

> *The fish the enticing bait sought out;*
> *And I was left lamenting*
> *The fate of that poor trout.*
>
> *I stood beside a brooklet . . ."*

MacMarshall driving a stolen tractor, I balancing behind on the rear axle. We hit a rock, I lose my grip and fall against the deep-treaded tire, get lifted up and over, scream, and Mac-Marshall stops the tractor with the offside tire poised over my neck. Did this incident, and others like it, really take place or had I invented them? MacMarshall, when asked, confirmed that they were true. On the other hand we often claimed to have seen the same ghosts, observed to the letter the same occult phenomena, dreamed the same dream on the same night. I lost the ability to unravel real and false.

"*What was that?*" he was gripping my arm.

I had heard it too—footsteps—but had kept quiet hoping that whoever it was would pass on by. Together we raised our heads from the straw and saw in the moonlight a man standing by the door, casting an eye over the barn. Was he looking for someone? We ducked down, but not quietly enough: the man looked up and staggered back in one staccato movement.

"Who's in there?" You could hear him taking receding steps into the yard.

"David and Marcel," I responded politely.

"*Who?*" and the man walked into the barn again.

"Davy and Marce," I said in normal frightened tone. "Marcel MacMarshall."

"What are you stupid wee bastards doing here?"

"Who's that?" MacMarshall said, braver now.

We rose to our feet.

"Pie Hogarth," the voice answered.

"Pie Hogarth! Oh hello Pie."

"Hello Pie."

"Hello boys. Camping out are you?" He took a look around. "Jesus wept . . . Well boys, I'm camping out myself tonight. Got any fags?"

"Smoked them."

"Where are the ends?"

"Smoked them."

"Are you on leave from the army Pie?"

"Yeah Pie, your brother told us you'd joined up."

"The brother told you the truth. And I'm not home on leave."

"Were you booted out?"

"Cheeky wee bastard, I'll scud your lug."

"Deserter?" MacMarshall deduced.

"That's it boys. I'll give you the story. But listen, what about you pair taking a walk up the Rowan's Dyke and picking up some fag ends. I'm gasped."

"The Dyke?"

"No chance Pie."

"I'm serious. Get off your arses you pair of cunts, before I kick you up the fucking road."

We hit the street again, bent double searching in the light of the moon for recycleable cigarette butts. Pie had cigarette papers to roll them in. We came back with enough for two thin cigarettes, having already smoked the longer butts well out of Pie's olfactory field. He had removed his raincoat and was wearing jeans and an army battledress jacket.

"Two drags each for you," he said benevolently, handing over the cigarette. "Only two."

"Why'd you desert the army Pie?"

"I'm wanted," he said exhaling smoke. "I'm a wanted man boys."

"What for?"

"What did you do?"

"Killed a man. In Italy."

"*Italy!*"

"That's right boys. He knifed my mate, so I fixed him, got him in an alley and chibbed him up. Blood everywhere. I had to desert. I'm a wanted man in four fucking countries."

Was this possible?

Pie Hogarth's adventures in civilian life were common knowledge and amounted to drinking fifteen pints of heavy a night and interfering, as the phrase went, with prepubescent girls. Equally well known was the relationship of the youth of our village to her majesty's armed forces, to wit, that countless mothers had received countless letters from disillusioned sons who, at seventeen, had signed up for nine years of heroics. And better known than any of this was that Pie Hogarth's whore of a mother, absentee father and wastrel father surrogate would never squander a sum of cash on buying their son out of the army.

"If you knew some of the things I've done boys, it would make your flesh creep."

We knew well enough to keep quiet when people started talking like this.

"And that bloke—he wasn't the first one I put underground."

"How many?" dutifully from MacMarshall.

"Three."

"All Italians?"

"No. Two Englishmen. Two creeps. Aye boys, I've changed. I'm a real hard cunt nowadays."

We played it by ear, just in case there should be a drop of truth in the swillbucket. Maybe, for example, he had murdered someone accidentally, say with a stray shot during rifle practice. That happened. Discussion of Pie's capacity for slaughter was abruptly curtailed by his change of subject.

"Christ I could do with a ride!"

We laughed.

"How's your big sister these days MacMarshall?" Pie's lopsided mug was concentrated vileness.

"Fine," MacMarshall answered with resignation, accustomed to intense interest in Sheila.

"I'd ride that until her tits were blue," Pie spluttered enthusiastically. "Just thinking about her gives me a hard on. Fuck it, I'm going to have a wank."

We turned away, burrowed into the straw and let him get on with it, but after only a short rendition of the familar noises Pie spoke up: "How's about one of you boys tossing me off, eh?"

"Fuck off Pie."

"Stuff yourself," and we laughed at the man's lunacy.

"Come on. Listen MacMarshall, if you toss me off I'll *suck* you off. Really Marce, I will. Come over here."

"You must be off your head," MacMarshall's laugh was less hearty than before.

"Leave him alone Pie," I said sensibly.

"Shut your fucking puss," Pie spat across the barn, "before I

[63]

shut it for you." Then ingratiatingly: "Hey Marce, come on."

"Leave me alone."

"Come on Marce. How's about it? You just toss me off and I'll suck you off. Okay?"

Pie rose from the straw and came on all fours towards us. We leapt and made a dash for it, but a shriek from MacMarshall told me he'd been caught.

"Skinny wee cunt," Pie was jabbering, "I'll stick it up your arse."

He had MacMarshall pinned to the stone floor, a hand gagging him while the other tore at his clothes, Pie's erect prick waving about. I grabbed his hair to make him understand that the joke was over but he caught me a stray punch to the balls and I doubled up breathless. MacMarshall's sobbing was echoing. The sheath knife was in the straw somewhere, stuck inside a half-eaten turnip, and the only weapon to hand was a rusty spade I'd noticed hanging on the wall.

I brought the spade down on Pie Hogarth's skull. After the first blow the rest came naturally to me and it was MacMarshall himself who finally stayed my hand. Pie wasn't moving, there was a fair amount of blood coming out of his head. Moonlight had entered the barn and you could see the blood beginning to stain the concrete floor. We stared at him and at each other, fighting or cultivating the urge to run.

"He's dead."

"Is he?"

"I don't know. Feel his heart."

"No thanks. Serve the bastard right."

"But it's me who gets the blame."

"No. We'll say it was the two of us. In self-defence."

Retrieving the knife and the turnips we left the barn without paying further attention to him.

It was a mystery that not one word was heard in the village concerning Pie Hogarth, his army life, his criminal life, his desertion or his death. MacMarshall and I passed a sleepless night in Johnnie the Pole's hut, alternately constructing water-tight alibis and threatening to denounce each other.

❧

"A half bottle of Four Crowns please, Walter."

Mad Walter, father of Cocky Dunwoodie and barman of the Sporran Tavern, shuffled to the cupboard slobbering his incantations in a peculiar mouth-music of the nose.

"By here lads . . . no' bad . . . grand! Champion! Aye min, the Four Crowns, the Old Tawny Port . . ."

He returned, twitching, with my purchase clasped to his waistcoat, but not before MacMarshall had pocketed two packets of Capstan cigarettes from the display case.

"And two cans of Pale Ale please, Walter," this cheerfully from the thief.

"Celebrating then?" Walter cackled, shuffling back to the cupboard and paying no attention to MacMarshall's exuberant reply.

In the spring when I was fourteen I fell in love with Shona Savage who made me tremble every time I touched her. She and I, half undressed, as naked as we had ever been, came blindly together in first love beneath the trees of an enchanted forest to which we gave not a thought. Dew on the grass, birds in the air, the river Esk spluttering down in the gorge where Mac-Marshall and I had swum, swallowed too much water, cast for trout and caught eels, discussed at dusk the glories of our future.

Her bottom got covered with broken flakes of leaves from the previous autumn, and neither of us found it amusing when I turned her over and dusted her clean. Saliva oozed from the corner of her mouth and I licked it away. When the breeze came I shivered from her tongue in my ear. A face I knew from the world of fantasy turned out to be the face drawn in passion of Shona Savage. Where before had I seen that swift eyes-left-and-back-again look, the mock-insane flash of eyes at difficult moments? And wasn't there also something in her face which made me think of Marcel?

I forced love to fight for its power over me: had I been able to unearth one credible fault in Shona Savage I would have given her up at once. I searched often enough for defects but critical appraisal met always with affirmation of my farthest fetched ideals. It was as if I, with the collaboration of God, had brought together in one person all the qualities I lacked in myself and revered in others.

There were few words between us, no precautions taken, and a taut silence afterwards, both certain of having seduced the other unscrupulously; yet it was clear that our action had committed us to each other for life. We lay beneath the silver birches for several hours, desperately entwined, the evening wind ruffling through unbuttoned clothes, in love for ever. And all the while fully sensitive to the presence several yards away of Shuffling Hughie the ubiquitous Peeping Tom whose ferocious dog had a nose for these events.

MacMarshall too had fallen in love: with Jennifer Raeburn, a city girl of immense sophistication who spoke three languages and actually had a job, although it was only in a bookshop. MacMarshall went for svelte women with inoffensive busts and curly hair. He had suggested, in my own interests, that maybe Shona Savage had an excessively pronounced arse and a pair of tits disproportionate to her stature: I had to tell him to watch his language, also his taste, and be careful about saying things he might later regret.

I met him by chance one night on the wasteland that lay between our village and the main road. He had some news for me.

"Intercourse has taken place."

I didn't believe it. He'd only met Jennifer a couple of weeks ago whereas I had known Shona for at least two months before any such thing happened. I pointed out that it was nothing to boast about—everybody got round to it one way or another, the

[66]

Chinese, the Americans, even the English participated. But not Marcel MacMarshall: this was an imaginative exercise devised to put him on a par with myself.

"You refuse to take my word for it? Okay, *look!*"

He unfolded the raincoat that was slung over his shoulder. I couldn't see anything at first but when we stopped beneath a lamppost it was clear enough: the lining of his coat had a dark wet stain, right in the middle. It was a brand new coat too, not exactly made to measure, but a fine piece of material all the same.

"That's blood etcetera," he said to erase conjecture.

"As in dogfish . . ."

"Fuck off. I love her."

"Sorry. I believe everything."

"It's grand isn't it?"

"True."

"It gets better every time as well."

"How many?"

"Three. Have a smoke?"

"Filter . . ."

"That's what she smokes."

"Where do you get the money?"

"She has money. By the way, I met The Gall on the bus."

"The Gall."

"Yeah. He told me Pid Price is attempting to break his record tomorrow."

"We're not going to that are we? Where's it to be?"

"Usual place after school."

"Are you going?"

"Might as well. For a laugh."

We said good night. Pid Price was a disturbed youth whose "record" consisted of roughly fourteen inches of shit, human excrement, maintained unbroken from the anus at a height of several feet, which last named effect was obtained by Pid sitting barearsed in a fork of the white oak in the Lane. It was an obscene performance really—no women were permitted to attend—but MacMarshall and I, in common with every genuinely inquiring mind, usually put in at least a token appearance.

Pid Price once kicked a cat to death and in return was punched senseless by Pie Hogarth's brother. He had lost his front teeth and had never replaced them. He was absent from school for protracted periods when they bunged him into hospital for electro-convulsive therapy. Only the intervention of Teak Thompson had prevented him from sticking a broken bottle in the face of Agnes Corrie the village slut, six months gone with her fourth, who had proposed in a drunken moment that Pid be locked away in an institution. And old Nancy Turnbull the midwife had sworn to police it was the voice of Pid Price that had demanded from behind a mask to know the location of her life savings. Black Bob Cunningham once incurred Pid's wrath—a brick on the head, thrown from behind—by surmising that black men were as good as white men. We had a name for people like Pid Price but I have forgotten it. The shitting contest—Pid versus himself—would be well attended.

Those, then, were the lovers and the social conditions from which we were preparing to depart. The Four Crowns Old Tawny Port and the two cans of Pale Ale were, as Mad Walter had guessed, to be drunk in celebration. It was MacMarshall's birthday and we had thirty years between us: the minimum school-leaving age was fifteen and we were contriving to say goodbye to education and to our homes in one grand coup. Parental signatures for passports had been obtained by lies about a grape-picking holiday in France. Expected back to resume our studies, we had no intention of returning until we had made our mark in the Ledger of Life, as MacMarshall's father called it.

For more than a year we had been earning wages singing in pubs and folk-music clubs in the city, Edinburgh, and were proficient on guitar and piano. The pubs were best, for over and above wages you were invariably treated to a night's drinking, gratis and for nothing: it was the public's way of expressing ap-

preciation and it helped to compensate for the regular humiliation and subsequent sacking when the landlord discovered that
we were well under age.

As our reputation spread from sailors' dives along the wa-
terfront

(*The Leith police
Dismisseth us*)

to student pubs around the university, we dropped a lot of the
sentimental stuff in our repertoire, began prolifically to compose
songs and changed our name from *The Wolverines* to *The Brothers
Karamazov*.

Stuck in school from nine to four, rehearsing two or three
hours every day and working the clubs and bars in the evenings
and at weekends, saving cash had been no problem. The funds
stood at more than one hundred pounds, which must have been
a lot then. On the morning of the day of celebration we bought
sleeping bags, a camping stove, an army kitbag and a map of
the world.

"Be careful with that," I admonished him.

"Relax," MacMarshall tapped his hip pocket where the new
map protruded, "or you'll end up dropping that bottle."

We were crossing the river Esk by means of mossgrown
steppingstones.

I had selected for the alfresco drinking session a spot at once
secluded and historic: the grave and tombstone of Camp Meg,
the Meg Merrilees immortalised (as if she needed their help) by
John Keats and Sir Walter Scott. She had been a personal friend
of MacMarshall's great-grandfather who had passed down the information that Camp Meg, so called for no other reason than
that she inhabited a hovel on the site of a former Roman en-
campment in our village, was two metres in height, a talented
doctor, herbalist and veterinary, and by no stretch of the imagination a lady "most akin to the witches of Macbeth" which is
how that scoundrel Sir Walter Scott put it.

Firsthand accounts notwithstanding, these pernicious misattributions persisted in the form of legend: Camp Meg was a sorceress. If you circled the tomb three times at midnight, knelt before the great stone and asked her to rise from the grave and speak to you, she would speak.

That was exactly what happened when Marcel and I put it to the test in the distant days of impersonating logs and persecuting people on murky nights. *Is that Camp Meg?* A voice replied promptly, *I am she,* and we ran in terror. Of course it may easily have been nothing more than the wind in the trees, that soughing into which so many voices have been read over so many aeons, transmuted by our twinlike brains into the plausible reply of an ancient gypsy, for MacMarshall and I were close in a way that, for all I know, is gradually becoming extinct.

It was to the future we were looking now as we laid out the beer and cheap wine on Camp Meg's tombstone. MacMarshall spread out the map while I opened the cans with a knife. A Pale Ale and Tawny Port cocktail. This is how you drink it: open the can all the way round and discard the lid; swallow half of your beer and top up the remainder with Tawny Port; cover with one hand and shake with the other.

Solemn, we surveyed the map paying particular attention to France. After London Paris was to be a major stopping-off point.

"The Bastille."

"It's been pulled down now."

"I reckon," he said reflectively, "that we'll be famous pretty soon once we get there. The French are old-fashioned about music, there'll be nobody like us in Paris."

We pointed in turn at places on the map, tracing possible itineraries, exchanging scraps of knowledge. Did you know that you need special vouchers to hitchhike in Poland? In the north of Norway the sun goes down for ten minutes and rises again. You can take a ship hundreds of miles down the Danube. In Spain they put you in jail for nothing at all, if they don't like the look of you. Do you know that song *Port of Amsterdam*? We'll go there.

There were few places we did not intend to visit, even the unpronounceable ones in Hungary and Rumania which Johnnie the Pole had assured us we would never see in his lifetime. No gate was closed to entertainers of our stature—it was only a matter of patience. The farther we travelled the greater our fame would become. There was no plan to remain poor strolling minstrels.

"Happy birthday," he wished himself, draining his cocktail; "I enjoyed that something *powerful*. Let's fold up the map and take a walk—I'm getting itchy feet."

We trespassed through the grounds of Newbattle Abbey and headed back towards the river, MacMarshall drunk and singing. I carried my cocktail with me, taking it easy. He put an arm around me and fell into a forced march.

> *"Over the mountain*
> *Over the Main*
> *To Gibraltar*
> *Through France and Spain . . ."*

"Where exactly," he interrupted himself, "is High Barbary?"
"Africa. But it's called something else now."
"Feel stupid singing these old songs.

> *A feather in your hat*
> *And your kilt abune your knee . . ."*

"Your dad said we should wear kilts. Sing stuff like that and make a fortune."

> *"Sailing down*
> *Along the coast*
> *Of High Barbaree!*

"You know, I look around this place . . . The people . . . What they're up to . . . I'm completely ashamed of being Scottish. I wish we'd brought the guitar.

> *O I loved a lass*
> *And I loved her sae weel*
> *But——"*

"Are you seeing Jennifer before we leave?"
"I suppose."
"Tell her we'll send money so that she and Shona can come and meet us somewhere, for a holiday. Say Athens or something like that."
"Good idea."

Our women had let us down badly, having neither interest nor faith in our musical career, agreeing with our parents that it was a fine pastime but not something to be taken seriously. Consequently we had begun to phase them out of our lives, taking every opportunity to be unfaithful behind their backs. Mac-Marshall took up his song again, the only Scottish folksong in our repertoire.

> *The men o' the forest*
> *They ask it o' me:*
> *How many strawberries*
> *Grow in the salt sea?*
> *And I answer them*
> *Wi' a tear in my e'e:*
> *How many ships*
> *Sail in the forest?*

Looking back over our shoulders we saw the *Welcome to Scotland* sign recede, as before us the *Welcome to England* sign drew near.

"You're in no man's land now," the driver shouted above the grind of his clapped-out lorry.

The first thing we noticed was that the police wore a different style of helmet. There was great excitement between us about being in another country, being out of our own. It had only taken three hours.

"Personally, myself," the driver volunteered, "I would sooner spend an evening with toothache than with an Englishman."

Out of gratitude and the politeness of the road, we laughed.

At dusk eight hours later we were coming into London, the whole journey done in three rides. We asked to be dropped off at Piccadilly Circus. The custom among the young was to sit beneath the Eros statue, talking, drinking from bottles, smoking, moving from group to group introducing themselves to one another, people of all colours and nationalities. We were surprised to see someone strumming a guitar, and our own attracted passing attention when MacMarshall, already fully at home in the West End of London, slipped it from the case and began to play. His singing soon got us noticed.

> *I am a travelling man*
> *I live in a hurry*
> *I leave in a hurry. . . .*

A young man sat down beside us, watching MacMarshall's fingers galloping over the strings. He nodded appreciatively and at the end of the song paid his respects and asked if he might have a cigarette. In turn we asked for directions to the Dover road. These he supplied with laudable precision and we gave him, in response to a request, the price of a cup of tea. Have some more cigarettes, we urged, exhilarated to be out in the world meeting people we could really talk to who saw us for what we were.

As it was a fine night we thought we'd walk to the Dover road rather than take the bus recommended by the man in Piccadilly Circus. Our concept of a big city was uninformed to say the least, and we spent three hours tramping through the bleakest streets imaginable to romantic youth before picking up a lift to Dover Marine where we bought one-way tickets to Dunkirk.

Hitchhiking was, still is and always shall be, hard work in France. We slept by the roadside two nights on the trot, stranded in that uninteresting countryside between Paris and the Normandy coast. For the first time in our lives we went twenty-four hours without food or drink, not a house to be seen where we might have begged a glass of water. Cars zipped by at top speed, often swerving to indicate a desire to run us down, and usually throwing us a smile and a wave—Oh look at the nice hitchhikers!—or a gesture of intense hatred. "No wonder the English despise them," MacMarshall noted. On the morning of the second day, while we lay half asleep on the grass verge, an old Frenchman pulled up and offered us a ride to Paris.

The first night in Paris, spent on benches in the street, Blvd. Kellermann in the Treizième, was also the night Marcel Mac-Marshall discovered the true meaning of all life and made it known to me. Laying aside his litre of rouge he stretched the length of the bench and patted a full stomach.

"This is it," he said by way of prelude. "You've just got to make yourself happy. The trouble is that nobody seems to know how to do it. I do though. And the main reason I'm happy is because I don't give a shit . . . about *anything*. For example, if a gendarme took his gun and shot me dead right now—say for sleeping on this bench—it wouldn't bother me one deek. In fact the prospect of it actually cheers me up. There's nobody as happy as me. You can't get any happier. And do you know what it is? I accept death. Not that there's any option, true, but you'd be surprised. My mother was always talking about dying—you'd think it was the worst thing that could happen.

> *And always remember the longer you live*
> *The sooner you bloody well die.*

Good song that. *Do you understand that song?"*

"Of course I do."

"In that case you accept death the same as me. You just don't realise it yet. It's amazing, isn't it, that the wine's so cheap here."

Another amazing thing was finding cafés open at six in the morning. We were up and off the benches at dawn when the old men with moustaches started sluicing the streets and the sewage stenches turned the stomach until you stopped noticing them.

We ordered coffee and brioches at the zinc counter, and when a little man ran in and downed a glass of spirits with his breakfast coffee we made signs to the waiter that we wished to do the same. To all appearances this was a friendly café; MacMarshall was in favour of offering our services as entertainers. We must do it without delay, it could mean an engagement for tonight.

MacMarshall's knowledge of the language was limited to an extent that compelled him on occasion to order beer, packets of cigarettes, loaves, in twos because he couldn't say *one*, so it devolved on me to conduct the business side of our foreign affairs. Since making our decision to leave home I had paid special attention to my French teacher but not to the strong Glasgow accent in which she butchered her subject: a whole generation from an area of thirty square miles grew up believing they had learned a foreign language.

We rehearsed what to say, agreeing on *Bonjour patron nous voulons chanter dans votre café*. I had to repeat it two or three times, but persistence and the visual aid of the guitar which MacMarshall held up behind me as I spoke, won through and we were understood perfectly. The patron relayed the information to his four customers. An air of levity, as if we weren't being taken seriously, was dispelled when the patron, strumming a make-believe guitar and pointing at us, got it across that we should sing a song right away.

We were used to these spontaneous auditions and had a special song, *The Hermit*, whose vocal harmonies and earcatching arpeggios were calculated to seduce a sceptical interviewing audience. Two glasses of wine were on the table before the customers' scanty applause had subsided. Immediate success! There

[75]

remained only the question of wages, what time we should report for duty, other formalities.

This time the patron had no idea what we were getting at; and it took us half an hour to admit that we were unwanted here in our professional capacity. The café didn't even stay open in the evening and he laughed up his sleeve (some days later when we began to get desperate) at the suggestion that we play to his lunchtime crowd. The patron would always listen to a few songs when we turned up for breakfast, and he always set up some wine, but his attitude seemed to be that we were engaged in some exuberant prank, mild participation in which gave him a certain amount of satisfaction.

One crisp afternoon by the Seine, Pont Neuf let's say, a singular young man wearing a silver top hat, white leather jacket and yellow trousers approached us in a manner both outlandish and charming: there were still a few yards between him and us when he suddenly began to tap dance, clicking his heels in the air from side to side, mastering well-balanced spins and arabesques, his hands clasped behind his back like the early rollerskaters.

MacMarshall had been drinking cold beer all morning on account of an unslakeable thirst and he had seldom been so drunk. Laying aside the flagon of bière blonde he got to his feet and fell in behind the bizarre figure, faithfully reproducing his clacks and ricochets, deadpan expression, hands behind back. I knew nothing of MacMarshall's skill at tap dancing; he must have learned it in secret.

Passersby began to take interest in the kangaroolike pair whose serious faces contrasted brusquely with their splayfooted skips and paramilitary ambulations. I considered the likelihood of MacMarshall having met previously with this character and rehearsed the whole thing for my delectation, but this was out of the question for he hadn't been out of my sight for more than five minutes since we left our native country. Onlookers got perplexed, fed up, and moved on as replacements arrived. Then

the pas de deux came to an abrupt finale at MacMarshall's failure to execute the splits. The two shook hands and MacMarshall
called me over to "interpret."

Jean-Luc was an entertainer by trade and, as far as I could
make out, an utter lunatic by vocation. When I shook his hand
he refused to release the grip and continued talking for a minute
or two, giving me to understand by means of mime that our
hands had been welded together by some extraterrestrial force.
He got it into his head that MacMarshall and I were Japanese, a
delusion he conveyed to us by sticking out his front teeth, slant-
ing his eyes and pointing maniacally at our faces. That we were
Japanese was unexampled as a piece of comic information: he let
this be known by clapping his hands like castanets, protruding
his tongue, clicking his heels and farting loudly at will.

On accepting the offer of a swig from our bottle Jean-Luc dug
into his yellow waistcoat, produced a plastic spoon and poured
himself spoonfuls of beer which he gargled prior to swallowing.
He indicated a wish to whisper something to me and when I
came close enough he bit my ear. All the same, the upshot of
this chance meeting was an engagement to audition for work in
a nightclub. Jean-Luc's friend had a club near Porte D'Ivry—
they badly needed performers. He had done his own act there a
few times, the tap dancing. There would be money in it for us,
not much of course, but was it ever much? We were all for
doing it right away, that very night, so we spent the rest of the
afternoon, at Jean-Luc's behest, drinking the foul Grand Pastis
de Marseilles and discussing the vagaries of our professions.
Marseilles MacMarshall he was called that day until it soured.

The place looked small for a nightclub. We had hoped for a
little grandeur, and Jean-Luc had led us to believe that the club
was a favourite haunt of the elect, but these little clubs often
were deceptive. It was done that way to confound the police and
the wrong sort of customer. This place had evidently taken
exclusiveness to great lengths for there wasn't as much as a sign
outside, just the number 59bis.

Jean-Luc, there was no sign of him either, and the bastard

had gone off that afternoon omitting to leave his share of the bill. He was probably waiting inside. They were his friends; he had got fed up hanging about when he saw that we were going to be late.

In we went after grooming ourselves and each other in a shop window. No reception desk. We pushed open a second door—babble of talking and drinking. A third door led into a dirty little bar where a hundred or more men and women were packed together. In a corner was a miniature stage, bare and sterile. It was a difficult passage through the crowd, made worse by the bulk of the guitar and worse still by the fact that we were the only white people in the midst of a throng of obvious foreigners, probably Algerians or Moroccans. "We'd better be good," MacMarshall said to me, "or we'll get our throats cut here."

"Jean-Luc," I addressed the barman, making gestures to signify Top Hat and Tap Dancing.

"Nous voulons chanter!" MacMarshall roared over my shoulder, knowing that phrase well by now.

"Chanter? Vous voulez chanter? Oui, bon . . ."

"Ça va? Do you mean it? Maintenant?"

"Oui," the Gallic shrug, "ça va. Allez-y . . ."

We got up on the stage and the cacophony dwindled.

"*Crystal Ball Rag,*" MacMarshall said in my ear as I tuned the guitar.

It wasn't what we'd planned to start off on but it was a raucous song with plenty of melody and MacMarshall did well to suggest it. We gave it an amount of heart, the audience took heed, and after the first verse we became our confident selves, MacMarshall gesticulating away and stamping his foot, me making the most rudimentary guitar work appear complicated.

No one applauded.

After the second song someone threw a lighted cigarette at us, then an empty cigarette packet. Other members of the audience followed suit. I noticed that MacMarshall's hands were trembling, I took a long time to retune the guitar, wondering if

I was going to be using it as a blunt instrument. Wouldn't be the first time, I mused, recalling horripilating venues in the Port of Leith . . . your balls always tighten when there's a threat of violence . . . your mind goes blank and you feel like running away . . . your bowels go loose when you know you're the victim.

I struck up a jaunty guitar tune, seized by a fit of do-or-die inspiration. MacMarshall looked disoriented: what song's this? He prided himself on knowing the instrumental introductions to all our songs, but this was a piece he'd never heard before, something I'd learned on my own purely for fun, knowing it was inimical to our repertoire. It was a tune from the nineteen twenties.

"*Tap dance!*" I urged him. "Do that tap dance!"

Two fat men shouted at us, another threw an empty glass. I kept playing and tried to smile as if they'd been throwing bouquets.

"*Tap dance!* For Christ's sake Marce, the fucking tap dance . . ."

MacMarshall, virtually in tears, did a few limbering-up exercises and glided into a tap dancing routine, tortured and stiff, nothing like the one with Jean-Luc but still a better than average performance.

The audience response was immediate. They laughed their heads off and threw more cigarette packets. These were followed by the contents of ashtrays, corks, glasses, sandwiches. A dwarfish man leapt onto the stage and attempted a pathetic emulation of MacMarshall's dancing at which the crowd exploded in appreciation, applauding him vigorously. They didn't seem to notice us leaving the stage, and they certainly didn't notice our profound self-disgust.

We were deported from France, Marcel MacMarshall and I, when the police nailed us for busking in the streets. In the days before the demise we had tried repeatedly to leave Paris, but every evening found us back in our repulsive hotel which was cheaper than the dirtiest youth hostel.

Our money didn't last a month, and had we owned an engagement book it would have remained blank. We sang in cafés and bars but received no hard cash in return—a spot of food, but more likely drink, was the most we came to expect. So against our will we took to the street in imitation of a blind violinist we'd seen during the endless walks up and down the great boulevards and seedy back streets.

It soon transpired that the quickest way to make money was to have one of us performing while the other took the humiliating role of bottler, rattling the hat under their noses, always merry and bright. "You must realise," MacMarshall explained in anger when I refused to do another bottling stint, "you must realise that we are beggars, we're just respectable beggars: *these cunts don't give a shit about music.* We've got to embarrass them into coughing up."

The reactions of the police were apparently arbitrary. Pack up and move, a gendarme would tell us when only half an hour ago a colleague of his had tossed us a couple of francs. Then we were picked up one morning with less than a couple of francs between us. We were taken to a large building where they dumped us in a room for several hours. When they came back it had all been settled. We were minors, maybe even escaped delinquents.

Marcel had an old great-aunt whom he hated but who lived in London, and arrangements were made for us to sleep in her spare room. We would redecorate her house if she would promise to say nothing to our parents. Within twenty-four hours of setting foot in Victoria station we had secured employment as factory hands. After a week's work we repaid our repatriation fee from our wages, which included piecework bonus and good attendance allowance. We then resigned our positions.

A week's notice was required when you resigned from the factory, but during this week MacMarshall's great-aunt suffered a heart attack while the three of us were attempting the *Daily Telegraph* crossword. We rushed her off in an ambulance but she died on the way to hospital. Up all night talking about death, we didn't feel like going to the factory in the morning so I telephoned our chargehand. We were severely penalised, losing both the attendance allowance and accumulated bonus earnings.

Later in the day a woman of thirty or so turned up claiming to be the niece of MacMarshall's great-aunt. We were against the idea but the woman, Margaret, was determined to move into our house, sort everything out and arrange the funeral. No one had consulted us so our indignation was momentarily heartfelt, but it was true that the phone had been ringing all day and people we didn't know wanted information we could not supply, so this Margaret moved in and took control.

Like the great-aunt, Margaret spoke a language that was new to us: *better class of person; not quite proper; it's time for elevenses chaps!* The very concept of elevenses was new to us, to say nothing of the word itself, but all the same she took to us in a big way, listened intently to our plans and offered sensible advice.

"I suppose you fellows don't drink," she said in the evening after she'd cooked us a meal.

"Now and again."

"Well, let's just have a teeny one," she said in the voice of a mischievous child, bringing out the great-aunt's brandy which we had been diluting nightly for over a week. "Soda, chaps?"

"Why not?"

"What an unusual idea," MacMarshall said, eagerly reaching for his glass.

Margaret had two children and a husband who was in the air force. She played the piano much better than I and she also liked to sing, although she seldom had the time nowadays. She was a tall woman, about the same height as MacMarshall, with a short mature hairstyle, small breasts and huge hips. In repose her goofy teeth stuck over her lower lip.

She said we ought to try to get work in London pubs. We could try the George and Dragon round the corner where the manager, Mr. Ben Bone, was a personal friend of hers. We could go there now and ask him. This suggestion swept off the webs of failure and death which had cramped our entrepreneurial style since the return from France.

From the way he patted her bottom and insisted on paying for everything, it was patent that Ben Bone would be sympathetic to any proposals made by Margaret. They stood talking conspiratorially while we carried the drinks to a table.

"Illicit intercourse?"

"Definitely. They must think we're kids."

"We'll make sure she asks about an engagement."

When they joined us Ben Bone said he was determined to give us a break, without even hearing us play, purely on the recommendation of Margaret whom he knew to have excellent taste. We didn't mention that she hadn't heard us either. But first he would have to clear it with his employers, the brewery. When, after a few beers and much teasing about our incapacity to hold strong drink, we made our excuses to leave the couple to their sins, Margaret strangely insisted on walking home with us. Ben Bone didn't think that was necessary—we knew the way home didn't we?—but she was adamant. Obviously she was in the process of giving him the heave.

Back home, brandy on the table, Margaret made disparaging remarks about Ben Bone, asked us what we thought of him and flopped down on the couch where I was tuning the guitar.

"He seems an okay guy," MacMarshall said, perhaps with an eye to a future reconciliation between Ben and Margaret, and certainly unwilling to put our engagements in jeopardy.

"Old fool," she laughed, pouring three glasses.

I went on tuning. With my ear close to the instrument and my eyes closed I didn't notice that she was meddling with the tuning pegs, surreptitiously raising and lowering the strings. When I caught her at it—a serious offence this—she laughed out loud, indecorously I thought, judging from her normal behaviour. I glowered at her. Then she suddenly tickled my ribs and my shock was such that I couldn't restrain my laughter. MacMarshall accused her of drunkenness. She giggled and called us silly boys, chucking him under the chin and saying what a handsome little chap he was.

Chap! MacMarshall surprised everyone by grabbing her round the waist and tickling her till she tumbled off the couch, squealing laughter, legs kicking, skirt all over the place.

"Give me a hand, she's a public menace."

"Don't you dare!" she screamed, the scream converting to hysterical laughter.

It was probably an accident but as I went for her arm she laid hold of my balls, said *Ooops,* but didn't let go.

And that, grosso modo, is how Marcel MacMarshall and I ended up eye to eye, kneeling mothernaked on his dead aunt's bed with Margaret spread out between us.

Troilism, he kept chuckling under his breath throughout the next morning, *Troilism* . . . He'd found the word in a newspaper in-depth report.

The next evening followed a similar programme, drinking and fucking, Margaret proposing the former and we making ready for the latter. All day she had kept us at a distance, gone out without a goodbye, returned with the kind of hello you expected from your sister. But after a couple of drinks her demeanour underwent radical alteration. She had us separately this time, setting up camp in the bedroom and receiving us in rotation.

This young man's paradise had us bored by the day of the funeral. Having buried great-auntie we borrowed money from Margaret and rented a room in the East End, miles away, promising to invite her round for a "meal" as soon as we were settled in.

A letter arrived at our new home from Josh, friend and fellow musician, who at seventeen had landed a respectable job in London and would be arriving from Scotland in his new company car.

He decided on arrival that he was going to be our manager. We were wasting our time, in his opinion, playing around in small clubs and bars and getting little money for our efforts: that sort of apprenticeship was a thing of the past. Nowadays one went straight to the big record companies and agents, Josh said, making a firm impression on us with his airy confidence in himself and in our abilities.

We were proud of being able to live solely off our musical earnings, even when it meant going hungry, but Josh was right, it was time to strike before we got too old for the game. Josh cancelled all but our bread and butter engagements and forbade us to play in the underground stations during the day, even though it was guaranteed cash, the London street music scene being fairly stable with an average hourly rate that rarely varied.

Instructing us to rely on himself for money, Josh hired a recording studio and began rehearsing us for our debut into show business proper, making us run through every song until the rough edges had been transformed into charming idiosyncracy. On the morning of the recording day he took us out to breakfast, dressed in the expensive blue suit, shirt and tie which he liked to wear when he was representing us, and smoking cheroots incessantly.

The first session was an unmitigated calamity. We sounded exactly like parakeets, the instruments like musical pots and pans. The studio people robbed us hand over fist with impunity—we were too overcome by failure to quibble about money—and Josh got into debt over it: alone among us he retained a spirited outlook, confident too that his bank would advance an overdraft on the strength of his secure position in the oil company. "Look at it this way," he said as we replayed the master tape, squirming at the incompetence, grateful that none but ourselves possessed a copy of it: "From this point on you can only improve."

"I made a list," MacMarshall told me, "of all the fucking *books* I've read since we came back to London. I do fuck-all except sit here and read. I'm becoming so intelligent I'm getting dissatisfied with my life. Listen to this: *The Jungle; All Neat in Black Stockings; The Dream of a Ridiculous Man; In Praise of Older Women; The Tight White Collar; British Churches; Swiss Family Robinson; All Quiet on the Western Front* . . . I just sit on my arse *reading*! And listen to that old harpy next door."

The harpy was of uncertain nationality, spoke a language I have never heard before or since and appeared to know no English. During the day she was silent, maybe she slept, but at night you couldn't leave the room without her making it known that she was aware of your movements. In the squalor of the unlit hallway you saw the glint of her eyes as she poked her head out the door to scan you, but you never saw her face.

The landlord said she was very old and had lived in the house for decades; she'd been a sitting tenant when he'd bought the place, always posted her rent rather than hand it over in person.

Late at night if one of us pissed in the wash basin to avoid trekking to the lavatory on the floor above, and turned on the noisy plumbing to flush the basin, she screamed at full voice, unintelligibly, but you felt it was sheer torment rather than anger; as if she had once suffered hellish torture involving a running tap. She'd bang on the walls, wailing, keening till we turned the water off. The first time it happened we ran naked to her door in the middle of the night assuming that she was being murdered; she gibbered and screamed as we banged her door but refused to open it. Then as we walked away we heard the door opening, but when we turned around it had been closed again. Eventually we learned to piss in the basin without flushing it at night.

She'd been dead for forty-eight hours when Marcel and I persuaded a policeman to break down her door. It wasn't as if there was a smell—we merely sensed her absence one night and tested her by turning the tap on gently. The pipes rattled in the walls, the only sound to be heard.

But that all took place much later. The sad harpy was yet in the land of the living and MacMarshall often felt her eyes through the thin wall that separated his bed from hers, felt her overlooking him while he read his books.

". . . *The Sign of Four*," he went on, "*Knowledge and Wonder; She Likes It Rough; The Great Gatsby; The Constant Nymph; Living with the Bears,* both volumes of that; *Poetry for the Young:*

> *So remember this my daughter:*
> *When all is done and said,*
> *You can take a horse to water*
> *But a pencil must be lead."*

The sound of muffled sobbing woke me in the middle of the night.

"Marce? What's the matter?"

It was dark, his crying frightened me.

"Marce, what is it—are you dreaming?"

"No."

His sobbing got interspersed with curses.

"You might as well tell me what's up."

"Oh, fuck knows. Listen David. We have to admit. We are failures. I've just about had it—when did we last have a decent meal?"

"Josh's. Sunday week."

"See! You remember the exact time. *Ten* days ago. We are beggars. I wanted to better myself, no, really, I did. But now . . . I could easily go mad, I know it, I could. I don't want to be a beggar."

I heard him sniffing, drying his eyes, calling himself names. There was no way of contradicting what he had said. The faith in ourselves which put an unusual vitality into our performances had dissipated, the straight road that had lain before us for so many years was developing turns and inclines, always uphill and endless.

"Is there any tobacco?"

"Yes, here. Why don't you turn the light on."

He was trying to smile but without much conviction. I knew too, from letters he'd been writing and receiving, that he was back in contact with Jennifer Raeburn and was missing her to the extent of idealizing her in conversation with me and speaking of settling down with her when his rambling days were through.

"We'll see what happens," I said, "when we record the Paris songs."

Josh, optimistic as ever, had shelled out more cash and arranged another studio session. This time, at Josh's instigation, always following his instructions and bright ideas, we recorded the songs in total darkness, seeing nothing but the green light that told us when to begin.

When the lights came on the first thing we saw was our manager, tie undone, beer in hand, fist raised victoriously, pacing back and forth in the glass-walled control room.

"Perfection," he said, just the one word.

And MacMarshall and I knew too when we had done our best: something would happen to us in midflight and we'd move together towards a plane on which voices and instruments became wholly attuned, no strain, in a supreme balance; a slight glance or movement, perceptible even in pitch darkness, would convey half a dozen precise instructions about what was going to happen next.

The best of the four songs was one of MacMarshall's, *Moonbeam* it was called, so good that even our great vanity didn't save us from incredulity. When you looked at the lyrics on paper, as I was then doing, they appeared banal,

> *The windows all black and green*
> *The people sleep tight*
> *Let's throw our clothes on the ground*
> *Let's stay here the night*

but when you heard them in the song they made you shiver.

Every agent who heard the tape was interested in doing business with us and our just deserts came scudding in from all quarters. No money right away, but infinite permutations of possibilities, all of them guaranteeing to put Marcel Mac-Marshall and me at the top of the world's hit parades. This we found quite offensive; it went hand in hand with treating us like puppets. We wanted to be filthy rich, true, but we were determined to avoid any further humiliation in our career.

From the start we persecuted the agents, ridiculed their bank account philosophy and their poverty of aesthetic, adopted an attitude of strict inflexibility. Daily we were introduced to smartly dressed men in their thirties, bejewelled creatures who drove limousines and smoked cigarettes such as you never saw in a tobacconist's. Weekly we were sent telegrams at our sordid little room inviting us to come and meet so and so from California, from Germany, come and hear some trite song they wanted us to immortalize.

We were forced to tell them that we didn't want anybody's trashy ditties. What did they mean by saying our own stuff was too good for the current market? We were singers, musicians, artistes. All we wanted was to issue an innovative collection of songs and let the money follow gradually. We had no interest in the hit parade; it was a confidence trick reeking of cheap talent and moronic sensibility. Now and then a good song crept in—we wouldn't object to that—but how could these people ask us to put our hearts into singing limericks about unrequited love?

So after many afternoons spent in glamourous offices in Mayfair sulking in our rags on long leather couches, we finally parted company with the last mystified agent. Josh, understandably, had grown progressively enraged: if only we would allow these people to sell us on the strength of one bad song, he reasoned, we would make our fortunes and then be free to do as we pleased. But the closer we came to financial success the more pugnacious we became in our intransigence. Josh shook his head several times a day, but he was well equipped to see the funny side of the story.

That was the week I came home to find MacMarshall packing the bag. We hadn't talked much of recent events.

"I'm going back to Scotland for a while," he said with a touch of shame in his voice. "You don't mind if I take the bag, do you?"

"Is it Jennifer?" I asked after the silence.

"Don't call her a bag!"

We laughed inanely.

"What about the music?"

"Write to me if anything good comes up."

"I will."

I carried his bag to the station. We didn't speak on the way.

"Right then."

"Right," he said taking the bag. "I'll fuck off now."

Un Fiore Di Campo

"Garibaldi is a state of mind."

Bologna novembre '77.

IT COULD REALLY BE MARVELLOUS so i'll wait you.

Oh yes!

I wish to see you walking in my streets . . .

Wonderfull!

I accept! I don't leave anything to say except try to come here for Christmas holiday.

I could not understand you, sure, I'm keep singing. In a chorus now (music for camera) you'll listen if you'll come as probably as we'll have a concert in that time.

Now it is cold here to snowing, but everything is warmer here, the weather, the people, the tastes, the touchings. And first of all we've got better stoves!!

I would really hope that you come. Are you convict? Listen then Davide, answer me quickly.

After you can tell me a day and *an hour* (during that day) and phone me at this day and at that hour and you shall tell me when you will. leave, and the time too, so I must be sure to remain in Bologna.

For sleep there are no problems.

My telephone is in the envelope and for call in this city you must dial alot of numbers, I don't remember but you can let you know them.

So I'm gonna sleep wishing you'll come on a fine journey. It's snowing Davide!! Good Night e sogni d'oro. Buona Notte. . . .

It is only four o'clock p.m. and already it is dark. My head is heavy: I've got a tempesture. This is doubtlessly winter. Dear Davide (this should be at the beginning of my letter!) listen, the best day I can imagine for your arrival in my city is on the twenty-third of decembre, cause I'll take two weeks from studies and I shall rest far away from the home of my parents and stay always with you.

But telephone to me on the twenty-first at lunch-time and tell
me when, more or less, is you arrival.
It's cold outside like never was before.
I'm waiting some friends.
But hurry up!
Wake you up
It's time for leaving
It's time for coming
The winter is grey
But if you stay
A little bit here
A little bit near
dear
My mind is so clear
I want see you sincere!!!

Now it is Christmas Eve. I don't know . . . I hope you are
well. I was waiting you yesterday so probably you won't come
and I am a bit unhappy. I hope there is nothing bad. Buon
Natale! (Happy Christmas, sorry if you can translate this . . .)
I'm gonna sing tonight.
I had Italian song I did want to sing for you.
I thought alot in these two days . . . now I am terrible, I will
smoke one cigarette.
If you want write me Davide, I was seriously saying I am happy
to see you and exchange letters. A friend came in and I'll keep
writing this letter still.
I'm actually writing nothing.
I'd like to know why you didn't come.
Better: I *want* to know it.
I'm getting bored myself. Shitt!!
I hope you are well. I hope you are well with me too.
I'm gonna get so stoned tonight I'll try to seem happy. So I say
much love. Sorry-me Davide, I want only to send my good feel-
ings.

Clorinda

Her letters had a subtle catalytic effect on me. During her months on the run in England we'd talked on very few occasions; her English was bad, my Italian primeval, her lover jealous. But when we sang and played music together Clorinda and I discovered each other right away and a mute sort of friendship began to grow.

Then she decided that she'd had enough of living with Randaggio, ten years her senior and, as I say, a fairly jealous guardian of his prodigy, and she started to think about going back to resume her education in Italy. Randaggio alternated between encouraging her to leave and trying to dissuade her. "I love her," he told me, "and she loves me. So why is living together so intolerable?" In the end he too, an American whose holiday in Europe had turned into a two-year stay, began making plans to return to his own country.

They were both friendly towards me and had spent evenings at my flat, together and separately, relating the story of their good life gone bad. He put it all down to sexual troubles caused by their age difference and her Italian Catholic upbringing, while she confided shyly to me that "good bed" was almost all that remained between them. He considered her too young to understand the depth of his feelings for her, she spoke of him as "extremely immaturity." It seemed not to be enough that they both *wanted* to part and felt the need for it: in the curious way of men and women in love they were determined to arrive first at a sensible reason for carrying it through, a reason founded upon the assumption that the other was chiefly at fault.

Randaggio was a puppeteer by trade. Clorinda, and sometimes Clorinda and I, supplied the musical accompaniment to his shows. Face intelligently expressionless, she sits in full view of the audience, playing her guitar and singing an ad hoc repertoire of silly songs and tongue-in-cheek tearjerkers. Randaggio bungles onto the stage with his prize puppet, the Universal Hobo: *"Hi kids!"* in the squawk quality of voice that amuses so many children. The puppet trots and lopes, falls on its face and recoils in a backspring, upstages both Randaggio and Clorinda; but you notice in her a facility for conjuring sudden beauty out of an array of apparently unrelated features when an extempore change in the programme makes her frown, smile, laugh aloud. *"Hi kids!"* in exaggerated Brooklynese, then *"Ciao tutti!"* over his shoulder to Clorinda. "Now lissen kids . . . ahem . . . I mean for Chrissakes ya gotta lissen and shut y' lousy little traps for a change. . . . Ahem! Ya gotta lend me y' little ears y'knowhadamean, 'cause I got somethin' tatellya kids . . . I got somethin' tatellya about *puppets!* Thank you, thank you. Now: the *foist* thing ya gotta know about puppets is what I'm tellinya here: *Puppets,* y' understand, *are-not-real-people.* Now look at me. Pretty, huh? See? *I* am a real person. But *this,"* the Universal Hobo begins to strut and preen himself, "this here is a *puppet.* . . . Take that ya bum!" he hollers, booting the sad dishevelled puppet around the stage and out into the audience, "take that ya lazy bastid!" He was an unparalleled success with the children.

Randaggio had already left for New York when Clorinda came to say goodbye to me on her last evening in London. I had arranged for her to go to Amsterdam to the home of my friend Sol Bartok. Sol had told me in a letter that he intended driving to Rome to meet a man whom he believed to be a saint and he had agreed—few would have refused—to take Clorinda as far as Bologna.

I was in the middle of repainting my kitchen when she arrived so she hunched down in a corner of the evacuated room, fur coat and black bandana giving her the appearance of a ruffled crow against the pristine whitewash, and she talked to me as I worked. It amused me how comfortable she always seemed to be in the squalor of my decrepit flat—a man of my years ought long since to have established himself—but at sixteen she was already a veteran of North London squatting life and an authority on basic building skills and house maintenance, social security offices, jumblesales, claimants' unions, community projects, shared kitchens and being trapped with one's lover in a depressing bedsit. She was looking forward to going home.

Our conversation turned naturally to Randaggio, whose absence as lover, friend and interpreter was nervously felt by both of us. "I have loved him," she said, "yust for buy to me this coat in London." I assumed her to mean that it was kind of Randaggio to want her to be warm, but I could never quite be sure, for whenever I spoke she misunderstood me, doubly misunderstanding my efforts at clarification, with the result that I left most of the talking to her. Given freedom to improvise, her English improved appreciably, but if you interrupted with a question or asked her to elucidate a point she reverted to stammered slang and irreconcilable pronouns.

When conversation ran out she produced a small piece of opium, explaining that she didn't want to risk carrying it through Customs. She cut it in two with the breadknife and we ate it with a cup of coffee. In the ensuing euphoria I finished painting my kitchen, had a bath and agreed to her proposal that she cut my hair. Thus spruced up and in high fettle I took her for a final walk through the neighborhood, rounding it off with a visit to my friend Cruikshank, Cruikshank the writer, for whom Clorinda had expressed a strong liking and admiration. Cruikshank was a likeable but enigmatic character to whom I had been introduced several years ago by Conrad Winchester. Conrad had recently engineered Cruikshank's escape from a sinister therapeutic community in which he had been forced to remain against his will; I had found him a room in a house nearby and he was now settling down to write the story of his bizarre experiences.

We were well received at Cruikshank's and he and Clorinda embarked without preamble on a mutually demanding discussion about Love and Evil while I read a chapter of his current novel which appeared to be dealing with just those concepts. Later in the evening Cruikshank presented her with a suitcase, "You can't check in your luggage in cardboard bloody boxes," and on the stroke of nine, punctilious of habit, he invited us to

a winehouse where we were to get "horrendously pissed."
Clorinda left the following morning and I heard nothing from
her for weeks.

Hearing one of her songs on the radio prompted me to send a
postcard and we began writing regularly to each other. A letter
in the morning from Clorinda, my name and address misspelt
and the envelope black with last minute postscripts, would set
me up for the rest of the day, bring out the best in me, often at
the expense of bringing out the worst as well. I might be
rereading her words while walking against a headwind up the
Holloway Road, talking to myself, and I might sing out to a
fascinated pedestrian,

> *Will you* miss *me*
> *Miss me* miss *me*
> *Will you wi . . . . . . ll you?*
> *When I am gone.*

Or her phrases, particularly the incomprehensible ones,
might spring into my head and impel me to act in a manner
inimical to my true character. "Davide I am poet-like so you do
one like surmise—*Shall you????*" What had she meant by this?
While pondering the question, laughing aloud more likely than
not, I stopped at the comical shop called *Raymond's Raiment*,
new and secondhand ware, observing that the proprietor had altered his unimaginative window display. There was a letter
stuck to the glass from the inside, the top part bent over to conceal the sender's address:

Dear sir,
Two weeks ago I purchased from your shop (Raymond's Raiment)
a new velvet jacket which cost me £8.25. On the first night I
wore it two people came up to me one after the other and offered
me £30.00 cash down if I would part with it, which I didn't of
course. I know a good deal. This is the third jacket I have bought
from you and I will continue to do so. Also two pairs of shoes.
Keep up the good work.

Yrs. trly.
Geo. Wilson.

[98]

The letter was a palpable forgery and would delude no one, but its charm coincided with something in Clorinda to exhilarate me on beyond the cordon of self-consciousness. I walked earnestly into the shop.

"Yes sir, good afternoon. What can I do for you today sir?" such bowing and scraping as one associates with ne'er-do-wells in Dickens.

"Good afternoon. Actually, I don't want to buy anything right at the minute," I told him importantly. "On the contrary, I'd like you to give me something. As a personal favour."

"Sir?" the obsequiousness simmering into quiet rage.

"Yes, I've come about that letter in your window."

"Yes? Ah, yes sir, the velvet jackets. Is it credit facilities you're asking about? That can be arranged. Now, at the moment we have most sizes in stock, most *normal* sizes that is, in a wide selection of shades, midnight blue, maroon, bottle green . . ."

"No, I'm sorry, you don't understand. I've got plenty of jackets, three or four I think, in fact one of my jackets is made of French velvet which is said to be the best. But I don't have to tell you that. No, what I'm after is the address of the man who wrote you that letter in the window."

"Well I can't very well do that sir," he smiled, indulging my lack of savoir faire. "After all," he turned away to rearrange a display of rainbow nylon socks and fluorescent underpants, "after all sir, my customers trust me to respect their privacy."

"Of course! I understand that! But don't you see? It's in your interest as well as mine."

"Tell me sir, you're not from the Board of Trade are you?"

"No," I said intelligently, "I am an anthropologist."

"Yes sir?"

"And what I'd like you to do is give me that customer's address at once. You did say he was a customer, didn't you? Now do you see what I'm getting at?"

"Not altogether sir, I must confess. But really, I have to be getting down to business now so I'll wish you good day." He threw me a devastating smile; the man would have been an ace with the East India Company.

"Please," I said solemnly, "listen to me. Hear me out. I don't wish to appear aggressive."

"Of *course* sir, of *course.*"

"On display in your window you have the work of a first-rate author. I have a natural eye for those things. Now I don't want to let a find like that slip through my fingers, do I?"

He shook his head in assent.

"I must have that man's address."

"Well I'm truly sorry about that sir, because the truth is I've lost the address. Misplaced it."

"I understand. I see. But I'll tell you one thing: I don't give up so easily. I'm going to come back tomorrow and try again."

"Sir, you'd be wasting your time. I'd be glad to help you if only I could."

"Oh come on—what's your price? Twenty-five pounds? Even a man of your integrity, your business acumen, must find it hard to make ends meet all the time. Fifty?"

"I'm sorry sir," he smiled hopelessly, palms upwards, "I'd gladly help . . ."

"All right," I conceded, "I'll leave it for now. But I hope you'll reconsider what we have been discussing."

I hurried out of the shop, turned towards Italy and threw the blame at Clorinda.

Ciao Davide. Sorry-me if I didn't write for so long. I feel terrible, I got so angry with some friends of mine, I really need to kill somebody.

Sometimes I think it not so terrible to know what means hate, cause I can't stand people who talks you always so sweet and in the deepest part of the fucking soul can't stand you.

Davide I feel terrible. I was happy to hear a letter from you.

Randaggio wrote me he's well, he is doing the theatre of marion-etti with his friend Kowalski in New York and he seems to be petty satisfied. He does not like anymore living in NYC and he says he is sad except but he found his art-work which is good and so he will stay there for now.

Yes I could be happy to see you in Dutchland and Svizzera but just this moment I cannot. Maybe I will have some holy-day in Eastertime. I will let you know it.

For two days I'm doing nothing but swearing all the time.

Today the sun is shining but my heart still is covered by snow.

I want to go to London!

Maybe in July I'll come. Will you wait me?

I didn't write to Randaggio from a long time so he told me I must be angry with him. I can't know what bloody he mean in saying this, so I won't probably write to him all the same.

I don't know what the fuck wants people with me.

I'm like I am. People know me.

I'm so bored!!

The only good thing is that I gonna do a concert.

Music still means to me a lot in communicate with people, so I've got another chance.

The amazing, Davide, is that in all those fucking stories I'm happy to be so terrible.

I think my Italy is still too much religious.

I should talk to the people about the "Good Faith."

I think is one of the most disgusting things we created in the world.

GOOD FAITH = ADMIT THE STUPIDITY LIKE AN HONEST ACTITUDE.

Sorry-me, maybe I'm still swearing words.

Bye-bye dearest friend, think of me somewhat, one kiss for every eye!

Write to me and have a good sleep.

I'm burning my energy in hate. BOOOOWUUOOO . . .

I still can like you a lot anyway. I have inscribed Randaggio's address on the other side.

April has come
to the red city
in 1978.

But it is late and cold and also raining too. I just come back from some dreadful place: better, I saw it awful tonight. (I'm still try to find an alibi.)

How are you?

I'm in a strange moon (not so ghastly).

I'm gonna find cigarettes . . . well . . . now I'm right.

I am studying alot now that my exams approach. I'm afraid. I don't know that probably they won't go right. I can always buy a degree.

I would lose an whole year.

Virgilio (to state my case-history) is so bad, if you know his works, but I am feeling good about Catullo who is extremely wonderfull.

There's one problem: I can't stand any kind of teachers, I think they are suspicious people, I don't mean to generalise but it is quite clear when they are in a school that they are teachers. They can't be people and they must say I am good enough for a piece of paper . . . well . . . I don't have other choice.

All the world is an honourable shitt!!

I'd like to live
In the jungle . . .

Do you recall this song written by Randaggio?

But at least here in Bologna when we hate the teachers we can bomb them with molotov. Sandro and Lisa and me have exploded our teacher's car, not the teacher only his machine, but there is one more teacher who might even get killed dead so he'll have to be very careful I think!

Do you know that I am seventeen nowadays?

I'm thinking if I should come back to London it would be a little shock.

I am writing something as a book about my Londonese experience (it's full of abuses!!). I don't know since so many scape-gotas. Ideologies about eating and shitting or paying some nasty guru.

I know the fact that your birthday comes soon, and Randaggio's too.

Happy birthday Davide, I would like to give you a present, I don't know, maybe I find a fotografy—sorry-me my macaroni English, I mean to say a picture of me and a wonderfull place in my little boring city. I saw Marthe and she talked to me about her omoxesuality, she doesn't interest her in anything else now, her big problem is Love.

Anyway I have a good time with her speeding brains.

Apart all these important but always external circumstances, I can survive.

Summer will be near. In the *Hot*. I need some of that sun after this froze winter.

SOLAR REQUIREMENT!!

Buona notte e sogni d'oro *Signor Loto* (which means your new name). I have thought of it. Ciao Loto.

She had invited me to come and spend Christmas with her in Italy but by that time my life had fallen into disrepair and I couldn't afford a holiday. It was true that I had a valuable trade at my fingertips—for several months I had been working in partnership with a mysterious countess who had access to plenty of opportunities in the construction industry—but I had lost my spirit of enterprise and capacity for hard labour; I worked only to cover the cost of my immediate needs. The attractions of manual work, and the rediscovery by many Londoners of the pleasures of a log fire, had impelled Cruikshank to set himself up as a supplier of firewood and he had generously offered me a profitable share in his business, but I could find neither the energy nor the enthusiasm, even for such a worthwhile cause as that. I slept a lot.

Clorinda and I continued to write to each other, the letters lengthening and the envelopes getting fat with photographs, pages torn from books, cassette recordings, newspaper cuttings, song lyrics and our own literary efforts. Stray Italians began turning up on my doorstep bearing letters of introduction, expecting in turn to be introduced to real life in London with free board and lodging thrown in. Having previewed the city through the eyes of Clorinda these unfortunate people were convinced that exceptional things would happen to them in London if they could only manage to hang on long enough. I didn't always feel guilty when I discharged them from my care and my household after the statutory week set down by International Law.

Then in midsummer a remarkable event took place. Cruikshank, who had been enjoying moderate success in the firewood business, decided to join, in a lay capacity, the ranks of a religious order and spend the rest of his days in quiet study and contemplation. It was the day after his twenty-fifth birthday. As a farewell gift to a trusted drinking companion he presented me with a sum of cash which he had deemed superfluous to the needs of the new life he had chosen. I wrote to Clorinda announcing my imminent arrival and received a series of postcards from various places.

Mr. Davide . . . Ciao Loto!
You're welcome.
Do it. xxx.
PS: This is no castle
of mine!

Isole Tremiti
Le mura del Castello
Les murs du chateau
The Castle Walls
Die Schlossmauern

NAPOLI. (*Da vedere: Museo Nazionale, Capodimonte, Palazzo Reale, Castel dell'Ovo ecc.*)
Ciao Scotshman,
Now here I am. Listen me more or less the date of this second coming and I'll be there.
Try seriously this time!

Goodbye, from Rinda. (This is an orible name you select for me. I think I prefer be called Pasta!!)

Arena Po.
1.) My old boyfriend is cursing in his lovely Naples dialect. Today is a marvel and I (in consequence) feel at peace with the world. Yesterday night I got truly drunk (he keep on swearing at me). His belly is gigante under the sun! My cicatrice of which I wrote to you is getting well. My friend says I should have it under the sun

Arena Po.
2.) like he is doing with his enormous pancha (belly). Yesterday I winned a chicken. My old friend winned three chickens. The flies are the worst enemies I've got here,

> *Flies in the buttermilk*
> *Two by two!*

Will you invite me to dance this dreadful TANGO? Sangue caliente .... clo-rinda.

My flight from Heathrow was subject to indefinite delay, and had Cruikshank learned of this he might have sped after me to retrieve what was left of his money, for it was on that morning that he apostatised for the second time. "I can barely comprehend," he wrote me c/o Clorinda, "your passive acceptance of my joining the Brotherhood; but didn't you suspect my mental health re. my alacrity in dispensing funds? It must have been undernourishment and whisky-brain. I have suffered an ordeal. I am broke. Please advise."

I boarded the plane and we got off to a false start after half an hour of taxiing: engine trouble, the captain said, and of course nothing to worry about; but I, who would sooner cross the Valley of the Damned on a kite than the English Channel in a jet, began to get edgy. For me, modern air travel is always an opportunity for uninterrupted contemplation of death. You can read a book or one of the bromide magazines provided by the airline, but when your mind is on death you can read it between every line. If there were only some arrangement with parachutes instead of the lifejackets which the stewardess was at that moment modelling for us, demonstrating how we were to save ourselves in the event of a forced landing in the sea . . . More bromide.

I took to brushing up my Italian, a language I learn mainly through songs.

> C'e un fiore di campo
> che e' nato in miniera
> per soli pochi giorni
> lo stettero a guardar.

Now translate, no need for complete accuracy, just the sense: Flower of the field born in a mine, for only a few days protected . . . lo stettero? . . . It is immoral to sing songs without knowing what you're singing. For years at school I sang *Good King Winston last looked out*. . . .

> Sfiorisci bel fiore
> sfiorisci amore mio.

We were in the air by the time I'd run through my song. The passengers were mostly Italians going home from a package holiday, so hilarity was minimal when the stewardess switched on the wrong recorded message, in English, informing us that we would be landing in Copenhagen in a quarter of an hour. The error was briskly corrected and we unfastened our seatbelts and relaxed—only to be instructed five minutes later to refasten them and extinguish our freshly lit cigarettes. Turbulence, the English captain told us: "Bit of turbulence coming up here." Really he ought to have added *Chaps* or *Old Fellows,* to finish off his sentence.

It was the normal bumpy ride at first, then the plane took a sudden dive, didn't stop diving, and you became unpleasantly aware of the velocity. Six hundred miles an hour.

"Madonna mia!"

Crossing themselves.

"Christ almighty . . ."

"Parco Dio!"

I sat petrified, my bowels dissolving, my mind on instant death, ashamed that to all appearance I was calm and British.

The plane righted itself. The bad weather cleared.

Our stewardess emerged chirruping from her little recess by the exit hatch: lunch was to be served forthwith. The Italian man sitting beside me, a fat business-type whom I'd been surprised to see making the sign of the cross, wanted to know if everything was under control. "Oh si, si," I said discreditably, shocked at the ease with which it came out. "Quite normal." I sounded like a Latin version of our captain, who came on the air shortly after lunch to draw our attention to the coast of France and to apologise, as if he had been personally responsible, for the spot of heavy weather.

Half a day behind schedule I arrived at the home of Clorinda's parents. She materialised at the top of the stairs, slim and stately, wearing an elegant nightdress, no longer the scruffy Rimbaud of London days. The bandage across her forehead, protecting the scar of an outlandish operation, only augmented the assured nobility of her bearing.

"Clorinda."

"I am happy to see you."

It was three o'clock in the morning and her family were all asleep so, finding nothing to say to each other, we took a walk through the city to an apartment she had borrowed for the duration of my visit. Changing out of her nightdress she had stood naked for a moment in front of me.

"Am I extremely ugly, Davide?"

"You're very beautiful, as you know."

She laughed and pulled a dress over her head.

"I am hoping you shall not rape me then," and she laughed heartier at what was obviously a piece of Italian repartee.

She took my arm and we walked at leisure through the empty streets of Bologna, saying little, the warm night receiving the silence.

"I must tell you one thing has been in my mind," she began uncertainly after one of the long easy silences that were to become our hallmark, "one thing I don't talk with anyone in Italy, and that is that I have had to come to an agreement with love."

"You mean come to terms with love?"

"I do. Come to terms."

"Agreement is better actually."

"Yes?"

"But terms is the usual way of saying it. Are you talking about Randaggio?"

"Yes I am. This which I am writing as a book of my Londonese experience, I am being forced to write this book because it give me so much pain to think about him and all that trial. But now I can come to an agreement."

"By writing it down?"

"Exactly. And I did want that you will read it if you can."

"Yes, I'd like to read it. I got a letter from Randaggio you know, just before I left London. He says he's thinking of coming to Italy in the autumn. To see you."

"Yes, he has written me the same. I don't write to these letters anymore."

"Is he still in love with you?"

"Perhaps."

"And you?"

"Well," she said like a woman thrice her age, "I think this never changes very much, so maybe if I shall meet with him I want to see him because I do love him in one sense the same. But I don't want to see him."

The only bed in the apartment was a double. We undressed on either side of it and lay down at a respectable distance.

"I think I see enough of you for tonight," she said, switching off the light, at once putting her guest at ease by setting our manners on such a tone of candour. "Good night Scottishman," and she kissed my ear in the dark.

La Città Rossa: reddish architecture and a Communist local government. Elsewhere in Western Europe, my mind included, were not the Communists considered revolutionaries? Here however the Party were the reactionaries, the Blimpish buffoons, always referred to contemptuously or as a monstrous joke. The atmosphere among the young festered of suppressed revolt, and the city during the day and early evening was redolent of Paris in '68. No European city had ever struck me as being so ripe for something entirely new. There were the concomitant sideshows, bombthrowings, enthusiasts and fanatics preaching, debating, inciting, at night on the Piazza Maggiore where young and old congregated to discuss politics, score drugs, demonstrate or simply meet each other.

My scant knowledge of history and politics was well out of place here, but equally out of place were those whose knowledge was limited to the same two disciplines. The people I met through Clorinda were revolutionaries of life, not merely over-politicized myopes, and they were younger, fresher, philosophically much older than their counterparts of the nineteen sixties. The main force working against them in this fairly wealthy city was heroin addiction, symbol of enslavement, the new religion of the masses. Every other person had, or used to have, hepatitis, caught from passing round a dirty needle. The Mafia of course are behind a trafficking that causes the pleasure-seekers and pain-fleers of Bologna to pay—and this is unique in Europe—more money for hashish than for dangerously adulterated heroin; and it is widely assumed that the government is behind the Mafia, or vice versa. Most of the kids have used heroin by the time they are fourteen, many have taken cures before sixteen and many others have died in sordid circumstances. At seventeen Clorinda had more dead friends than I had living ones at the same age. Anyway, as she (an abstainer) said to me, it keeps potential agitators well out of the way.

Day after summer's day we walked the streets and I came to know the city, its endless archways, its few bars and many superb restaurants. The best food in all Italy, they told me, and the most beautiful women, beloved of Fellini. The picture postcards did not lie in their eulogies of Bologna's three T's: Tits, Tortellini, Tower, this last oblique like the one at Pisa, miraculously standing in spite of gravity, revolutionary zeal and the occasional earthquake.

In the mornings Clorinda went to her parents' home, meeting me after lunch in Piazza Maggiore, "We have an appointment in Majority Square at three o'clock p.m.," where I would be introduced to her friends. Lisa and Anna, both seventeen and blatantly sexy, forever being pursued by older men, invariably showed up laden with plunder, elegant toiletries, cashmere sweaters, silk blouses, which they shoplifted from exclusive stores—where their eminent families no doubt had credit accounts. Two on a bike they ride around dressed like tramps, but if you meet them in the evenings they are silky and opulent and carry soft leather shoulder bags containing cocaine, contraceptive works, spare panties. They sit on either side of Clorinda, pressing gifts and kisses. I am generally excluded from this triumvirate, but Sandro, author and bomb expert, has a passion for all three which seems to have been fully reciprocated. Sandro's latest plan is to defraud big businesses by means of his extensive knowledge of the workings of their computer systems, and in this he is to be assisted by Marthe, a militant lesbian who is anxious to resume a one-night affair she had with Clorinda. Marthe ignores me too obviously for me to like her much—she takes Clorinda aside and whispers—but Marthe's girlfriend chats away to me in French, perhaps only because she is jealous.

Late afternoon and the abating of an intoxicating sun calls for an aperitif, so we head towards Pierino's café, really only two tables and a wall outside that you may sit on, where we drink a pleasant but vicious potion, recipe secret of course, devised and concocted by the proprietor himself, a nonagenarian former anarchist whose name it bears.

"Due Pierini per favore."

The old man and his wife laugh at a foreigner ordering such things, and they both repeat the phrase, no doubt attempting to mimic my accent.

"To your health Mr. Davide."

"Salute Clorinda."

I like the Italian habit of calling people by name as often as possible

"You do enjoy this drink?"

"Benissimo . . ."

"Un altro?"

"Aye lassie."

"Aye lazzee . . ."

Then, in all likelihood, a luxurious silence. The long letters had obscured the fact that we hardly knew each other at all and we often had little or nothing to say, our talk coming in bursts of prolonged concentration followed by death from natural causes. Clorinda talked the way Jack Kerouac used to write, as if commenting on a mass hallucination which she was witnessing, the beauties and horrors of which were too ineffable to attempt to portray in finished sentences. The thankless task of trying to say everything.

Three or four aperitifs of the kind served up by Pierino put you right in the mood for eating: some fresh hot bread, say, and a bottle of cold white wine, any wine, who cares, bread and wine, staff and comfort of life, to set the glands salivating. And just as you're draining off the last of the wine the chortling waiter—admirer of Clorinda, so we eat here for next to nothing—waltzes in with a second bottle half-wrapped in a white cloth, cool and beaded with droplets of liquid ice coursing down the glass, refills the glasses and sets up the first course which is always tortellini alla panna, al dente as never before, a fat cream sauce that demands immediate attention. It's all over in a minute. What next? Nobody can argue with this man's entrecote pizzaiola, a piece of meat big enough to choke a moose, red sauce streaming from the gills on the solid reek of garlic. Add broccoli with sauce hollandaise and a few croquette potatoes, a salad on the side to cool the tonsils, and you are well into the kind of snack that ought to be universally compulsory. All we lack is a litre of red, why not order a famous one this time, a Barolo, fine name that, you can repeat it indefinitely. Polish off that lot and you will be perfectly content to accept whatever cheese is set in front of you, goat's hair and all, if you know that it will be followed by a ripe peach and a half bottle of Lachrymae Christi. Clorinda and I begin on the innumerable coffees and grappe with which we shall drink ourselves sober.

She sits at my side in a mixture of horror and uncomprehending admiration, eating nothing but pizza margherita, and only a half portion at that. How is she able to drink so much without eating? Clorinda doesn't like food—it rather disgusts her. Eating is something she does reluctantly, she is almost anoretic and would rather take a vitamin pill in the morning, believing firmly that this is how the evolved human of the future will feed himself. To avoid expressing concern requires a good deal of restraint on my part. Look at this food, lass! We may be starving by next week.

"I don't mind too much to starve of hunger."

"I'd as soon not," I said, wiping my mouth with a square metre of napkin.

"Andiamo Davide, I shall take you to the osteria."

"Good idea, I'm thirsty. Beer . . ."

We took to the streets, singing harmonies, throwing cigarettes at each other, and made for the osteria, an Austrian-style drinking place with thick wooden tables, bench seats and a very heterogeneous clientele. On the way I suggested a detour:

"We must go and take a look at old Garibaldi and his steed."

"Garibaldi! Cretino . . . you crazy Scottishman."

But she let me have my way and we set out to pay homage to

his statue. Garibaldi is my hero, although his exploits have always remained somewhat vague in my memory. The rest of Italian history doesn't exist for me, ancient Rome included, but Garibaldi, Giuseppe Garibaldi, or at least the *idea* of Garibaldi, has been a cataclysmic influence on my inner life since earliest years when engravings of his head and shoulders impressed themselves upon me from the pages of school history books. He was always eluding death by the skin of his teeth, in France, Italy, South America, New York City, Sardinia, Sicily, and always returning to the fray with an army of irregulars falling in behind him like cats after a herring basket. In Sicily Garibaldi and his men were outnumbered twenty to one, yet they were still a huge success. And he was a first-class seaman too, a fisherman's son.

I stood reverently before the great statue of my hero, Clorinda laughing at me. How could anybody be against Garibaldi? I tried to explain it to her, that Garibaldi is a state of mind, an area of sensibility, a hero, not merely a man or an influence. Garibaldi is a *country*, I said as a last resort. But it all amused her disproportionately.

After some glasses of beer and local gossip at the osteria, midnight usually found us back in our apartment, shoes and most of our clothes discarded against the heat, the coffee machine bubbling in the kitchen. We were friends, Clorinda and I. We talked all night, even in our sleep, and we slept together for the sensible reason of the double bed. We held hands, lay close now, kissed good night, but it was not sexy.

Romantic: that was the opinion of Cruikshank who had written to thank me for the few lire I had sent in response to his disturbing letter. And could Clorinda avoid drawing her friends into the romance of her life? Viewed from any angle it was nothing less than romance in the grand manner. Precocious to the tips of her long brown fingers, tight gypsy skin that turns black in the sun, ferociously proud of her Neapolitan origins, singer of opera and lieder, guitar picker, troubadour of the astonishing folk music of Naples with its stab and caress of incomprehensible dialect, Clorinda, renowned concert performer from age thirteen, young Communist howling the polyglot lyrics of revolutionary ballads at Party rallies and demonstrations, by fourteen a disillusioned feminist (*Some of that feminista is worst than my mother!!*) and at fifteen a runaway street musician busking through Europe while at home they released her first record; travelling with Randaggio who stole her away with his mendicant puppets, Randy Klein of Brooklyn, the *Fourteenth Ward* whatever that may mean, called Randolph in London and in Italy known as Randaggio which is almost as bad as being called randy in England. And she manages on the wing to acquaint herself with every crucial idea, book, song, philosophy, relevant to our century. . . . Clorinda is pure romance, a legend whether she likes it or not, an allegory of herself, an unconscious disciple of Garibaldi. Yet in spite of all this she has, like many musical people, a stringently logical mind and excels at mathematics. She has no tolerance for claptrap and would be outraged if she were to read this.

We held hands, talked in bed, kissed good night.

Both of us, then, were severely culture-shocked to find ourselves precipitated one night into that bizarre domain which lies along the borderline between fine intellectual rapport and the crudest physical passion: as I understand it, a perplexing no-one's-land made up of the world just under the skin, halfway between the Sistine Chapel and Barbican Underground Station, a wayside shrine on the road to the heart of darkness.

She stirred in her sleep, woke up and opened her eyes. I was waiting.

In the unspeakable privacy of a pitch-dark room your flesh may assume the properties of warm liquid gold and mercury while hair may appear to you as silk, or threads of skin, or soiled straw; teeth may become tongues, hands faces, fingers gain sight and language disintegrate to accommodate new concepts of speech in the syntax of gibberish.

And then in the darkness her face was visible. We knew what we were doing.

It comes to you slowly, eventually with a wealth of detail, that you are fucking not only your friend Clorinda and everything she stands for but all her contemporaries and kin and future offspring as well, her entire genealogical tree, the whole microcosmic population of Bologna and hence the world ancient and modern in all its senseless charm of crossbred idiosyncracy, from Upper Holloway to the arid Coast of Dead Ned you are fucking *history,* fore and aft, from the first day of creation to the present dark night.

An alarm clock rang in one of the apartments on the far side of the courtyard. "It is a sign," she whispered, "that we shall go to sleep again."

Lovers in that haloed dominion are hardly likely to share profound spiritual union in the aftermath of such an experience, but neither are they likely to feel alone. Her hand resting in mine like a warm orchid, I closed my eyes and listened to that great white silence which in my mind is a hunting ground for the disembodied thoughts, in limbo till they find an ear, of people like Marcel MacMarshall, Suzanne and Conrad Winchester, Garibaldi, Sol Bartok, Cruikshank and all the rest of them.

Next morning I woke up to the sound of her singing and playing her guitar. Except for the odd smiles we exchanged here and there it was as though nothing more extraordinary than usual had happened.

"I think it's hotter than ever today," I said.

"Caldissima."

"A cold shower perhaps?"

"Cretino! I'm not Dutch."

"You mean Deutsch?"

"I do."

"You say German in English."

"Ah yes. In Italian it is tedesco."

We got half-dressed, washed each other's hair and walked out to let it dry in the sun.

"Where shall we go?"

"Wherever you enjoy, Davide. I don't mind to be someplace."

"What would you do if I wasn't here?"

The city was waking up, expectorating last night's phlegm, spitting it out on the brand new day. We made our way through the traffic and got into a side street, walking nowhere.

"I tell it to you," she said, giving one of the odd smiles. "This is a schematic relation of a day in my city: I always am at home from the morning until seven o'clock p.m. in the afternoon, writing my book and eating nothing except drink some tea. When my brain is then completely blow-up I go outside to a tearoom where my artistic friends, my Artist Friends, have noise discussions about the stupid particularity of their torment-life, and I normally have a favourite place in these metaphysics. And I can usually see someone invite me to a short dinner in exchange of some violent, sexual vulnerable words. Then I shall . . ."

She broke off as I nudged at the shoulder of a passing man who had offended me by staring at her in that repulsive manner for which certain Italians are notorious. I slandered his mother loudly but he kept walking.

"You must ignore them, Davide."

"But don't you find it insulting?"

"Well," she shrugged, "if I would be alone maybe I get a punch to the face for speak like that."

"Are you serious? In this town?"

"Sure." She smiled calmly, a little bitterly. "It's very popular."

I began to make it a point of honour, singling out the offenders well in advance and jostling them viciously except where strength of physique or numbers called for special discretion. Why, I asked Clorinda, didn't the real men of Italy come out in solidarity against these people? A proper trouncing in true macho style would be the quickest and perhaps best way of making the streets safe and pleasant for women. She guessed that most of the men suffered from the same brand of misogyny, and she ridiculed my naivety.

"And there is one thing I can know: Italian men are terrified with the vagina."

"How do you mean?" Had she got the wrong word?

"Well . . . I'm bit embarrassing to talk" (another odd smile) "but I have discuss with my girlfriends and they know the same. The Italian men can be usually very weird about touch your cunt, or kiss. Like it has disgusting them, you know . . ."

"Is this true? You know how they talk about Italian men in England. Virile and so on."

"That's England, Davide, but not in my brain! It is Italian men have make me feel bad with me, till I had discuss it with my friends and see that these men are very scared babies and nothing else."

"From now on I shall attack whenever advisable."

"Don't be a stupid Scottishman drinkard."

"Oh all right. Listen, shall we go in here for breakfast," I said, my attention drawn by the aroma of espresso to a window stacked with buns and pastries.

"If you want it."

"And you can continue your—what did you call it?—the schematic relation of your day."

"I will," she squeezed my hand, "dear hungry eating-man."

I set up a plateful of sweet croissants, two large coffees and a bottle of beer, and sat down beside her at the table outside.

"So what do you do after dinner when I'm not here getting you drunk?"

"I will tell you: after eaten I've got my little walk to a club where the most broken bands have their ghastly performances, when I pack up my rubbish and go directly to the osteria for a final glass of wine. I have a very movemented life after all. Even if the number of cicatrice on my face has arrived at three I've got an incredible number of lovers, sometimes I feel as a basket-ball. And I have in these last weeks a specimen of love story with an photographer of interest—the amazing of it is that I can't be knowing what I feel to him and I am silent all the time when he shower on me his big passionated love. . . ."

On the evening before my departure we sat out on the balcony and I played the guitar while Clorinda sang a much-postponed serenada to the ancient man and woman who sat nightly at a table in the courtyard below, emptying bottle after bottle and castigating one another into the hours of the morning. From their accents Clorinda knew they were from Naples, city of her birth, and she sang accordingly.

> *Angelare*
> *Angelare . . .*

They invited us to join them. The lady, seventy-nine years old, sat on my knee at once and began kissing me on the mouth, biting me and roaring with laughter at the favourable compari-son I made with her husband. He patted the belly that was heaving out of his shirt, curtly reprimanded her for being a flirt and resumed his chivalrous courting of Clorinda, dropping in a few words of English he'd picked up during the war, *my darling, a cup of tea, I give you my heart.*

Bologna.

I feel quiet sad while I'm watching the typemachine.
Wandering.
I should try to tell my real feelings.
It's too easy to call them sadness. It's like something more bright in its deepness, nearly not possible to explain with words.
You're invited to join the new moment. I could say I love you, but still it is not my meaning . . . or probably this is the best meaning, just love!

I'm sitting in my room. Everything is friendly with me here, they caress and flatter me, it is good to have so many encouragements . . . I can start write to you and everything will be pleased.

I've been writing all night my book since I left you eight hours before, but now I have to stop. The pressures are too heavy to don't notice them.

You come at first . . . my heart is suggesting me . . . it is fine! I'm quite calm while waiting my fate (stop the world and take a seat to watch it).

I'm wait in a religious silence my feelings to tell me what happened. It's good to be lonely after being with you an whole long time . . . I need to realise and make everything mine. I've an whole life with its comings and goings.

I'm tired it must be already 2 . . . I don't like to give my thoughts to some nasty dreams that I will never happen to remember.

I love this night. I feel such nice confidence with my conscience! It is always wonderfull to feel love with some people . . . Love is action . . . deep action for me . . . makes the blood shaking in my veins . . . one of few opportunities to talk directly with myself.

I'm getting heavy and boring. I can't feel stupidity, all I can think tonight seems necessary.

I will miss you in my lonely nights of writings. I am crying of happiness, I want one day to see you and explain with you much better than I did. Even if I have to fight with you and myself. I can't believe what is not truth tonight. Sometimes it is like getting used to sufferings . . . anyway it's good to suffer when it comes straight from the senses to make your brain alive again.

Life is realising, never before, I saw it so clearly, tonight I am sure of it. I will!!

There is no more time to hide myself. I'm blooming as a flower . . . opening me petals to send you my parfum. . . . Let it come until you!

Buona notte e sogni d'oro. Tomorrow I go away to Viareggio.
My love looks after everything.

Viareggio.   *Darsena vecchia*
Ciao Davide, here we are me and   *Old wet-dock*
Lisa after a day in the sun, I   *Vieille Darse*
feel wonderfull, we've been really   *Alte Dock.*
done in together well. Now we are making a little round "buying" (in our way). We already "bought" an overhaul and a
packet of Crystal Ball and a pair sandals. What great is living so
thiefly!!! (Like a thief).
Pastarinda.

Tonight I am strange and lonesome and don't know what I can
begin with writing, but I want to however. I had a wonderfull
reaction from your recent letter. I did like it very much.
I don't remember much about London—what's happening is
demonstrable: I just can remember a few things and it is awfully
sad cause it seem to me that in one sense I didn't live at all for
an whole year in that city. I remember the night when I cutted
your hair, and with Cruikshank that marvellous orator, like one
of the few days of friendship except with Randaggio.
I started again to study from one month right now, and as I
keep go on I feel like wasting away my times. How queer to
have two different lives, a world crazed with useless school and
another one with friends and music etc. etc.
They don't have anything together.
May I leave this school?
I'm happy in my city anyway!!
I'd like to explain once more how warm and beautiful is this
city for me: it's good walking in the evening.
Sorry-me for not say yust what I mean.
I know now that I saved a very short time for you when I lived
in London. At this time it seemed that every other relationship
but Randaggio was superficial and cold. I do hate the English

with remote cups of tea. I have never understand why they call you for a cup of tea when they don't have nothing else to give you . . . oh this doesn't mean to be friendly or kind: it's just bad news in me!

But perhaps you don't want to listen all my insults against these people today.

I took a bath.

Clean and pure is a good feeling.

Write one day dear and have a good life.

Late at night. I'm not anymore a "Revolutionary Student Loafer." This complicate everything. . . .

I'm not anymore an "active political soul with class-conscious-ness."

No rule no more in Bologna city.

I am a lady tired of ideology, that's all.

Those who have understood that our *pseudo*-revolution is dead are completely empty . . . just society people with their society gathering full of heroin, violation, any kind of delinquency.

I, myself, am a bit scared actually . . .

Sure Mr. X., there is logical connection between Communism and delinquency. It wouldn't sound so different to me even if a priest is marked by a Communist symbol.

Who has got courage to say?

Mafia? . . . Mamma mia . . . io scappo!

I am surrounded by junkies and hard music but I'm still not ready for this kind of heavy and soft voice stuck with heroin-ideal. You know what reminds me these people? They seem to ask for some water, a bog and some toilette-papers.

I feel in peace with the world this night.

Here I am on a different day. I received from you today a letter . . . smart my dear . . . your Italian is growing just smart. Do you know what means this word of yours "tanghero"? It is a boor.

When I opened that book and saw your picture I got shocked! What a criminal lamp in those eyes. . . .

It seems you have just come out alive from the electric chair!!
Well, I gave up again with writing to Randaggio long times ago, but he keeps send me his unbelievable letters. I think he write in series. I have a letter just exact the same as you received. He is a pretty-artistic-mind-full-of-fantasy (to spare in case of friend).

L'AUTUNNO È ARRIVATO,

NOI SIAMO SEDUTI NEL PARCO

(PARCO DIO)

LA GENTE CAMMINA INDISTURBATA. . . .

Do you remember yourself this poem? On the same serviette I found our song to the Italian peoples: A basso il pappa/ a basso la casa/ a basso le mutande.

Also my words on the arse of Catullo.

Bologna is wondrous in autumn: full of stabbed hearts.

Not one wall is being left.

I will compel my father to photo-copy the songs you want from nuova compagnia etc. My parents are gone for one week and Quando il gatto non c'è i topi ballano.

I feel terribly good in this house without my parents, "the authors of my existence."

I am looking for a job. My school is not all started yet but this year must be my last! I am sure they will send me away after two weeks. I am certain of this because two big companions of mine are in the class and we will be inevitably nasty.

My brother invite me to eat lunch. I'm not hungry at all. Ciao Davide. *Clo* is probably the best surrogate of my name. Ti mando un bacio grande, grande così:

Here is your slight telegram of affection.

My heart keeps knocking to the door saying: Give me some cares, bad girl!

My recent journey of Naples-Bologna was quite and warm.

Napoli left me smile-flying away upon some clouds. I did sleep for one hour and I found myself standing on the sunny Bolognese grounds.

Happy to walk in my streets again. I think maybe once more you shall walk together with me on this tarred-soul.

I saw Alberto and Sandro in the afternoon and I hear all the news concerning, with others, a house we shall obtain in the countryside and the prospect of my writing publication etc. etc. bla bla bla.

Alberto talked with his publication-company in Milano so they wait to read my robbish too.

And tomorrow Alberto will be back to Milano saying that at last he will get there my stuff sooner or later.

Now I don't have anything else than write again my story and give it in Alberto's hand. (Good luck!) I feel scared about seeing my attempted-tale upon a white clean paper-book.

I am assailed by many fears!

I feel mad as if I am a fearful child.

Any-how it means that my friends did like it . . . which seems the only thing to make me extremely happy and full of new hopes.

I don't know why I should feel so unprotective.

I could wish to talk but you are so miles away, fuck-in-hell!!

No more words. A silent cry is here to come.

Next morning woke up late.

Feel in the right mood for write again my efforts.

I should have talked to you much about it more.

I could convince only Sandro that I am a strange animal . . . I can be totally evanescent . . . only air and love.

I'm normally interested in love.

What normally people try to feed me (damned prevaricators!) is never always good enough . . . I know the food I prefer . . . I might eat *you* up in one minute!!!

(There isn't a disease worse than the podagra: a flaccid meat eating a leg chicken sitting upon a chair.) Podagra means to say: "Gout in the feet" . . . This morning I have received two letters.

The first from a guy in TURKEY!!

I actually couldn't believe my eyes, I couldn't remember having any kind of a relation during my 17 years of life with a Turkman called ADNAN!!

I started to read this letter which is in disgraceful English (worse than mine to notice!) saying: I would like to tell what are your hobbies. The word "hobbies" already irritated me, I stopped to use it at five years old. My father and mother used to say: Clorinda has funny hobbies—one is singing and the other is fencing!

The letter from him keeps saying, "Do you enjoy the pop-music? I very like the pop-music. I'm very affection Italian peoples."

And at the finish, "Please can I have your foto, loves from Adnan Banabak, Iznip, Turkey."

I went mad thinking from where the fuck he got my address of my home.

After three hours of meditations I had to go back to my early thirteens when I used to join such a club for friendship all over the world.

And it is likely that after five years I might get this corresponder in Turkey.

(I wonder what I had in mind to have to ask for a Turkish corresponder?)

Adnan called me Klorinda!

I surely will write back to him, I can't know what.

The second letter was from Miki who is now in the Sudan, but I yust couldn't read the letter cause I've been attractive by a marvelous photo of her—NAKED! Not bad actually, well done Miki.

Queste tutte le nouve . . . fatti diversi . . . informazioni utili
clorinda.

P.S. Is it true there is cafés in Switzerland with signs say "No
Italians allowed"? I did read this in the journal.

The Green Man

"It's no go the Yogi Man, it's no go Blavatski,
All we want is a bank balance and a bit of skirt in a taxi."

(from "Bagpipe Music," by Louis MacNeice.)

ALEX CRUIKSHANK was the only real writer I knew in London. Down on his luck, evicted from his home, he had accepted my offer of a place to work and sleep and for a number of months we led a fluctuating life of odd jobs, occasional wealth, exuberant discussion of the pincer movement we had in store for world literature. So a singular gap was left when Alex, with only two hundred guilders and a new portable typewriter, took off for Holland to write *The Amsterdam Book* and enjoy the hospitality of our friend Sol Bartok who had set up home there.

It was true that Cruikshank had been the epitome of abjectness over the weeks prior to his migration, borrowing cash from everyone he met, scrounging drinks from strangers, complaining of his lack of success with women and writing, selling his typewriter and usurping mine; but even at his worst, when he sat for hours in a heavy silence punctuated by his annoying habits of foot-tapping and whistling under his breath, when he left grey tide-marks round the bath, clipped his toenails on the breakfast table, failed to aim correctly while urinating, Cruikshank was always ready to be ejected from torpor and resume his usual persona of optimism if only someone would rise to the occasion and give him a boot in the arse.

The boot might be anything from the offer of a glass of beer to the suggestion that he embark on a new novel or irrational literary project. Cruikshank liked fat novels in the English tradition and pints of black stout in the Irish. He was one for novels with dense plots, nuance of selectivity, astuteness of characterisation, but I never found anything resembling these in his own works, for Cruikshank wrote his books discursively, as he talked in fact, always with three characters only, all of them blatantly unvarnished Cruikshanks.

It was Sol Bartok who emphasised that there are a minimum of two Cruikshanks, clearly defined, the man and the author;

and that both, needless to labour the point, are struggling to meet, or perhaps avoid, one another. There is the writer of digressive extravaganzas: and the man who admires above all literature the well-constructed novel. The man who yearns unsentimentally for a life of comfort and respectability yet allows the writer to drudge at his chaotic desk, night after night into morning, conjuring up books which no one will buy in that writer's lifetime. *The Amsterdam Book* was going to change all this. A third Alex Cruikshank, something of an irrevocable synthesis of the other two, was expected to emerge and spit it forth. These facts, by the way, come straight out of the horse's mouth, culled from his old diary-novels, *The Cruikshank Papers*, which I am shamelessly plagiarising.

It had been agreed that I should come to visit him once he'd established himself in Amsterdam, but many weeks passed before this became possible. A long holiday had been my intention, but the usual money troubles forced me to procrastinate again and again. Eventually, at a time when our work in the building trade had suffered a total recession and I had enough money to cover only a rather ascetic holiday, I decided to go to Amsterdam almost immediately, just for a few days.

Correspondence from Cruikshank and from Sol Bartok had indicated that there was great intellectual activity at number 5A Limburgerkaasstraat, but so far I had been sent no carbons from the projected novel, not so much as a chapter heading. Alex usually showed me his work hot off the platen for my delectation and critical appraisal, so I assumed that he was still in the preparatory phase and I made no mention of the book in my letters.

Then ironically, on the very day that I had set aside for organizing my trip to Amsterdam, who should turn up on my doorstep but Cruikshank, himself and certainly no other, although it did take a second glance to ratify this. He had a new hairstyle, carried a walking cane and was wearing a polkadot cravat and a Panama hat. His only luggage was a peculiar valise which would have been unobtrusive had it not been painted

bright yellow. It bore the legend, in bold black lettering,
B.I.F.

"Goed'morgen mijn'heer!" he said, raising his Panama hat.

"Alex! Welcome. Come on in. What's happened to you?"

"Oh nothing much." He smiled mysteriously and I noticed
that his accent had altered. "Actually," he said more seriously,
depositing the yellow valise and removing his coat, "quite a lot
has happened. I'll tell you about it later—when I've done my
exercises: running on the spot, *be-gin!*" and Cruikshank began to
run on the spot, raising his knees high and trying to keep a
straight face. "I feel grand!" he yelled above the sound of his
boots on the bare floorboards. "Anything for breakfast?" He
collapsed into a chair in the kitchen, cast his eyes about and
amiably fired rapid questions, "How's business—still getting
your face dirty? How's money? *You* were coming to Amsterdam?" he laughed warmly. "Christ I'm exhausted. . . ."

"Did you come on the night boat? We'll go out for breakfast
as soon as I've had a wash."

"I could do with a wash myself. No, I flew in this morning
but I've been up all night."

"Flew? Has somebody died?"

"Not exactly. I've got a job." Cruikshank sniggered as we
stood over the grubby sink washing and brushing our teeth.
"Don't bother shaving," he said, slapping the loose change in
his pocket, "I'll treat you to one at the barber's. And maybe we
should get a bottle of something for after breakfast. . . ."

"This is all quite intriguing, Alex."

"It is," he agreed. "But let's get out into the fresh air. I
could eat a mangy pup."

As we were leaving the house he suddenly remembered something.

"My action bag!"

"What?"

"My briefcase, I must take it with me," he muttered importantly, sprinting back up the garden path. "I have to make a
few calls today."

"What sort of job is this," I asked when he returned with the yellow valise, "where you fly to London and make calls on people? And what does that mean?" I pointed at the bold initials, *B.I.F.*, in four-inch capitals. Cruikshank laughed, irritatingly, like a cynical adept at a beginner.

"I'll tell you about it over breakfast. *Haa!*" he suddenly shouted at the top of his voice in the style of the old Cruikshank; this was enough to turn the heads of passersby and effect a change of subject, but he insisted on making a thorough job of it: "By gad, sir, I'm so happy to be back in London! Rare place! And to be walking here, this perfect morning, with yourself, down this street . . . Ahh," he sighed, "a few deep draughts of carbon monoxide, just what I've been missing. . . ."

"How," I asked tentatively as we breezed along the Holloway Road, "is the writing going?"

Cruikshank twirled his stick, coughed at length and spat into the gutter.

"I have renounced literature."

He started whistling and manipulating his walking stick like a major domo, now and then striking out a rhythm on the yellow valise.

"What about *The Amsterdam Book*?"

"Oh, I wrote it a couple of weeks ago. Finished, over. *Dood*. Eighty thousand words in six days," he sang mechanically, "Monday to Saturday, written from the entrails of creation in the netherlands of the mind, a hyperborean work written not in blood but in cold sweat. . . . Anyway I haven't even read it through, and I never will. Money is what I'm interested in now. Spondulicks. Literature is a racket."

"Maybe you've written a classic, a bestseller."

"Maybe I have. I'll never know. I've lost all interest."

"So you've given up writing for good?"

"Why not? Am I a troglodite? All the best writers give up before they reach their peak: literature as we know it is nothing more than the work of talented trogs; the ideal writer is the man of action who would not waste valuable time buggering about with pen and paper. . . ."

Cruikshank continued in this apophthegmatic vein long enough to tire of it, then he grew nostalgic about his early days in Amsterdam.

"There was, sir, a time when life, the writer's life, took one by the scruff of the neck at daybreak and carried one in fear and trembling, or ecstasy, I don't know which, but one was transported right through to sunset and then on, into and out of the night, and disposed of peaceably until another sunrise grabbed at the shirttails to whisk away body, heart and soul for the next day's play amid delight and spectacle. . . . You observe a change in my speaking habits?"

"Well. You've developed a foreign accent."

"Have I? Well never mind. I no longer have control over what I say. That's another reason I gave up writing."

"Emptying out the baby with the bathwater."

"You're probably completely right. But the truth of the matter, sir, perhaps even the sad truth, is that time has passed and I am changed."

We reached the Seven Steps café and sat down at a corner table.

"The days are *not* long past when I was to be seen, scarf about mouth, collar against damp, shoes flapping apart, pounding the cobbles of winter Amsterdam in cold pursuit of the daily crumb, the freeman's cigarette, the bum's beer. You know that side of me well enough . . ."

The waitress appeared and Cruikshank set about ordering his breakfast: orange juice, a kipper, coffee, toast and marmalade, and what he called a Full House, comprising bacon, eggs, sausages, tomatoes, bubble, a fried slice.

". . . I lived in unashamed poverty, delighted to have so much time to myself, collecting wood from the streets, *I*, a former firewood magnate! scavenging discarded furniture to burn in the stove that supplied totally inadequate warmth to my room—whose only virtue was being a *kraakhuis*, no rent to worry about. Breaking the timber into suitable lengths gave exercise and greater warmth. It burned faster than I could chop it up."

"Why did you move out of Sol's house in the first place?"

"Difficulties. Leah got fed up with me, said I was affecting the harmony of their marriage, but I think it was really my scrounging that did it. She could never refuse me a few guilders, it went against her beliefs, so she had to get rid of me on some other pretext. She got Sol to ask me to leave. It was quite funny. He also said that it was time I struck out on my own, which was probably true. 'Alexander,' he said the day I left, 'I feel towards you the feelings of a Sheik towards his eldest son.' I'm still on the best of terms with both of them and I see them just as often, but they've never come to my place."

"I'm not surprised," I said as the waitress covered the table with plates of food, "it doesn't sound so attractive."

"Oh it isn't. Or rather it wasn't: I don't live there anymore," Cruikshank mumbled through mouthfuls of kipper, "although whether the place *is* unattractive or *was* unattractive has nothing to do with my presence or absence. . . . Ah, this is excellent, you don't get this sort of breakfast in Amsterdam. Yes, I never bothered to notify you of my changes of address because it was better that my mail went to Sol's. Safer. Nothing was safe in my house. More coffee?"

"Thanks. Is your new place better?"

"It is. Have a sausage if you like, I'll never eat four. There wasn't anything as technologically advanced as gas and electricity in the old room: when I wrote at night it was by the light of the stove flames. But to get back to the point of what I was saying," Cruikshank dipped his fried slice into an egg yolk, took a bite and noisily slurped up some coffee, "the point is that it's all a piece of history to me now. Maybe it didn't even happen at all."

Finishing off our breakfast, we strolled along a back street to the barber's, a real barbershop with a striped pole outside. Waiting to be shaved I asked Cruikshank about his new job.

What was the meaning of the *B.I.F.* insignia on the peculiar yellow valise?

"Bureau for the Investigation of Future possibilities . . ."

"Next please!"

"I am one of their agents," Cruikshank called over his shoulder as he sat down in the barber's chair.

On our way back home he took from his wallet a plastic-covered ID card which showed a picture of himself against the backdrop of a map of the world. On the other side it said, *B.I.F.,* Alexander Cruikshank, Gentleman Traveller, Authorised Representative of the Bureau for the Investigation of Future possibilities. What possibilities was Cruikshank helping to investigate?

"All possibilities, my dear sir. That's the beauty of it. There's nothing, concerning the future, that we do *not* want to be involved in. But first off we're striking at the most important areas, on the understanding that Art is the strongest influence on Life."

"I hope you're not inventing this as you go along, Alex."

"No, no, it's all true. We want to represent artists, musicians, actors, singers, writers even; and later we want to involve politicians and big business because we'll probably need their support at some point."

"Is the *B.I.F.* a political party?"

"No. Or if it is they keep it secret. I'm here in London, return airfare and five star hotel courtesy of the *B.I.F.,* to put out feelers, make contacts, open a bank account and P.O. box, take a few photographs of people we are interested in, maybe sign up one or two promising talents."

"*Gentleman Traveller,* that's a nice touch."

"D'you think so? I suggested it myself when I got the job. They asked me what I wanted to be called."

"I can't help being sceptical though."

"I don't blame you. I was the same myself."

"Are you well paid? And how did you get this job anyway?"

"I don't know if I'm being paid well or not," Cruikshank's

face screwed up in perplexity as he dwelt on the thought. "Let me tell you from the start."

We were back at my flat, Cruikshank in the act of breaking the seal on a bottle of Southern Comfort he'd picked up on the way. He poured out two large measures, opened a carton of Dutch cigarettes, made himself comfortable on the couch.

"I was recruited to the *B.I.F.* about three weeks ago. My boss is a Norwegian called Geissler, forty-odd but looks much younger, whom I met in a bar where I was cadging a glass of pils. He suspected me of having talent, *taahlent* he calls it, and offered me a job painting his office. That coat," Cruikshank indicated, "was my wages for painting the office. You may laugh. I was cold and it was well worth it. Then he made a deal to give me free food and drink while I did some layout work on the magazine that we're putting out to publicise the organisation. Layout work, which I'd never done before, is said to be my special taahlent."

"And is it?"

"Could be. I enjoyed it. Geissler believes that the feeling generated by the mere *idea* of the *B.I.F.* will make people discover their own and each other's latent taahlents, cause new taahlent to emerge, create fresh bisociations and so forth. But he does talk a certain amount of cant, for example, that the prime purpose of my trip to London is 'To give support to the Pound Sterling'; that we exist chiefly to promulgate a concept called 'He-She,' which I don't properly grasp; that we are a powerful international consortium. Maybe we are, I don't know; he's evasive about facts, brushes them aside and reprimands me for pettifogging. *Aahction,* he's always saying, *we must take immediate Internaahtional Aahction!*"

"He didn't ask you to bring any packages through the customs?"

"No, no, I was on the lookout for something like that. I just asked him for some wages at the end of the week and he produced the plane ticket and hotel voucher. That's what is so unusual, there doesn't appear to be anything suspicious going on."

"Maybe he's setting up some bank fraud."

"Yes, I considered that as well when he asked me to arrange banking facilities in London. One of the other agents was despatched to Copenhagen with the same instructions, but it all seems to be aboveboard. We even got a few thousand guilders on loan from the Amro bank on the strength of a flat owned by our office manager, a Dutch guy. Geissler persuaded him to convert his flat into our office. . . ."

"What are the other agents like—are they cranks?"

"A preposterous suggestion, sir! Actually I don't really know. I've tended to lie low and reap what I could. Whatever's going on underneath, the *B.I.F.* has pulled me out of the hole I was in, so I'm happy. The Dutchman strikes me as an excellent bloke, very thoughtful and fair-minded. The others are arty people, a couple of actors, a musician, a photographer. A girl turned up from Paris—she's to be the company secretary, speaks seven languages, including Russian and Chinese. Just before I left she drafted a letter to the Kremlin, Minister of Culture, to inform him of our existence. . . . I really don't know. Maybe we *are* an internaahtional company with huge resources. Geissler talks of offices in Paris, Stockholm, Frankfurt, Zurich. 'See me in Rome next Wednesday,' I heard him say on the phone yesterday, and he's always going on about internaahtional aahction, 'What time is it in Bangkok right now, Alexander?' I laugh at him, and he laughs with me, but half an hour later it's, 'Have you read today's *New York Times*?' or 'I wonder what price gold is fetching in Singapore.' "

Cruikshank laughed to himself, shaking his head, and poured another glass of Southern Comfort which he downed at a gulp. Pouring a third glass he settled himself back on the couch, still chuckling.

"You have to admit," he said pointedly, "that it makes a change from starving artistry. And in a way I believe in the organisation. The most powerful thing," Cruikshank sat up straight on the edge of the couch, "is that everybody has been overwhelmed by Geissler's enthusiasm and energy. They have

[137]

unmitigated faith in him, in his ability to make us internaahtional figures. I get carried away by it myself sometimes."

"Do you think he believes it himself?"

"That's another question. It's hard to know what he thinks.
But I really don't mind. My only objection to him is that nobody ever gets paid in hard cash."

"But how does he get people to work for him? Is everybody
getting five star hotels and stuff?"

"No. This is where his taahlent comes in. Geissler has the
ability to sense, within minutes of meeting someone, the precise
nature of that person's ambitions. He then convinces them, and
it seldom takes much, that they need only put themselves into
his hands for all dreams to be realised. It's all a question of
realities."

"Or bullshit."

"Or bullshit. He talks a sort of pure mathematics, generates
an atmosphere in which the *B.I.F.* is *already* in virtual control
of the world. The others believe in him, it's as simple as that.
Geissler tells them that they are Life's True Aahctors, the spear-
head of the first True Internaahtional Aahction . . . and they
work away happily towards this end."

"Maybe it's a front for some sort of intrigue, you know, a
covert governmental operation set up to pry into the lives of
writers such as yourself. . . ."

"Former writer! But yes, that did cross my mind at first,
especially with the interesting initials. Geissler says he was
inspired by FBI and the fact that *bif* means something in Norwegian slang. It probably means practical joke. Amsterdam, as
you know, is full of loons."

Cruikshank reached for his yellow valise and extracted from it
a large desk-diary. "I really ought to have made some calls this
morning," he muttered to himself, noting something down in
his diary. He replaced the diary in his valise and refilled his
glass.

"Last week," again he smiled and shook his head, "I started

having qualms about Geissler. So I asked him what shape the organisation would be taking in the coming months. He said that in six months' time the *B.I.F.* would no longer exist. So why were we doing it then? Ah, the *B.I.F.* was only a starting point, a springboard. . . . So I asked him what was coming next, and he answered straight out: 'That, Alexander, will be entirely in accordance with your own desires.' Ha!" Cruikshank drank deeply and chuckled, as if he had just been retailing a pack of lies. "But let's forget the *B.I.F.* for the moment. What are you up to these days?"

When I dropped in to see Cruikshank at his hotel overlooking Hyde Park, two days had elapsed and great changes taken place. He had grown disillusioned with his job: no bank would open an account in the company's name without proper business references and registration; nobody was interested in being represented by, or investing money in, the organization; most importantly, ready cash was not forthcoming from the Amsterdam Office to cover his day to day expenses, despite Geissler's promises to the contrary.

On the bright side, Cruikshank had fallen in love with a married lady, a former acquaintance. He could think of nothing else and talked about her constantly, outlining plans they had already made for a new life together. But this happiness had only compounded his disinclination to be active in commerce.

Geissler, an international phone-call enthusiast, had been ringing Alex every few hours demanding bulletins on "Investments" and up to date commentary on the state of the Pound. I listened in on the extension to one such call:

"You *must* support the currency Alexander," I heard him exhort in a curious accent that was as much American and Irish as Norwegian: "You *must* baahlance the Pound if the U.K. is to be with us . . ."

"But what exactly do you want me to *do* with the bleeding Pound? I don't even *have* a pound . . ."

"Get out there on the streets maahn! Make contact with the people, the True Aahctors, show them what we are offering . . ."

"Yes, but when will some money arri———?"

"By the way," Geissler interrupted with aplomb, "I am recalling you tomorrow, we need you here to supervise the magazine layout. But for the moment here are two telephone numbers, one in Paris and one in Liechtenstein. They are booksellers: get on the phone and take immediate aahction as soon as we finish talking. We want to send each of them ten thousand copies of the magazine, sale or return, call me back on this at six thirty local time. Oh and Alexander, remind me to discuss with you the Intertimer."

"The *what*?"

"I am speaking of my blueprints for the Continental Intertimer. I will see you tomorrow at headquarters."

Geissler, in executive tradition, had hung up at that; and Cruikshank, doodling pad alive with notes and numbers, scarcely the price in his pocket of a phone call to Brixton, turned to me in anger and asked how he, Cruikshank, with his scant knowledge of foreign languages and sound knowledge of human nature, was supposed to approach reputable booksellers with the proposal that they undertake to distribute a magazine they had neither read nor heard of, a magazine entitled *Aspects of Action,* which in all probability was still on the drawing board.

"You could always resign, Alex."

"Yes I know. But then I'd have nothing to go back to and I'd lose the return plane ticket. These things are important at the moment."

The phone call to Brixton, which Cruikshank could ill afford, concerned his new lover, Angie. She had a husband to desert and a small son to take with her. Cruikshank intended to abduct the pair of them back to Amsterdam, for which project he would need more time and more money, and now here was Geissler recalling him almost penniless to head office. A brief call to Angie, during which I left the room, confirmed that she was ready to leave at a moment's notice as soon as Alex could arrange for their journey. This efficiency impressed me.

"I can't go back to Amsterdam tomorrow," he said to the mirror, where I could see his eyes sparkling and laughing while his mouth distended in concentration. "Have you got two hundred pounds?"

"I haven't."

"Do we know anyone who might?"

It was a rhetorical question. Cruikshank paced the room for a long time before being struck, suddenly inspired by the *B.I.F.* credo of immediate international action, with a solution to his problem.

"*This* is how I'll do it: I'll recruit *you* as a Gentleman Traveller, give you the plane ticket and a letter of introduction . . ."

"Wait a minute Alex . . ."

". . . you'll get a free holiday in Amsterdam," he enthused, "you can have my room, you can see Sol . . ."

"And work for the *B.I.F.*"

"Well," Cruikshank said expansively, "you might enjoy it. I did until yesterday. And you'll certainly enjoy meeting Geissler. *Good character for a book.*"

"Would I get any wages?"

"You'd get *something.*"

"Let me think about it for a minute. How long do you want me to deputise for you?"

"Oh not long! I'm not going to hang about. Three or four days at most. Geissler's bound to send some money by then. And if not I'll go home to East Grimpe and borrow it from my old man. So you'd definitely see me in Amsterdam by Saturday. With my new family. Will you do it? We could have a rare time. . . ."

"Okay, give me the ticket. I'll go tonight."

"*Good man!*" Cruikshank shook me by the hand. "Great, great!" he thundered, dancing round the room. "I'll write the introductory letter now. And remind me to give you the key to my living quarters."

"Are you sure," I asked as he sat down to write, "that this is in keeping with company policy?"

"Unquestionably," Cruikshank said without hesitation, his pen scudding deftly from line to line. "Internaahtional Aahction. They'll love it!"

With everything settled his joie de vivre returned and he had room service send up a bottle of Moselle. We drank toasts to future possibilities and to a successful elopement, then Cruikshank took a deep breath and placed a call to Liechtenstein.

I landed at Schiphol airport at dusk and took a taxi into Amsterdam. Instead of going direct to Kamer Cruikshank, the name he gave his garret which stood two feet from the moon at the top of several flights of one-in-three gradient Dutch stairs, I got off at the Leidseplein so that I might walk down a street that traversed the canals, the concentric canals, to a bar I knew on Damstraat. Crossing a bridge to whose rails were chained the familiar massed bicycles of Holland I recalled my own Amsterdam days, my first visit—was it *eight* years ago?—which marked the beginning of a protracted period of haphazard wandering in unconscious search of a corner of the world that did not contain the ghost of Suzanne Winchester. It was from this bridge that I had torn up a certain photograph and dropped it into the canal to drift as far away as possible. I stopped on the bridge and watched the lights on the water. There was a quotation I had paraphrased from one of Albert Camus' works:

> Holland is a dream, sir, a dream of gold and smoke, smokier by day, more gilded by night. . . . For we are at the heart of things here. Have you observed that the concentric canals of Amsterdam resemble the circles of hell? The bourgeois hell, peopled of course with bad dreams. . . . Here, we are in the last circle.

Unaware that the last circle of Dante's hell is inhabited by traitors I had sent the quotation to Cruikshank with the suggestion that it might make a suitable inscription for the title page of his new novel. And now he'd written the book in a week and forgotten it overnight, perhaps even consigned it to the waste-paper basket. But probably, I thought, he's given it to Sol Bartok for safekeeping: which would say something about all the "I have renounced literature" stuff. That phrase in itself was sufficient proof that he had not.

I sat down at the bar and ordered a glass of pils and a Dutch cognac, rough stuff but ideal for people like me. This bar was once a meeting place for young people but now it was full of old men polishing off their glasses of jenever and smoking cigars. I wondered if Sol Bartok was still engaged in literary pursuits. In contrast to Cruikshank's tirades, written at speed under the sway of any number of drinks and drugs, Sol's books were cool slim volumes containing, in aphoristic form, the loftiest ideals of the spirit. The great life of the mind, that was Sol's demesne, the meeting of intellects, while Cruikshank assiduously boycotted all meetings of intellects and turned up his nose at all spirit that was not bottled. Still, they got along well together, the Sheik and his eldest son.

I had a last cognac and headed off through the pedestrian precincts, traversing as always the canals, Singel, Herengracht, Keizersgracht, Prinsengracht. The night was damp, with fog no doubt over the Zuider Zee and fast approaching. I reached my destination and slunk into the warmth of the *Gouden Haan*.

This was Sol Bartok's favourite eating house and salon where he often held court, talking away to three or four people at once, in as many languages, Hebrew, English, French, Dutch too if his arm was twisted. Sol is a wise man from the Middle East, a catalyst among truthseekers, self-styled authority on the geography of the roads to freedom. Our disagreements were always of the finest quality.

In the days before I knew him Sol, born on a kibbutz, had been a captain in the Israeli army during the Six Day War. After the army he took up experimenting with hallucinogens, encouraged by the discovery that these drugs stimulated his natural capacity for telepathy. He had been aware since childhood of this gift but had never been eager to discuss it with others. He began to develop power over people, mainly through an ability for predicting or anticipating their thoughts and actions, but also by being able to *instil* thoughts into the minds of others so that they would behave in whatever way he desired. Sol swears that he never abused these powers beyond compelling people to offer him loans or invite him to dinner; but in the end he made the mistake of owning up to it. To his horror the authorities had him locked up and put under sedation. When they let him out he made arrangements to leave for Europe. He settled down in Switzerland, then Spain, and continued to rub away at the doors of esp.

I first met him five years ago in Madrid where I had been given the use of a flat by a Scottish couple who were sympathetic towards my literary ambitions. With no rent to pay I had enough money to live on for six months, in which time I hoped to complete my second major work, and one lazy day I got talking to Sol in the Prado where he was sitting making sketches in front of the Goyas. He was living in Madrid with an American girl called Joyce who had persuaded him to abandon his pursuit of psychic phenomena and "all that crap." She was a broad-minded but down to earth girl with a passion for therapeutic emotional abreaction, which discipline became in turn Sol's chief preoccupation. Fired by her lust for Truth, equalled only by his own, Sol threw himself vigorously into refuting his former beliefs and joined with Joyce in what he was later to call "a run on Reality," in which all spirituality and mysticism was ridiculed as an evasion of personal emotions and an escape from the basic laws of life.

Our meeting in Spain resulted two years later in Sol coming to stay with me in Wales where I had landed a marvellous job as a tractor driver. Most of my wages came in the form of a rent-free cottage and free food, but I was writing, I was politically naive and I wasn't complaining. In my house in Wales Sol had met and instantly befriended Cruikshank who had come down from

London for a holiday in the countryside. The famous attraction of opposites had never brought together such opposing poles as Cruikshank and Sol Bartok: they talked all night and claimed to understand one another perfectly, but to me, listening in silence, they were like an electric guitar and a tuba vying simultaneously to produce the finest rendition of a sonata intended for solo violin. By this time Sol's innovatory relationship with Joyce had ended in pain and resentment, each accusing the other of running away from the Truth, and Sol was in a half-world of loneliness, promiscuity, drunkenness and a token return to the religion of his forefathers in which women and their opinions are taken none too seriously. "A career in literature," Cruikshank instructed him, "is all that remains for the likes of us."

Then Sol met Leah, an Israeli girl, his twin, he liked to call her. Leah was a dancer of the dances of India, a practitioner of Yoga and meditation, a Sufi who wore kohl on her eyes and rings on her toes and could administer all sorts of massages and odylic potions. Sol's irrepressible love of the mystic returned at full throttle with his love for Leah and they were married within a month, here in the city of Amsterdam.

Amsterdam. On their most recent visit to London Leah had taken me aside and told me that Sol's aim was to make the city of Amsterdam beat in time with his own heart. . . .

But Sol was absent from the *Gouden Haan* tonight. The waitress told me that he was still a regular customer though; in fact he was using the café as a venue for weekly seminars he was holding, Work Evenings they were called, in which he made his wisdom publicly available. I'd been wondering how Sol was making ends meet. The waitress drew my attention to a poster on the wall, handsomely drawn in Sol's own hand, advertising Work Evenings with Sol Bartok, "Living with the Numinous." He was only charging five guilders a head.

Cruikshank's Kamer, when I finally got there after navigational errors caused by the hashish in my dessert, was an abomination, a living midden. I retched from the stench alone while trying to get the light to work: the moment I gave up trying, it switched on of its own volition. What appeared to be a moth-eaten carpet was in fact a blanket of cigarette butts spread over the floor space, while the ashtray, a giant one, was empty and spotlessly clean. Perhaps Cruikshank was using it as an eating bowl.

Could one person possess so many pairs of dirty socks and underpants? I retched again and opened the window, more of a porthole really: it looked out on a brick wall four feet away. The bed, a monkish pallet, stuffing protruding like pubic and underarm hair, was stained with the bloods and juices of medieval times whence it must have originated, and the polyester sleeping bag bore blackeyed cigarette burns. Did Cruikshank intend to live in this room with Angie and her child? There was scarcely room for one person to stretch out. No wonder Cruikshank had laid down the unprofitable pen in favour of international action. And he had even mentioned cheerfully, handing me the keys, that the Kamer was "a real improvement" on his previous room in the *kraakhuis* where he'd chopped wood and written by firelight.

There was a chair, an armchair which seemed to serve for a garbage can, heaped up with empty bottles, banana skins, dirty clothes, restaurant takeaway containers lined with mould. What could anybody do here but close their eyes and die at once. I opened the bottle of rum I'd bought on the plane, took a swig, lit a cigarette and puffed vigorously into the room against the odours of old boots and rotting dreams. The electric fire came on, all by itself. Laying my cigarette in the clean ashtray I scooped up the contents of the armchair in both arms, held my breath, and dumped the lot into a cupboard under the sink.

As I was doing this a mouse ran over my hand. Ah . . . *the Mouse* . . . that must be *the Mouse*, Cruikshank's mouse, sole sharer of the dawn torment. Alex had told me about this mouse, a fearless creature that ran over his boots as he wrote and turned up on his pillow in the mornings. Unless of course there were other mice in the Kamer.

I dusted off the armchair and swept the cigarette butts into a corner using an old scarf. It wasn't a bad chair when cleared of the soiled clothes and bed-sitter detritus. Shaking the squashed cushion back to life I came across a dogeared ledger of the type used by small businessmen to record their transactions. On the cover in bold script: *The Amsterdam Book*. I flicked the pages. He'd written it in longhand, pencil, probably unable to redeem a pawned typewriter.

After a day's travelling and a decent meal I was in good fettle to approach the book. The room was warming nicely, an advantage of its smallness, and its native smells were being replaced by those of tobacco smoke and dark rum, some of which I sprinkled around to accelerate the process. I found a glass by the sink, washed it and polished it dry on my spare shirt, poured a gill of rum, lit a fresh cigarette and settled down with *The Amsterdam Book by Alexander Cruikshank*. Beneath his name he had inscribed, perhaps in a moment of depression, "Order of the Typewriter and Notebook 1st. Class (Posthumous) Amsterdam, The Nether Regions of the Soul." On the title page was the quotation about the concentric canals and the circles of hell, and an effusive dedication to myself and Sol Bartok which he had cancelled out on second thoughts.

It was four in the morning when I finished the book. Cruikshank had written nothing like this before. All his former influences had gone out the window along with any number of obsolete versions of himself, and in this respect alone it qualified in my mind as a work of genius: it heralded the birth of a new voice. Yet it was hard to decide whether it was a masterpiece or a shrieking embarrassment.

The voice was not one I recognised as belonging to my friend, and none of the events described or dramatis personae was known to me beforehand, so I was able to eulogise and condemn as the mood took me, just as one would do with any author, forgetting altogether that we had spent hours, Alex and I, discussing precisely this book in the days when it was no more than a theory. He had selected its title before he had as much as visited Amsterdam. I wondered why he had chosen Amsterdam:

would the same book have resulted had he gone to Barcelona or Ushuaia?

Written in the hackneyed but deathless form of Man in pursuit of Being, the book had very little to do with Amsterdam except when the narrator chose to hit you on the head with it, the whores in their windows and the arterial canals whose sludge permeated the nights, as he squeezed from the tinsel city a startling world in his own image. I experienced for the first time what it meant to *be* Cruikshank with his unrelenting self-doubts and dissatisfactions; his hatred of the spurious and his longing for commonplace pleasures, which combination made him an Uitlander among ordinary people and an outcast among outsiders.

But he had already repudiated the book, hadn't even read it through on completion. Six days' hard labour then goodbye to the barren leaves. Had Cruikshank found himself in this work or buried himself? It was nothing to do with me, really. It was his own run, as Sol liked to say.

I got into the sleeping bag and fiddled with the light switch. The mouse returned as soon as the light went out.

At midday I arrived at the *B.I.F.* headquarters. Two men and a woman, all in their twenties or early thirties, were sitting round a desk in a large room that resembled a photographer's studio. Asking for Geissler, I was told that he was in Geneva opening a bank account but was expected back at any moment. Who was in charge then? I had an important message from London.

A bald dwarfish man was called in from the adjoining room and we introduced ourselves. This was Torben, the Danish actor. He shook hands with me, withdrew his hand quickly and opened Cruikshank's letter of introduction. As Alex had foreseen, his tactic of recruiting and despatching forthwith was warmly applauded as if he had pulled off some crucial deal. The other two men, Willem the Dutchman and Brian, an Australian photographer, joined with Torben in welcoming me formally to the organization. The woman at the table was introduced as a German cabaret artiste who wished to be represented by the *B.I.F.* and was investing accordingly. I chatted briefly with her while Torben made rapid calls to Geneva, Copenhagen, and to London where I heard him congratulate Cruikshank on his achievement.

I was provided with a yellow valise identical with Cruikshank's and was asked to fill in a faded mimeographed sheet which had a small space for your name, rank, photograph: the rest of the sheet was for listing your talents. Filling the page with truth and fiction I returned my dossier to Torben who placed it in a cardboard box beside several others.

The Australian photographer, with camera and tape recorder, left the office saying he needed to get some pictures and interviews for *Kings of the Streets,* an article to be featured in the *B.I.F.* magazine *Aspects of Action.* I joined Torben and Willem at the table where they were putting together the pilot edition. The German cabaret artiste, who looked more of a junkie or prostitute, and was very likely all three, rose to leave. She was anxious to know how soon might she expect to be called for auditions. When your files have been processed, she was told. May she have a receipt for the fifty guilders she had invested? Of course: Mr. Geissler will settle everything when he arrives from Munich. I thought he was in Geneva. At the moment he is about to leave Geneva for Munich.

I leafed through the paste-up prototype of the magazine which Cruikshank had been told yesterday to sell to the booksellers in Paris and Liechtenstein. The text had been typed out in atrocious English, the lingua franca of Amsterdam, on a plastic portable machine which stood in the corner of the room on an inverted orange box. For all its elevated subheadings, *The Philosophy of Action, He-She Tomorrow, Eye Music, The True Actors,* the magazine was little more than a glee-club newssheet.

Cruikshank, probably the only *B.I.F.* executive with a command of correct English, had been put in charge of the layout department while the others, Torben, Willem, Geissler, supplied the copy: chiefly Geissler, whose pandemonic style and unorthodox vocabulary was evident in the work of his subordinates.

So far I had witnessed only the secular workings of the Bureau. The magazine, however, while sticking to the same areas of international finance and action, dealt with the topics in a manner decidedly occult. Geissler ranted about the gold standard in terms of "He-She," a concept which the others had absorbed fluently, if not intelligibly, into their own articles. From the gold standard Geissler moved on to the Golden Age which would come into being when the True Actors of Life, embodiments of He-She, congregated under the aegis of the *B.I.F.* and gave their wholehearted support to the currencies of the world. This morbid interest in world finance seemed a suspicious characteristic in men who were rather obviously not wealthy; and their spiritual approach to the subject did not inspire confidence.

Furthermore, most of the pages of the magazine were blank except for titles and headlines: *B.I.F. Versus F.B.I.; The Cosmic Traveller; Prime Ministers' Phone-In; Interview with Rothschild.* As it stood it was an utter washout. Still, I told myself, the game's the thing. Maybe they *were* wealthy, maybe I'd get some wages for my troubles. And even if I didn't, I was obliged to stand in for Alex until Saturday so I ought to get down to business. Come on men, let's get this show on the road.

"What would you like me to do, gentlemen?"

"Have you the talent for layout?"

"I'm afraid I haven't."

Cruikshank's absence had been traced as the root cause of the magazine's slow progress.

"Perhaps," the timid Dutchman suggested, "you have the *hidden* talent for layout."

"We have discovered this in Alexander," Torben murmured encouragingly.

"No," I said with some firmness, "I can't even draw a

straight line with a T square. Maybe I could write an article."

"Yes. Would you like to read an article I have written today?" Torben asked quickly, as if he'd rather I didn't write anything at all.

"Yes, why not. I'll read it immediately."

The hit-or-miss spelling was permissible, but over and above the double, triple and quadruple negatives, and the rules of Danish grammar applied to the English language, the article was refined nonsense. Entitled simply *Off the Street*, its only recognisable point of reference was the nebulous "He-She" concept. Was this an example of automatic writing from beyond the grave?

"Your English could do with tidying up. It isn't quite clear what you're getting at, see here, '*I hadn't never always dreamt before.*' This sort of thing will confuse your readers."

"Yes, of course," he said understandingly in his quiet voice that made you want to strangle him. "This is what I am intending. We must confuse your minds," Torben struggled for the right words, "so as . . . so as to make their minds think in, in *positive* terms about *all* possibilities."

When he emphasised a word Torben's voice went quieter still.

"You could be right," I said, fearing instant discharge from my new job, "but on the other hand it may get mistaken for a printing error. Or people may get fed up trying to understand you."

"Yes, *exactly*. We must feed them up, feed up their minds. I agree. Let us look at the unfinished articles," he said, picking up the prototype. "I have been appointed editor until Mr. Geissler returns. We shall decide an article for you. Now . . . would you perhaps take over the *Interview with Rothschild*? We need two thousand words and some pictures for the spaces."

"Fair enough," I answered briskly, getting into the spirit of unbridled fantasy that pervaded the organisation. "Which Rothschild are we after? Because I believe there's more than one."

"Of course," Torben crooned in his mild aggressive way. "The *chief energy,* that is what we want."

"Have we his telephone number on file?" I asked, astonished at my own seriousness and the ease with which I adopted the first person plural.

"I believe," Willem spoke up, "that the file is disorderly."

"Ah yes," Torben purred, "Willem is our office manager. He is in charge of all office transactions."

"I have stopped arranging the file since Alexander has gone to open London. I am trying," he smiled modestly, "the layout."

"Do we *have* Rothschild's number?" I asked Willem soberly, sceptically.

"Perhaps Mr. Geissler has it," he said with apparent conviction.

I'd liked Willem from the start. He seemed, as Cruikshank had said, an excellent bloke, warm-hearted if a little naive. He had brought me coffee and sandwiches and had enquired after Alex's health. If the *B.I.F.* carried a fall guy it was Willem, for he was supplying the premises, the company car and the phone with its heavy load of long international calls, as well as the security on the bank loan.

I opted for a spot of immediate international action myself and, with Willem's phone bill in mind and my own possible embarrassment at heart, placed calls to Rothschild banks throughout Europe, calls personal to Rothschild himself for which we would not be charged unless the operator succeeded in getting him on the line.

None of my calls was accepted. I asked Torben for advice on the next move.

"Mr. Geissler will perhaps take over the Rothschild interview. There is also *The Cosmic Traveller* to be composed."

I spent the rest of the afternoon working on *The Cosmic Traveller.* Torben gave me some notes he and Geissler had made and I proceeded to discuss the economic theories of Ezra Pound in the light of major breakthroughs in the treatment of psychosis and recent advances on the international "He-She" front. Willem confessed ashamedly to not understanding my article, but Torben nodded approvingly and placed it in the cardboard box.

My last international action of the day was to phone Cruikshank's hotel while Torben and Willem were out visiting a client.

"Alex? *B.I.F.* here."

"Ah! How's it going?"

"Pretty loony."

"Isn't it. How does Geissler strike you though?"

"Haven't met him yet. He's in Geneva. Or Munich. Expected any time . . ."

"Ha ha."

"Listen, when are *you* expected back?"

"Well, tomorrow I suppose."

"With Angie? You got the cash?"

"No on both counts. She's coming later, everything's grand on that score, it's just tricky with her husband right now. But I managed to borrow some money this afternoon, enough to get me to Amsterdam. So I'll see you sometime tomorrow."

"Good. I won't last long here. I wrote an article on 'He-She' today."

"Immediate Literary Aahction!" Cruikshank yelled down the phone. "You win a medal and a coughdrop."

"And I found the Book last night."

"What boot?"

"Book. Your book. I read it."

"Really?" He sounded sincerely incredulous.

"It's brilliant. No wonder you ran a mile . . ."

"*Ran?* What are you talking about?"

"I don't know why I said that. I didn't mean anything by it."

"Hm . . . Well maybe I'll take a look at it if I've nothing better to do. Which seems likely."

"Listen, I can hear our colleagues on the stair. I'll see you tomorrow."

I was at my happiest, after a strange day's work, strolling under the trees by the canal on my way to Sol and Leah Bartok's place at the end of the tramline, a spacious house which, like the Bartoks' hospitality, is legendary among travelling people with intellectual or artistic aspirations. There the Truth is discussed at all hours and levels, seldom without the accompaniment of plentiful food and wine, music, wholesale sensuality and mild drugs, for Sol and Leah are not interested exclusively in the life of the mind.

5A Limburgerkaasstraat. I rang the bell.

The great Sol, as if sprung up through a trapdoor, stands smiling in the hallway, arms heavenwards in benediction so that his robe of black satin, really a smoking jacket, opens like a stage curtain on his nakedness, displaying it to the street. The inimitable Sol, my first sight of him for a year, wizard of the infinities, atlas of the soul, inhabitant of regions astral, prophet of the new hedonism, prodigious lover of all things intangible, the prime minister of mirth, leader of the elect, His Most Holy and Invisible Oneness Sol Bartok, Ludi Magister, prince of the spirit of Amsterdam.

"Hei . . . gh . . . he . . . igh . . ." he hums in quiet delight, head to one side, drawing syllables like chewing gum from the mouth.

"Sol you religious old bugger! I hardly know you without your beard."

I went to embrace him but he laid his hands on my shoulders.

"*Wait!*" he looked directly in my eyes. "I, I mean *we,* my wife and I, have been expecting you. Follow me . . ."

"How come? Did Alex ring you?"

"Alexander? No, he is busy writing a book about me. Leah! Leah!" he bellowed at her as usual, "we have a . . . *visitor.* Come here!"

Expecting some behaviourist prank or pious ritual I followed him into the lounge: long purple candles and exotic rugs lent it the appearance of a temple of Eastern worship. Leah came in from the kitchen looking, as always, at once sensual and ethereal. Sol looked on intently as we hugged.

"You can . . . *fuck* . . . her later if you want to."

"*What* did you say, Sol?" I turned on him.

As far as I could make out it wasn't a joke. I looked at Leah who was smiling airily at this remark from the normally jealous and, reluctantly, monogamous Sol.

"Don't listen to him, David. Sol wants to make us laugh. Come and sit down. How are you? We knew you would come today. Or tomorrow."

"So I've been told. I'm very well, Leah, but what's all this about?"

Both of them were smiling, as if they had some good news which I was soon to share.

"*Divine Prestidigitation,*" Sol sang out nonchalantly, like an inquisitor going playfully against the rules to give clues to the deserving.

The phrase was familiar. I looked to Leah, puzzled by Sol's happy smile and averted eyes. We were sitting round a low table and she was pouring wine into wooden goblets or gourds.

"Your letter," Leah said helpfully, "was full of Signs. Sol understood the Signs. He is making a journey."

"Which letter?"

"Divine Prestidigi*ta*tion," Sol prompted.

"You haven't joined the *B.I.F.* by any chance?" I asked him, getting bored with the riddle.

"*B.I.F.?*" He pondered it. "*Bif!*" he squeaked out through his nose, then, after a pause: "*Fib!*" Then again, "*Fib!*" but this time loudly, like Eureka.

"Look Sol, just tell me what's happening, will you? You know I'm not very evolved."

As I spoke I remembered a letter from Sol some weeks before in which he had asked me for the names of the Muses and their respective arts. He often requested information of this sort to save a trip to the library. In my reply I had facetiously included a tenth Muse, Sol Bartok, Muse of Divine Prestidigitation.

"Remember!" he raised a finger, dilated his eyes: "*Prestidigitation.* Press-the-digitalis!*"

"Yes I know what you're talking about now. But so what, Sol? What's this journey you're making?"

"Sol," Leah said cheerily, "is on a voyage to the perimeters of experience. You must explain it to David yourself, Sol," addressing herself helplessly to him, "because I'm not very good at explaining things."

As she spoke these words to him Sol leapt to his feet and balanced on one leg, screwing up his face in disdain, hands spread before him in a gesture of deprecation, uttering quick gasps as though in pain. Not until Leah had finished her sentence did he relax this bizarre stance.

"What's going on, Sol?" I asked, as a long-suffering victim of Sol's ontological experiments. "Is this something to do with your Work Evenings?"

He didn't answer but pointed at the stacks of books on his desk: *Hafiz Complete Works, The Cabala, The Song of Songs* in Yiddish/Dutch, *The Koran, Swedenborg, Pseudepigraphica,* and two huge lexicons, all lying open with notes in the margins.

"Sol, he works harder than anybody," Leah explained.

The phrase sounded more his than hers. He moved closer to me round the table. I began to suspect that all wasn't well.

"From now on," he told me in a solemn whisper, "we do everything by the book. We go by the book. *You,*" he said pointing, "have been sent here. *I* sent for you. You are the Keeper of the Book."

I looked wonderingly at the intelligent face, deep brow, wide eyes, permanent beard shadow, as he handed me a thick volume from the pocket of his smoking jacket. It was the Old Testament in Hebrew, which I am not qualified to read, far less keep, but he was insistent. Was this a new, more crackbrained regimen for the apprehension of Truth or had Sol gone over the top? There was something different in his eyes. I knew he had given up hallucinogens years ago but I asked all the same. He told me not to be frivolous.

I left the room to go to the lavatory, and when I came back

Sol had assumed the full lotus position and was jerking his head from right to left and muttering away:

"Verso-Recto-Verso-Recto-Verso . . ."

"Leah," I said authoritatively, "if you don't tell me what is going on I'll assume Sol has gone crazy."

"Don't worry," she said calmly. "Would you like some dinner?"

And I heard Sol change his mantra to:

"Red-Green-Red-Green-Red-Green . . ." still flicking his head to left and right.

"All right then," I said, "let's have dinner."

"Are you hungry Sol?" Leah asked on her way to the kitchen, and as soon as he heard her address him, Sol ceased his head-jerking, sprang up and went into his posture of total horror and revulsion, again relaxing it when she stopped talking.

"Sol," I asked him when we were alone, "what exactly are you doing?"

"Moving upwards," he said casually. "Always upwards," he stressed. "Following the angels."

"Tell me about it in plain language."

"Sure. All right. Listen: *One day in Autumn the Mullah Nasrudin was walking* . . . No, no, no, no, no. Upwards, we are moving upwards, following the angels."

He formed his arms into wings and began to flap them pathetically, smiling, moving round the room in short skips. Leah returned and Sol approached her, swaying back and forth, rotating his head, eyes swirling, circling in front of her face.

"Here David," she said to me, "have a cigarette and *relax.*"

"No thanks," I said producing *halfzware shag* and papers. "I like to roll."

"He likes to roll!" Sol repeated delightedly, reenacting the head-rotation procedure with me, his face an inch from my own. *"He likes to roll!"*

"For Christ's sake, Sol!" I shouted at him. "What the fuck is all this pantomime?"

"*Wait!*" he ordered with a flick of the wrists like a magician saying abracadabra, abruptly curtailing his gyrations.

He left the room and came back with a small trunk.

"This," he said confidentially, "is my Pandora's Box."

He glanced sideways at Leah who smiled at him and poured out more wine. I drank my glass quickly. Sol hadn't touched his at all.

"Here it is," he said to himself, drawing from the trunk a green hat, a Borsalino, probably a gift from one of his house guests, the sort of token people leave behind.

Sol placed the hat on my head, then took a pace backwards.

"You are *The Green Man,*" he said to me in sheer wonder, pointing, like a child at a circus. "*The Green Man!* We must always follow The Green Man."

The hat was certainly green, so was the jacket I was wearing. I thought to say something funny, make Sol laugh, find out if he was *able* to laugh.

"Don't follow me:

> *I am not Mahomet,*
> *Far from it . . ."*

"*I* know that!" he said, indignant. "You are The Green Man. *The Green Man,*" he repeated incredulously; then confidently: "You are The Green Man."

He dipped again into his Pandora's Box and handed me a sheaf of papers, opening up his robe to conceal them from the eyes of Leah who had settled down to reading a book while the dinner was cooking. The papers comprised a short story of Cruikshank's, my Divine Prestidigitation letter and a series of Polaroid photographs of nude women in lewd poses, one of whom, I was shocked to discover, was a former lover of mine. I looked up from the photos to see Sol, over by the curtained window, brushing his face against a hanging plant. The Green Man was smoothly superseded by The Green Plant. We must follow the plants, that was it.

"I wish I could talk to you, Sol. I think you need some kind of help."

"Well," he said with sudden enlightenment, "when you can't get help from a man—*ask a dog!*"

At that exact moment, God, in his infinite cruelty, caused a dog to bark loudly in the street outside the window. It took all my strength to prevent Sol, quite naked by now, from rushing into the street to seek help from a dog.

"Ah," he said in my arms, giving up the struggle as abruptly as he had begun it, *"The Green Man . . .* We must always follow The Green Man."

"Sol," I said, squeezing his shoulder, half in affection, half in rage, "I wish I could understand you."

"Why can't you?" he shrugged amiably. *"I speak all languages.* But right now I must go to bed because it is raining."

True enough, it was raining.

Sol got into his smoking jacket, flapped his wings and began moving up the stairs. Halfway up he turned to me, raised a finger and spoke with great meaningfulness,

> *It's raining*
> *It's pouring*
> *The Old Man*
> *Is whoring*

then off he went to bed, murmuring indistinct conjurations.

I had imagined Leah to be humouring Sol, out of inherent terror of him, but in our subsequent conversation she assured me that he was breaking into important new territories of the mind. She agreed that it was a "wild run," but felt that we lesser people were obliged to bear with Sol and not condemn him before we had understood what he was up to. It wasn't till much later in the conversation that she dropped the information that she was in love with another man. Did Sol know of this? Of course! We have no secrets from each other.

Maybe that's all there is to it, I thought as I walked home to

Cruikshank's Kamer: Sol loses his lover and his sanity follows her out the door. Was that possible? Whatever the case, it didn't tell me what to do to keep Sol safe from hospitalization, possible maltreatment and probable repatriation for being in the country illegally. But for now he was asleep, peacefully as far as I could tell from his face.

We had a lot to talk about, Cruikshank and I, when we met the next evening.

I spent the day at the *B.I.F.* office, tidying up my article and meeting my boss Geissler. He stormed into the office at midday with the news that "Switzerland is in," showing off a photograph of a skyscraper in Zurich which he claimed was our own property, and distributing to his staff ballpoint pens and matchboxes bearing the logo of a famous Swiss bank.

Geissler wore jeans and an army combat jacket and his receding hair hung down around his neck. His yellow valise was plastered with travel stickers. He shook my hand warmly, stood me up against the wall-sized map of the world, and began taking photographs. I asked straight away if I might have some money. "Torben! Willem! Give this maahn some money! Our new colleague must have some caahsh. Alexander has done well. Is he back? We must take urgent internaahtional aahction while our luck is holding. Willem!" he shouted, snapping away with his camera, "you must send a telegrahm to Rome, to Zeffirelli: we want him to start next week on a film for the archive of the *B.I.F.* experience. Torben! Have you taken aahction on the Continental Intertimer? Oh come on, maahn!" Geissler said, slapping me on the back and putting down his camera. "Yes, I *know* I was in Switzerland myself, but I cannot have time for everything. Get on the phone to Rolex immediately. We want two hundred thousand guilders advance on the *idea* for the Intertimer. How much," he said, turning to me, "is that in Swiss francs? Never mind. Tell them Torben that we'll post the blueprints in the morning, as soon as Alexander has finished them."

I slipped away unnoticed while Geissler was making a phone call.

Cruikshank had arrived early in the afternoon. When I got back to the Kamer he was in the armchair reading the closing pages of *The Amsterdam Book*.

"I've just quit the *B.I.F.*," I said, "and poor old Sol has gone mad."

"I quit the *B.I.F.* myself, the moment I got carried away by this significant work." Cruikshank closed the book, tapped it with his fist and let out one of his piercing howls. "And if the truth be told," he quietened down, "I never worked for the *B.I.F.* at all. I was a skilful imposter. But what's this about Sol?"

"Well, it looks like he's gone round the twist. I know it's hard to tell with Sol—maybe you should just see for yourself: you've spent more time with him lately. But with me he just talked in riddles, called me *The Green Man*—does that mean anything to you?—and invited me to fuck Leah."

"Never heard of *The Green Man* except the pub in East Grimpe. Not really Sol's territory. As for Leah, I know there's this bloke she's supposed to be in love with."

"She mentioned that."

"Hm . . . Sol's a bit funny about it. I doubt if he likes it very much, but it was at his suggestion that she went ahead and got it going. A few weeks ago when he was reviving the old sexual freedom stuff, screwing everybody he could get his hands on, Leah's best friend included."

"Anyway, I told her we'd come over this evening."

Walking again across the breadth of Amsterdam to what Cruikshank called the Fun Palace on Limburgerkaasstraat:

"D'you know," he said to the air, "I think that maybe I am a genius."

"I'd be inclined to agree with you. When I read it last night I . . ."

"Oh I don't mean *this*," Cruikshank interrupted, pulling *The Amsterdam Book* from the pocket of his raincoat. "The writing of it does have something to do with what I'm talking about; but the book itself," he said, tapping it again with his knuckles, "well, it's only a by-product. And an irrelevant one at that. Whether I keep it and have it published, or throw it away, makes no difference to me. In fact," his eyes flashed beneath the streetlamp where he'd stopped and gripped my arm, "in fact I think I *will* throw it away. A proper gesture!"

Cruikshank laughed up his sleeve, took a pace forward and tossed *The Amsterdam Book* into the air. In the silence of the night we heard it fall, schluff, into the canal. He was smiling broadly, well pleased with himself, as he might look after draining the first pint of black stout following a period of abstinence.

"A proper gesture," he summed up. "Cruikshank est mort, Vive Cruikshank. Let's get going."

He swung his walking cane and adjusted his cravat, his face an optimistic light gliding along the banks of the Amstel. I had been finding it hard to say anything.

"Did you plan all this in advance, Alex?"

"No! Not at all! I was going to give the book to Sol for his Pandora's Box. An important relic, *what*!"

"So what sort of genius are you then?"

"Well . . ." Cruikshank screwed up his face with the word, "I don't really believe in all the genius crap, but what I meant was this: I feel, for the first time in my life, that I am at the perfect centre of my own powers. The book was a prelude to this state, and recognising Angie as the person I want to live with (which came as a surprise) was a result of it. I would've seen her differently before—what I mean is, I would have failed to recognise her. Now, I can master anything I choose to; and I know exactly what not to choose. That doesn't mean I'm growing complacent, or that I know everything. On the contrary, it just means that I'm no longer searching for something in life, butchering my brains, trying to write like an inspired lunatic, wasting my time on things like the *B.I.F.* Genius, in my

[162]

opinion, is nothing more than the ability, the knack really, to see the thread running through the beads. I've lost interest in the meaning of life, I don't care *what* it means: I just want to live it," Cruikshank concluded with a quick smile, "and investigate its possibilities."

"*The Green Man!*" Sol said breathlessly, in the enraptured voice of childhood, the moment he set eyes on Alex Cruikshank.

I didn't receive even a perfunctory greeting when I walked in and saw Sol, pointing at Cruikshank, wrapped in his smoking jacket amid the wreckage of what had once been furniture. Electrical wires hung from the ceiling, a window had been smashed, floorboards pulled up. Sol claimed responsibility with lordly gestures at the debris and at himself. I asked him how things were going. Upwards, he said. We must follow the angels, the plants and The Green Man.

"Alexander," he said almost in awe, "you are *The Green Man!*"

"Sol, you're off your bloody bonce," Cruikshank said soberly, putting an arm around him. "Talk some sense and tell me what's the matter."

From that point on Sol refused to address us in a language we could understand. He talked volubly in Hebrew, or he mimed, contorting his small muscular body into horripilating postures and making rhythmic gasps of pain alternated with empty laughter.

Whenever Leah opened her mouth to speak Sol crouched in horror, frantic hands pushing her very existence from him.

The question was what to do with him. Cruikshank and I agreed to sit it out in the hope of a change for the better.

He got worse.

Three of his disciples from the Work Evenings turned up and decided to stay for a while, Zennish novices who were accustomed to outlandish modes of behaviour in their master. They sat for two hours, literally at his feet, seeming to understand every flicker of his eyes, every charade; then without warning, in the peculiar Zen tradition, Sol smacked a female novice full in the face.

We tried again to get him to talk, asked him in private whether there were problems in his married life. He wrote down on a sheet of paper: Leah is the Ideal Woman, and handed it over with a nod and a smile. Leah was still holding on to the story about the outer edges of experience.

Cruikshank moved to take Sol in his arms but Sol pushed him away, miming his opinion that all physical contact was repugnant.

I tried explaining matter-of-factly that if he were to go outside, which he had repeatedly expressed desires to, he might be arrested and put in hospital. I reminded him that he was an illegal resident. I pointed out, in case he was unaware of it, that he was acting in a way that drew attention, that might frighten other people. I told him that he must never strike anyone again. Sol listened intently, respectfully, thought for a while chin in hand, then responded at length in Hebrew.

He had typed something on a sheet and pinned it to the wall: "Before this revelation everything was enveloped in a kind of mist. And the whole reason for this, as I see it, is that people are under the misapprehension that the human brain is situated in the head: nothing could be further from the truth. It is carried by the wind from the Caspian Sea."

From time to time he would expose his cock, holding it meekly in the palm of his hand, as he had apparently done earlier in the day at his café, the *Gouden Haan*.

We sat for an hour or more, strangling in the silence, waiting for a miracle as Sol mimed his way through a series of incomprehensibles. Then he lay down and curled up tight, refusing all attention. He stayed that way for a full ten minutes.

From that submissive position he suddenly leapt into the air, pointing, shaking, and shouted happily: *"The Green Man!"*

The words were directed not at Cruikshank or me but at a

traffic signal out in the street that was visible through a tear in the curtain. We all faced the direction indicated by Sol's out-stretched arm which hung there as if floating.

The Green Man, nine inches tall and clearly a real green man, changed to a flashing green man on the pedestrian crossing.

Sol was too quick for us. All we caught were splinters of glass as he threw himself out of the window. It was fortunate that we were on the ground floor. I got outside in time to see Sol pick himself up and rush across the street towards the green man, already a red man, throwing kicks and punches at all who stood in his way.

They got him almost immediately. We convinced the doctors that Sol had been messing about with drugs, so he was allowed to remain at home in his own bed, heavily doped on the kind of sedative that stays in the bloodstream for a week or two. He was snoring within the hour.

Cruikshank and I took to the streets sometime after midnight and wandered along Marnixstraat towards the Leidseplein. Angie had telephoned Sol's number with the news that she and her child would be arriving in three or four days, and Alex was caught between joy and sorrow: he was finding it difficult, with Sol Bartok lying in purgatory half a mile away, to talk about the new life that was opening up to him.

We turned down the Leidsestraat which cuts straight through the four concentric canals, Prinsengracht, Keizersgracht, Herren-gracht, Singel, into the final circle of hell. Crossing the great square, the Dam, we sat down mechanically on a bench. We tried talking.

"Have you got somewhere to live with Angie?"

"I'll find a place. No problem."

"What do you think you'll be doing with yourself."

"Nothing much," he said half-smiling. "Get an unoppressive part-time job. Take the kid for walks in Vondelpark. Write cheerful books."

The cold quiet of the night was broken gently by the sound of a music-box which plays on the hour from the clock above Peek & Cloppenburg's department store.

Au clair de la lune
Mon ami Pierrot.
Prête-moi ta plume
Pour écrire un mot.
Ma chandelle est morte,
Je n'ai plus de feu:
Ouvre-moi la porte
Pour l'amour de Dieu.

Throughout that lonesome tune played on the loneliest of instruments, its haunted lyric passing across my mind, I gazed like a moron at the neon sign saying *Peek & Cloppenburg.* Lack of sleep and the draining effect of prolonged contact with insanity were beginning to unbalance me.

Peek & Cloppenburg . . . the long name and the short, the ghost of Pierrot, Cruikshank & Bartok, *The Amsterdam Book,* the *B.I.F.,* the concentric canals, merged in me and congealed into one tortured hallucination, presided over by the unique yet ubiquitous Green Man: and Sol and Alex were now Peek & Cloppenburg, advertised in tall letters, chieftains of the Dam, death of night watchers above the last circle.

Historia Felicitatum

THE COUNTESS AND I are in business together, the roofing business: we repair leaking roofs, faulty guttering, blocked rainwater pipes, in brief, everything related to keeping the weather at bay from above. We learnt it all from a book.

Our clientele is drawn from the well-appointed intelligentsia, who prefer to engage an outfit that has a bit of style rather than face the traditional British craftsman who is not much fun, seldom a conversationalist, and with whom they are ill equipped to deal in spite of their professed solidarity with the working classes of the world. With her extreme personal charm and revolutionary views, secrets to no one, the Countess attracts and fascinates these clients—described by Clorinda as *radical souls in reactionary bodies*—who, of course, are forever requiring roofing work to be carried out on their extensive properties or on those of friends to whom they have recommended us. Is it because they assume that she, and I who am slightly left of Joe Hill, would never stoop to overcharging a fellow traveller?

Bodger, the Countess' dog, the Roofing Dog, sits always at the foot of the ladder except when he gets tempted away by the prospect of something to eat. Due to the Countess' embarrassment about robbing people hand over fist it invariably devolves on me to ask for the cash, no cheques please, when we have completed a job; and this is when Bodger comes into his own, crouched by my side, hackles up, snarling as the money is counted out, snapping vigorously at the hands that are supplying him with the finest meats.

We enjoy roofing even though we know very little about it. It is pleasant to sit on a roof in the sunshine, reading aloud to each other from the instruction manual, doing everything step by step. Bodger however, barking down below, loathes the life of a roofing dog, and the chief complaints levelled against us by our clients are of the "Bodger has bitten little Emma again" sort.

Enemies of great wage differentials, we work on a basis of vague equality, calculating our fee for a day's work on an estimate of our employer's salary (not forgetting his tax dodges, realisable assets and bank interest), doubling it up because there are two of us of course and slapping a further percentage on top to accelerate the redistribution of wealth.

It's a healthy life, there's plenty of money to be made and it's an ideal job for someone with no particular skill or talent to offer. For the most rudimentary practice of roofing in Britain it is essential to understand the function of the slate-ripper and to master the technique of manipulating it: the slate-ripper is a long iron implement from which two hooked . . . but I am forgetting that this is supposed to be a love story.

The Countess and I had a kind of love story interwoven with the pursuit of our trade. In fine spring weather, after a hard day, our pockets fat with earnings, we would select a suitable pub where we might slake away the slate dust and discuss the evening's itinerary. It had to be a place where we would not be refused entry on the grounds of dress, dog, dirty faces, and one that sold traditionally brewed ale, pints of which the Countess liked to drink with a glass of *pastis* and water on the side. So we usually found ourselves in workingmen's pubs ("When will you learn to say working*person*?"), spit and sawdust efforts with darts tournaments in the background and all around you the bellicose exchange of sporting and political opinions lifted from the pages of *The Sun* and *The Daily Mirror*, newspapers so popular that each man had, protruding from the jacket pocket, his own private copy of one or the other of them.

The Countess takes a lot of teasing from men who find roofing a strange occupation for a woman, particularly an attractive woman, but she is a specialist, not to mention charmer, in dealing with hecklers. And Bodger too is delightful company in a milieu abounding in pork scratchings, steak and kidney pies, peanuts and sentimental drunks who are eager to part with these in exchange for an opportunity to pet the doggie. Bodger wolfs down the proffered morsels and submits frigidly to the perfunctory stroke for only a moment before sounding a warning growl and show of fangs; insistent strokers, desperate for approval, always get bitten by Bodger and laughed at by their mates. Others, who raise a fist in mock attack at the first snarl, are relieved when Bodger cringes and slinks off to cower beneath the Countess' chair, smugly gratified when Bodger grovels back afterwards to reingratiate himself with the food-bearing offender: who, deducing that man has conquered nature, offers the broken-in beast an especially large morsel followed by a heavy dose of petting. This time he gets bitten with no warning whatsoever.

Well drunk by seven in the evening we would leave the pub and start thinking about diversion, but first we had to go home and wash, change into clean clothes, investigate some new restaurant. Then perhaps we would go to the cinema or theatre and round off the evening with a midnight visit to Hampstead Heath where Bodger was allowed to run wild and chase the sinister eccentrics.

Brought together professionally by financial distress the Countess and I soon became very good friends. Although she herself was more or less impoverished, she had a wide network of acquaintances who were not. These people, it seemed, were always complaining about how difficult it was to get a tradesman when you needed one; so the Countess, always keen to learn about and gain more control over her environment, set herself the goal of acquiring various technical skills. By the time I met her through an advertisement in a short-lived magazine called *The Practical Catalyst*—"Person wanted for hard work and early retirement. Must not be feeble. Must like dogs."—she had gained proficiency in carpentry, plumbing and bricklaying. On the phone she explained to me that roofing had emerged as the most profitable and satisfying trade. Moreover there was a huge amount of work to be had in this field. Was I interested? I made it clear that I knew nothing about roofing—"Jolly good, neither do I."—and arranged to meet up with her. Expecting a crank I turned up well armed with healthy scepticism and discovered the Countess to be a remarkably intelligent young woman, if a little odd.

She poured two glasses of home-made sloe gin, introduced me to Bodger with the dishonest assurance that he would not bite, and began at once to discuss business. There was this man who by means of a substantial inheritance had become rich against his will and was anxious to become only moderately comfortable again. Most of his wealth was in the form of run-down property which, because of the tenants therein, he was unable to sell. He had already reduced their rents to nominal sums and had promised to rehabilitate their homes: it wouldn't do for people to think of him as some kind of slumlord. Why didn't he simply give his property away? His trustees, whatever they were, wouldn't allow him to. The major portion of the work was roofing. She had already done a bit of roofing but really it was a job for two people: there was a lot of heavy work, it could be dangerous working alone, and besides it was very lone-some up on a roof, especially without Bodger. Anyway, there was this book . . .

I read the book that evening and we started work two days later. Soon business was so brisk that I was often able to offer casual work to the likes of Cruikshank and later Randaggio when the Countess took a week off to go mountaineering or potholing. And slowly I came to know her—as a person who saw much and said little. Every new piece of information about her past led me to ask questions, and after a few weeks of desul-tory talk in pubs and on rooftops her extraordinary life took some shape in my mind.

Born in Italy to an Irish mother and Polish father, she was raised by a nanny in Peru and spoke no English until she was six. Meanwhile her parents had been circling the globe at speed, squandering the family wealth in ill-advised speculation and fi-nancial intrigue. Then they all settled in France. There was talk of gold smuggling and gunrunning. There was a private casino. Then the Countess was sent off to school in England, having just accustomed herself to speaking French. She ran away from school at sixteen and got married to an Australian actor whom she divorced two years later in order to marry a university lecturer from Buffalo, New York. Then a degree in oriental languages at an American university. There followed her political days in England where she marched, sabotaged, spoke out, as outraged as any oppressed proletarian and twice as articulate; but she retired in disgust to the Hindu Kush to live with a tribe of nomads. She stayed there two years and wrote a book about them, by which time the nomads were beginning to strike her as being just about as bad as everybody else. Repulsed in a desperate attempt to enter Tibet she returned to England with her husband and divorced him. On this overland journey she was accompanied by a very young and perhaps docile Bodger whom she had rescued from being stoned to death on the streets of Kabul and who entered England unobtrusively, drugged on sleeping tablets, curled up at the bottom of a small suitcase.

The Countess settled down in London to renew friendships and seek a tolerable means of earning a living. She learnt a few skills, she placed an advertisement. But she wasn't altogether satisfied, a fact I deduced from the number of times she tried to interest me in a project requiring that we go to Patagonia, to a specific region where the language is a mixture of Welsh and Spanish, and set ourselves up as sheep-shearers.

Our friendship took us to bed one night on a weekend camping trip, and afterwards we spent many nights together and many days of kissing and cuddling on rooftops. I doubt whether we were ever wholly serious about our romance but there was a positive creative force in it that made me delighted to get up and go to work in the mornings, convinced that something bright would come to pass.

Wide awake one night after the late cinema we drove into the deep south of London where my old friend Julia Einstein was giving a party. Bodger, as always, was in attendance, nosing the gearstick at inappropriate moments and barking loudly when he spied a policeman or another dog.

WHEN Werther met Lotte she was in the kitchen cutting a loaf of bread. I beat Werther on all counts: for a start, it was in Julia Einstein's bathroom that I met Loyshka.

Now did this event take place yesterday or was it more like a couple of years ago? It doesn't matter. . . . I knew quite a few of the people at the party—Julia of course; Sol and Leah Bartok on holiday in London in the days before the advent of The Green Man; Cruikshank and his then lover Renata; Conrad Winchester, long divorced from Suzanne but still in optimistic pursuit of truth and beauty. I wonder if they noticed anything, these witnesses of so many turning points and blind alleys in my life.

Asking for Julia I was directed to the bathroom. I didn't see Loyshka right away, all attention being focused on Julia Einstein herself who was talking earnestly while sitting in the bath soaping her breasts. Several girls, Julia's old school friends, were standing by like ladies-in-waiting. I recognised Elena with the blonde curls and lisp, Rachel with the tinted spectacles and the haughty bitch who said "No men in this bathroom."

But forget the others.

Loyshka. What is she like? I am a lover, I see everything at one and the same time. I cannot describe everything. Besides, when was anything ever conveyed about hair by the colours of pine trees at night? Do believers in God gain automatic understanding of quantum jump?

"You can have mine," Loyshka said from a corner of the bathroom when I asked Julia if I might have a glass of wine.

She looked like a schoolgirl, out of her depth among the grown-ups. Probably someone's younger sister. Her outstretched arm with the glass of wine in her hand, cheap Spanish, and the nervous laugh when she said she didn't like alcohol—these first contacts were secondary to the unusual ambiance in which she appeared to me, an actual *light* coming off her skin. I am not one to cry Miracle when the dead are revived or to wax pensive over the Shroud of Turin, but I believe that the word saintlike passed across my mind. "All legend," says Sol Bartok, "is built on rock: let no one talk of love who has seen no such light."

The sight, sound and brightness of her were at that moment ingrained into me, proleptically, as if I already knew the confluent course our lives were to take and wanted to remember exactly how we had begun. Still, despite the quick glance and second glance—was that *fear?*—the harmony of certitude as when one grasps a law of nature, she had only spoken a dozen words from which a gravid brain had inferred a great deal. I accepted the glass, sank a draught of the sweet liquid vileness, spontaneously emptied the rest over my hysterical friend Julia Einstein and left the bathroom as if I had important things to attend to.

In a large room downstairs that had been cleared of furniture to accommodate dancing I sat with a glass of beer and thought of Loyshka's face, nothing else. The Countess, sitting on the floor with Renata and Sol and Leah and Julia's young son, was restraining Bodger from doing mischief to the too trusting child. I wondered if Loyshka had come with a man, and if she had, what I should do about it. It would be easier to talk to her when the place had got a bit crowded.

"Fear eats the soul," I heard Sol Bartok say. It was the title of the film we had just watched. "This is the direct translation of an Arab proverb."

"Yes," the Countess said, "it was about an Arab working in Germany. Sit *down* Bodger."

"Why is your dog so horrible?" little Matthew kept asking.

"He's *not* horrible. You're not a horrible little Bodger-dog, are you? Bodger just has . . . interesting habits."

"Alex and I saw that film," Renata said, "but the audience really spoiled it, you know, people laughing at the sad bits and . . ."

"It is a great mistake," Sol put in, "to show people anything remotely approximate to the truth. No, listen," he insisted, raising a hand to quell objectors, "what the public want is excitement—and they are willing to pay well for it: murder, rape, torture, these are the things the public enjoy, not to say deserve. When I finally come to power," he declaimed, pausing to swallow about half a pint of red wine, "I shall condemn the public to thirty years of solitary confinement . . ."

"Sol, don't talk so much," Leah said, in Hebrew, but everybody understood and laughed.

". . . which most of them have coming anyway," Sol added quickly. "I will now stop talking for fifteen minutes. Come and entertain me, David my boy."

We sat in a corner and I mentioned Loyshka to him. What was Sol's opinion on the notion of love at first sight? Were such things possible?

"Well," he cocked his head, raised an upturned palm, "it is certainly impossible for anything to be impossible. Where is she?"

"She's upstairs."

"So why are you talking to me about it? Leah!" he bellowed across the room, "Leah! I need some affection."

"That wasn't fifteen minutes," she said, sitting down beside him.

I drank up my beer and left. On my way upstairs I collided with a lady from the Seychelles Islands who engaged me in urgent conversation. She was drunk.

"That man," she jerked a thumb, "just told me I'm getting *fat*. Do *you* think I'm fat?"

"Well," said I, sizing her up on the stairs, "you look fine to me. But maybe I should subject you to closer scrutiny."

"He really upset me, that man."

"Right then, let's get this out of the way."

She stood at ease while I hauled her sweater up and over her breasts. What was I doing here, I ought to be hurrying on my way. Was I drunk too?

"Not bad," I heard myself say appreciatively, undoing her

jeans and slipping the zipper down to where green panties creased brown skin, pondering the result of Loyshka appearing at the top of the stairs and the Countess at the bottom.

The lady from the Seychelles giggled.

"You seem to me to be in excellent shape," I ventured, rummaging hamfistedly in her pubic hair.

"What are you doing?" she giggled, holding on to the banister rail with both hands behind her back.

"The Grand Tour," I said, and it was all taken in good part.

Having achieved this degree of intimacy in so short a time it was clear to both of us that we were not made for each other: we kissed, shook hands and continued respectively up and down the stairs.

More guests had congregated in Julia's bedroom, standing around in the usual groups of threes and fours. I had no idea that Julia Einstein had so many friends, notably handsome young men: they stood by watching their hostess as she tripped back and forth from cupboard to wardrobe, dressed only in a longish T-shirt, trying to decide what was the best outfit to wear. Loyshka was standing by offering advice and encouraging Julia to get dressed quickly. Stuck for something original to say I gatecrashed their conversation with the suggestion that Julia simply get rid of the T-shirt and leave it at that.

"After all," I said expansively, "what's a party for if not . . ." and my sentence trailed off, pulled up by Loyshka's smile.

"Have you met?" Julia asked.

"Yes," we said simultaneously, although really we hadn't been introduced.

"I was just saying," Julia whispered, "that I'm after that young, *person,* sitting over by the door. May I enlist your help?"

"Fine," I said. "Loyshka and I will go and warm him up."

"I don't think we'll need to," Loyshka said, tugging my elbow. The young person was watching Julia as she bent down to open a drawer. We walked over and sat down beside him on a large cushion.

"How did you come to know Julia?" I asked Loyshka after a few moments of discreet staring at each other.

"We went to school together. Is that your dog?" Bodger had followed me upstairs and was sniffing at the sandwich in my hand.

"Certainly not! It belongs to the lady I came with."

"Oh."

"My friend."

"Mm. What's the dog called?"

"Bodger."

"Was that the lady with long blonde hair and cowboy boots?"

"Yes."

"It's a nice looking dog—*hello Bodger!*—isn't he nice."

"If Bodger belonged to me I would shoot him."

"What? Why?"

"No, I wouldn't shoot him. I've no idea why I said that. Come back Bodger!"

If she went to school with Julia that made her five years younger than I—five older than she looked—perfect once you took my immaturity into account. And look at the sunrise eyes—can they be yellow?—and the body moving beneath those fashionable rags. Her blatant good looks made her easy to describe at first, small waist, busty, slick shoulders and solid hips, perfectly red sculpted mouth, not at all pink, teeth that really flashed, clear of complexion and brighteyed as a child, all the classic stuff, elegant hands (I imagined my own paws weighing up her breasts) and filtering from her this translucent rainbow, and in her voice too there was a glimmer.

Julia, fully dressed, sat casually beside us and was duly paired off with the man of her choice, who looked as though he'd waited a lifetime for just that event.

"Julia told me you're writing a book," Loyshka began after a break in our talk during which I felt her body heat warming my arm several inches away; and simultaneous with an abrupt lull in conversations around us she spoke out clearly: "Is it a novel you are writing?"

Every eye turned to meet the author.

"Book?" I said uncomfortably. "I'm a roofer."

The silence persisted, everybody curious to hear the conclusion. I felt myself redden.

"*Is it a novel?*" I mimicked cruelly, but no one as much as tittered. "You," I said in her ear to throw the others off the track, "are the most attractive girl I've ever met. Let's go downstairs and have a drink."

"I'm sorry about that," she said on the way.

"My fault. I shouldn't be embarrassed."

"No, you shouldn't. And," she whispered exaggeratedly, to cheer me up: "I *would* like to read your book."

Opening a wine bottle, Loyshka fetching glasses, I remembered she didn't drink.

"You don't really want wine."

"No. But," and she kissed me, and I kissed her, gentle as air, and something was sealed.

"And do you have some kind of occupation?" I asked intelligently when two intruders rolled into the room.

"Yes, I'm an advertising manager, at least I will be on Monday, I just came back from Paris where I've been for two years and I answered an ad in the *Times* and got this job with the Filmic Worldscape Anthology which is a book, and I have my own office near the London Dungeon, you're welcome to visit if you're ever around that area . . ."

"Don't meet many advertising managers. Were you one in France too?"

"Oh no," she said as if I should have known, "I was at university, Vincennes, studying drama but I'm also interested in film, that's why I took this job, meet some people, and the Anthology only comes out once a year so I thought I'd do it for a year then maybe go back to college, am I *talking*?"

"A fair amount."

It didn't take a Paracelsus, or even an amateur gypsy, to perceive what was taking place behind our eyes and chatter. We might as well have talked elegant balderdash: it would have instructed and delighted just the same.

The Countess showed up with Bodger in tow. She'd had enough and wanted us to leave immediately, it was long past her early bedtime and poor Bodger hadn't had his supper. I introduced Loyshka while Bodger snaffled another sandwich from an oblivious kissing pair. Responding with polite restraint to Loyshka's effervescent greeting the Countess went off to fetch her leather jacket.

"When can I . . . ?"

"Yes, I'll give you my number, and my office . . ."

"I can get your number from Julia," I chirped innocently, not wanting to be caught so redhanded by the Countess who, because she doesn't believe in jealousy, gives you hell for making her feel it.

"No," Loyshka said seriously, "I'd rather give it to you now."

I was standing at the door of the dancing room, looking for Cruikshank and Renata in order to say good night to them, when another friend of mine walked in. He was gazing around in wild surmise at the abundance of attractive women present. He wanted a woman to dance with, but how could he be expected to choose one among so many?

"Dance with her," I said without hesitation, pointing at Loyshka who was standing across the hallway, whose kiss was still wet on my mouth, whose phone number was neatly written on my cigarette papers. "Loyshka Kittson: Conrad Winchester."

The Countess' silence as we drove home gave me plenty of time to think. My only worry was that Loyshka might turn out to be a pervert; for, with the exception of the Countess herself, I had lately been meeting nothing but the kind of ladies who liked to talk enthusiastically about, say, Ouspensky and then somehow manipulate the conversation round to, say, buggery; and no matter how compatible these two things may be they were highly unsuitable to my needs. I was growing increasingly simple in my tastes, turning into a simple sort of man who, like Alex Cruikshank, wanted little more than to settle down with a simple woman and get on with things. Now the great thing about simplicity is that it cannot become predictable, and we aspiring simpletons share many characteristics with the beasts of field and forest. We show agitation when the full moon rises, but not always. . . .

"What was that girl's name?" the Countess broke into my thoughts.

"Loyshka. Did you like her?"

"No."

"Why not?"

"She seemed a bit of a twit to me. Are you going to see her again?"

"Yes. What do you mean by twit? It seems a bit strong for someone you hardly spoke to." (*Don't* defend her, you fool.)

"Well, a bit poncified you know."

"You mean wealthy and middle-class."

"Suppose. I can't imagine my having anything to say to her. Let's drop it."

"Okay. Bodger, will you please get your snout away from my ear."

Talking about Bodger: I read a wonderful article in a newspaper about a playful Alsatian who, after a lifetime of child-guarding and utter devotion, attacked and ripped the throat from his master—*and for no reason at all!* This article, I remember thinking at the time, offers a fine illustration of my notion of simplicity. True, the newspaper was a few weeks old, but all the same it was a first-rate article. Rastus, the old Alsatian dog, was put to death immediately. Serve the master, Rastus old fellow, bring his slippers—the disgusting ones—heel Rastus, give auntie a paw Rastus. Rastus accomplished such tasks for twelve years with the simple intensity he brought to his every act. Had he discovered, somewhat late in life admittedly, that the master was unsurpassed among hearthside nincompoops, no leader of men or dogs? Is that why he tore the master's throat out?

[181]

Not to stray too far from the point: I was advancing, or perhaps reverting, to the desire for a simple life that included a simple woman who had no more than passing interest in Ouspensky and buggery; and now here was Loyshka in whom I already had great faith. Nothing simpler.

As we drove across the Chelsea Bridge I wondered whether she was dancing now with Conrad Winchester. It would be a terrible and ironical state of affairs if something were to happen between the two of them. But I had faith. And Conrad and I were friends now—we were well equipped to deal with those things. I thought of Suzanne, who has a different surname now and lives out in the country with her new husband and her four children. Why on earth did she leave Conrad? He believes that he frightened her off by insisting upon seeing her as she really was, is, and by never relinquishing his desire for absolute honesty and emotional freedom. Maybe he is right. Conrad is often right about such things. And who could know better than I just how much Conrad means to Suzanne?

The torments of men and women. I thought of Loyshka, whoever she was, and my blood ran freer. Try as I might to invent them, there were clearly no more barriers between myself and everything I had ever desired.

So we met a week later in a coffee shop. I had done my best to look presentable but next to Loyshka, haute-coutured to the lobes of her ears, I resembled a well-turned-out scarecrow such as an enterprising farmer might enter in a competition.

"I'm the worst dressed person in sight," I said, looking round the room.

"Are you? So you are." She found this very droll.

"I didn't know it was this sort of place."

"Sorry. You don't mind me dressing up do you? I've been thinking about you every single . . ."

"I should think so too," I snarled between kisses. "Do you know that I love you?"

"I knew it!" she shouted, throwing her arms about me and upsetting the coffee cups, to say nothing of the other customers and the staff. "It's so wonderful! I love you so much, let's get married shall we? God I don't even know your surname, let's go away somewhere—I'll get more coffee, you don't fancy marriage do you? It doesn't matter very much so don't worry. I don't care either. No sugar. Black or white?"

"Let's have two of each to celebrate."

"Good idea."

She came back with four coffees, none of which got tasted.

"My flatmate said—*should I be telling you this?*—she said that I'm not to spend the night with you and spoil everything."

"Well," I collected myself from being taken aback, "in that case you must spend the night with me and not spoil anything."

"Yes good . . . good . . . good. That way I can keep my promise to her and she won't lecture me, shall we go somewhere this evening?"

"Before we go to bed you mean?"

"How far away is your bed?"

"An hour. We could have something to eat first."

"What a good idea! I haven't had an appetite for months, where shall we go?"

"There's a bogus French restaurant just round the corner."

"My uncle probably owns it."

We walked slowly back to my flat after dinner, alternately silent and overflowing with things to say, important details. Here and there we stopped to look at ourselves together, running our hands over each other's bodies, unbuttoning clothes and slipping inside, cool fingers on hot skin, hot tongues through cool dry lips.

I had washed my bedsheets that afternoon but hadn't had time to dry them. We rushed out to the launderette and got there just as it was due to close. Me and Loyshka, close together on the plastic chairs waiting for the sheets to dry.

But no one had thought about contraception. We slept fit-
fully yet luxuriously, merging and separating, and in the morning she told me she wanted a baby.

"But," I hesitated, "do advertising managers have babies?"

"That's not what I am!" she pouted in outrage.

"What are you then?"

She was parading the room wearing only her bra, examining
my personal effects while I lay abed full of merry japes and
thoughts of fatherhood.

"Well I'm me for one thing. And I'm the most intelligent
woman you've ever met."

"Undeniably," I agreed, surprised that it hadn't crossed my
mind before.

"So what are *you* then, a roofman or whatever, is that what
you are?"

"I am a destiny," I said with dignity.

"*Wot?*" she rasped, a Cockney fishwife.

"I am a destiny."

"Ohwh . . . a destiny," she mused, wriggling into her panties. "Well if you are a destiny," she stood up and stuck her tits
out, "then I'm one as well."

"Grand."

"Kiss me," she pounced, "you man of destiny."

"If only," I inhaled her frangipanic breath, "you'd wanted a
baby last night."

"I didn't know till this morning," she told herself pensively.
"You have to think a lot about things like that."

She got up and slipped a dress over her head and down, curls
springing free, hands popping out from the long sleeves.

"Will you come back to bed now that I've watched you putting your clothes on?"

"Willingly. But advertising managers have to be at their offices in the mornings."

"Ah well then. Out you go and make some money."

"For our future."

———

After that first night in my little hovel, most of our time together was spent in the kitschy elegance of Loyshka's house, a plush horror, a smart address which fairly pealed with clashing colours, gadgets, smoked glass, transparent telephones, automatic chairs and a split-level kitchen designed along the lines of Tutankhamun's tomb. I was cheered to learn that the house belonged not to her but to one of the myriad family millionaires who had lent it to her when she returned from France. I even grew to love the place as if it were a log cabin on some idyllic shore, which in certain respects, as Cruikshank pointed out, it was.

It was there on the fake brass fourposter that I first examined her from top to tail in search of defects. I couldn't gracefully accept my own good fortune. Her magnificent flesh: I stared for a long time trying to analyse physical attraction. She had asked if I believed in auras:

"Because," she told me, "you've got one."

"That's all rubbish," I said, keeping quiet about the things I'd seen on the night I met her. "But you have a first-class imagination."

There were few things upon which we agreed, but somehow the more precisely we expressed our love, desire, ideals—always in quite different fashions, she saying one thing and I saying the opposite—the clearer it became that we were appreciating the same quality in each other, sharing the same passion, learning the same music on different instruments.

I was shocked by how quickly it became a totality, an absolute such as we are given glimpses of in the holy books and the chronicles of overpowering love. It is towards this state, I thought, that the fornicators are hopelessly striving; of this that the searchers for peace retain prenatal memories. These pious and high-minded notions caused me to turn instinctively to Sol Bartok who wrote back to me: "Put thy new house in order, for the God of Love has set aside his arrows and taken receipt of the neutron bomb. He moves with the times, He evolves. . . ."

The extraordinary became the rule of my life, I rediscovered everything. Love was no longer a luxury to be sought at leisure in between maintaining one's household and one's head above water. To watch me striding out in the morning to seek my daily wage, having enjoyed say three hours of enlivening sleep, you would imagine me to be a disguised prime minister or celebrity on his way to engage courageously in the important business of the day. You would imagine this immediately from my bearing. Yet it is no secret to initiates of these pages that I am but a common labourer masquerading as a craftsman. But to watch me masquerading as a craftsman you would imagine, from my absorption in my work and the reverent manner in which I apply myself to it, that I was one of the few true artists, a maestro who had rooted the very bed of life to express its secrets through his chosen medium.

Everyone who meets me professionally senses at once that I am not what I am, but they can seldom put the finger on what it is that gives me my curious godlike appearance, as if I knew everything, which I do, but had chosen to remain taciturn and inscrutable. Yet I have little influence on others except to make ears prick up momentarily when I enter a room, and my sole revolutionary act consists of being the neon refutation of that which is not grounded in the mysteries of common sense. For and because, let me say it now, true love is the privilege of megalomaniacs, those who love themselves *above* all others.

The first night I made love with Loyshka I trembled like a shot deer. I couldn't tell whether she was trembling or not, I thought she was, then I realized it was me, then I realised that I couldn't tell the difference. . . .

Many weeks later, on the top deck of a London bus of all places, she smiled at me, no reason, and I was struck by something almost suprahuman in her face. A whisper movement of the lip, eyes lowered, surreptitious clasping and unclasping of her hands, altering her being like a change of subject: these things put me on the track. Her apparent capacity for ecstasy is what I called it.

That's what was on her face one cold morning in Scotland

when we stripped off our clothes and plunged into the freezing stream; and when we swam together in the middle and surfaced together chest-high in running water, the same look was still on her except that it had spread and deepened, boiled up against the killing cold of the water, and emanated now from her fingers, her eyes, lips, from her electrified hair and the tips of her breasts. We laughed about the cold, hugged it away, swam to the riverbank and danced ourselves dry.

After that day I noticed the look, the inchoate ecstasy, much more often, saw it quite clearly, until I took to believing that the force was so strong in her that she had to concentrate much of her energy on keeping the ecstasy down lest it should take her over altogether.

When I tried talking to her about what I saw, we usually got caught up in those lovers' gazes in which neither fully understands what is going on, or why he is looking, and in which neither can avert the gaze. We would embrace, surface and breathe, dissolve into a molten weld so that when she rose and walked across the room the embrace seemed still to contain the distance between us. Yet in the same minute she might rummage in one of her dozen handbags, baskets, purses, portmanteaux, whip out a dirty scrap of paper and say, for example, "Listen to this Mr. Davy:

> *A remarkable cure for the gout*
> *Was discovered by Mr. C. Trout*
> *Who went fishing one day*
> *Between April and May:*
> *It was found in the boot he pulled out!*"

"Discovered by what person?" I'd ask, perplexed, wondering what on earth had prompted her not only to write it but to recite it at that particular moment.

"Mr. Trout. I made it up."

"Hm . . ."

The way her ecstatic look flowered away into uncontrollable laughter:

"Do you like it?" This eagerly, expectantly, flopping to the couch and kicking off her shoes in one rabidly sensual movement of her whole body.

"It isn't a bad poem."

"I wonder" (her laughter escalating against my straight face) "if there's a C. Trout in the phone book."

Yes, there was. She, Mrs. C. Trout that is, listened in bewilderment to Loyshka's "communiqué in verse from the seaside."

"Loyshka, that woman will have sleepless nights."

"You're right. I'll call her back and explain."

"Maybe that's worse."

"Maybe you're right. *You* do it."

And the controlled ecstasy would return when the chuckling faded.

It was something Sol Bartok too had noticed. A Visible Event of the Soul, he called it, reborn in her with every breath she drew. These generally pass unnoticed before unpracticed eyes, rather like political skulduggery which is concealed from the public to obviate instant revolution. But Visible Events of the Soul have a persistent habit of emerging, the truth being escapologically accomplished and always freeing an arm here, a leg there, two arms and a head. . . . That's how Sol talked about it.

"Do you believe," Loyshka asked me, leaning across a table laden with food and wine, "that there are *basic differences* between men and women?"

I laughed as she swayed tipsily, propped on one elbow, her free hand absently stroking her décolleté.

"Listen pigface," she enunciated, seating herself demurely, "I'm asking you a serious question."

I felt her foot sneaking into my groin.

"Women often have better cleavages—ouch—and better intelligences. *More wine?*"

"You only want me for my wonderful body."

"I know. I'm a disgrace."

"God I've been drunk since the first sip. Give me more. Pass el bottle. Mucho pissedo. Can't lift the vaso."

"You promised to stop addressing me in Spanish."

"That's true. *Trew!*" she repeated in a Scottish accent intended to be an imitation of my own. "*Grand!*" she went on, tossing back her head and pouring a glass of wine down her throat. "That's how you drink Mr. Davy—did you know that?—and you say *Grand!*"

"Differences," I remembered, "between men and women——"

"Yes well what I think," she interrupted enthusiastically, "is that there are either heaps of differences or none at all. Or maybe just one."

"Babies!"

"Oh don't make fun of me."

"Sorry. But you always bring the talk round to babies."

"And you always try to sidetrack me. Now why is that?"

"I think it disturbs me," I said looking at her eyes, shocked after the fact at the veracity of my statement.

"But why? The responsibility? I thought you wanted us to have children."

"Well I do. I don't really know what I'm saying. It isn't the responsibility that scares me it's, well, maybe it's not that I don't want to have children but simply that it scares me. Yes, that's what it is."

"Maybe that's the difference."

"Between men and women?"

"Yes. If it's true of us, and we're man and woman. What rubbish I can talk!" she said in conclusion.

Often in the middle of conversations like this our eyes would meet and we'd break off in midsentence as if we'd been overheard purveying malicious gossip or caught spying through a keyhole. Or maybe it was that we had both speechlessly recognised some symbol or phenomenon whose existence confirmed the hopelessness of trying to render intelligible the lover's world within. Quiet.

Then hand in tentative hand we disembogue unsteadily from

the kitchen into the huge sitting room. Loyshka loses her skirt on the way.

"I look nice," she says to the mirror, "in my shoes."

"Yes. Listen, I . . ."

"Yes, you must."

Against the walls, across the table, wonderfully undignified, standing, crawling, divesting garments as we roll, movement in movement, mouthfuls of carpet, thudding our way up the stairs (Isobel lives here too and she might walk in), lusting from room to room, what a noise we can make, we will fuck in the fields, on the streets, on the beaches, to the last gasp we'll detonate ourselves on land, in the air and on the high seas, through inner and outer space . . . we will always surrender.

Leeched in sweat beneath a duvet, limbs indistinguishable, her head appears on my shoulder and her old voice comes back.

"Hello," she says.

Loyshka liked giving presents to everyone. Look around the room: stacks of books, records, a toy bear, a new hat: she liked to bring presents when she came to see me, anything, whether I liked it or not, just to celebrate. On the walls, flattering sketches of a highly idealized version of myself, gifts from the artist. When Loyshka takes up a pencil to draw she looks like a four-year-old at the cinema, transfixed, but with the face of an ascetic. If you speak to her it breaks the spell.

In a village on the island of Crete she sat two hours, silent amid the drunken café noise, working over a portrait of an old man who was sitting at our table. When the drawing was completed she came back to life and passed it over for the old man to look at. He grew increasingly delighted, antique laughter, stamped his foot, rabbited away to his friends in toothless dialect and passed the sketchbook to me.

It was one of her best, nothing was missing from it, it breathed. The old man was a local character so his portrait attracted universal attention in the café and was circulated from table to table, even to the tourists. Loyshka was embarrassed by

the unqualified approval, but she too could see what it was—
that the old man had been immortalised, and probably just in
the nick of time.

Someone suggested she give the picture to the old man,
someone else overheard and agreed. I could see that Loyshka
didn't want to part with the drawing; unusual for her; perhaps
that is why she deferred so readily, barely allowing herself to
reprimand the old man when he began folding it up into
eighths to make it fit in his breast pocket. She took his hands,
retrieved the drawing and showed him how to roll it up properly.

"Why did you give it away?" I asked later as we lay on our
backs looking at the denseness of the Milky Way, the prolifer-
ation of stars in a Greek sky.

"I don't know really, I didn't want to. He was quite an unpleasant old man actually."

"He didn't look very ripe with wisdom."

"But it was strange, I saw so much in his face. Things," she
said thoughtfully, "that he probably doesn't even know about or
think about. And so many lines, wrinkles, all burned into him.
He must be over ninety. There was something . . . oh I don't
know . . ."

She cuddled into me and began sobbing.

"Loyshka. What is it?"

"I feel so sad now . . . I'm so stupid . . . it's just that he,
that old man, looking at him made me feel so, oh I don't
know."

"He was a sad old bugger."

"Yes. But I didn't like him."

She dried her eyes on my shirt, sighed and gave me a kiss.

"I don't want a boring old drawing of *him*," she whispered
lightheartedly: "*I want a baby.*"

"Now?"

"Sometime. Not right now."

I could see her smile in the dark.

———

Back in London we had our first fight, the only battle really, when Loyshka discovered that she was pregnant. It had happened earlier than we might have planned, but we were nonetheless joyful about it—it was like becoming an adult for the first time. I grew happier about it daily, pleased to relinquish dreams of footloose adventure and look to a future of warmth, love, the pleasure of the heart: which is what I used to dream of while leading a life of footloose adventure.

Loyshka too was radiantly full of herself for the first few days, until it dawned that she was going to be bonded to a child for God knew how long, tied to a love that would preclude for some considerable time the realisation of her other dormant ambitions. The advertising manager game was a temporary aberration, an edifice constructed to keep herself moving in the world at a time when all her personal involvements had come to nothing. What she really wanted to do was be an actress and resume the studies she had begun when she lived in France. She was typically stagestruck. As for myself, although I enjoy watching plays, I can seldom abide actors and actresses when I meet them in person: it is an irrational prejudice which I am still trying to understand. But Loyshka—anything remotely connected with Theatre made her heart jump and her face light up.

So when she told me she had decided to have an abortion, it was her future career that I picked on as the keystone of argument. Against my will I heard myself thundering out the usual points of view about women and children.

"It's you who are scared now, Loyshka, scared about doing something irrevocable. If you really wanted to be an actress you wouldn't be a bloody advertising manager."

"I *know* all that," she said helplessly, "I know that very well. But I *can't* have a baby. I'd resent it and you'd hate me for that."

"I suppose you are right. And it does have to be your decision."

"Well?" she looked up at me, expecting understanding at last.

"Well kill it then."

"Oh," she screamed at me, "oh you *bastard . . .*"

"Well."

"*What?* How can you say something so disgusting to me?"

"How can you want to kill our baby?"

"Mine, not ours."

"All right. Your baby and your stupid career. I hope you're better on stage than you are in real life."

That's when she threw the knife at me. I ought not to have left it lying around. A lucky shot, it stuck in my shoulder like a decoration, made a tiny wound. The blood came slowly, warm on my shirt.

"Go away Loyshka. Get out. *Out!*" I shouted.

"You're bleeding, oh . . ."

"So will you be if you don't *fuck off!*"

I held the knife in my hand until she left.

It was only two days later we learnt that she wasn't pregnant at all: a mixup at the clinic, sorry about that, a human error. Loyshka telephoned with the news.

"Good," I said, "that is good."

"Listen. I want to tell you that you are the only man for me, and I am the only woman for you. Whatever happens."

"Even when you can't tell the difference between wanting a baby and an abortion? And when I throw you out of my house?"

"Even that. Yes. Do you love *me* like that?"

"Yes. I wish I didn't."

"I'm coming over. Now. Don't go away."

And she rang off. But when she arrived it was clear that something had been lost.

For a week we hovered like dogs round a master's grave, doing the things people do when they have suffocated their love and know not how they did it. Continual reassurances on the phone: *Do you love me?* a question we had never thought to ask before. Turgid conversations snatched in cafés while she was between calls as an advertising manager, conversations terminated always in fake resolve with a dead kiss and a forced smile of au revoir. Black arguments if we made love; then frigidity, impotence, horror. In ten days we fell from endless delight in each other to dread at the thought of spending a whole evening together. This left us the famous choices of the tightrope walker: advance with confidence, fall a long way down or get off. So we agreed to part. No more phone calls, no letters, nothing, ever. It had been my suggestion, but Loyshka had almost to push me out the door.

— 2 —

AFTER three sleepless days and nights of intolerable physical pain and loss of all appetites I set about adopting a fresh, if not new, outlook on how best to get along.

I rerouted my energies into a life of colourful promiscuity and made sure that I was never left alone for more than a few hours. It was reminiscent of earlier years with Marcel MacMarshall when we used to set a time limit of three hours in which to *negotiate* a pair of attractive girls; if we failed in this we were then pledged to take up with any girls who would have us, no matter how much we disliked them. It was a covenant we'd made to broaden our knowledge of human nature.

A normal day now consisted of saying goodbye in the morning to a lady called Christina, turning up at Maureen's flat for rapid sex on the wing before she went to college, and then maybe trying in the evenings to ingratiate myself with the Countess who always booted me out at ten o'clock when she went to bed. Perhaps because of my involvement with Loyshka and the Countess' with a man called Ralph—to whom she was imparting her roofing knowledge—we had ceased to enjoy harmonious relations and had wisely decided to work separately for a while to avoid the potential dangers of having violent arguments on rooftops. Late at nights I could catch Greta when she came home from her waitress job. Greta and I had a chaste friendship except on the nights when she felt unutterably miserable: then we might fuck each other into a stupor and in the morning discuss our worthless lives. Love, according to Greta, real true love between man and woman, indeed between all people, was the only meaning left in life. I remembered a book I'd read and told Greta that Love was nothing more than a poodle's chance of attaining the infinite.

The roofing business, not unlike the personal relations business, was now strictly a means of support. I was so lacking in motivation that on the rare occasions when I went to work I doubled the usual extortionate rates. My work, which I had once loved, became a quintessential expression of intense hatred. News of this began to spread and rumours were circulated to the effect that I was a capitalist and unworthy of decent employment. People began to ignore me in the old haunts where formerly I had been a reliable source of cheerfulness and good fellowship.

Then Cruikshank, who had stood by me admirably, joined his religious order and gave me the money to go and visit Clorinda in Italy.

I returned from Italy in much better condition and with the realisation that my salvation lay somewhere in the past. I composed long interesting letters to forgotten friends, renewed contact with former lovers by means of lies like "I had a dream last night in which I realised that you have been the great woman in my life." Surprisingly it worked out well, and soon I stood at the centre of an extensive network of correspondence. People turned up from all over the world to take advantage of my grateful hospitality. Encouraged by this I wrote a letter, my first in years, to Suzanne; but I received no reply.

I grew more promiscuous in every way. The Countess too, having decided that Ralph was *too feeble,* had cast him aside and become promiscuous and had publicised the latter fact to good advantage. Loyshka Kittson was shocking friends with her promiscuity I was told by Julia Einstein, who almost got an unexpected slap in return for the information. And Marcel MacMarshall in one of his rare letters—on notepaper headed

M. MacMarshall & Co. Painters & Decorators (Estimates Free)—let me know that he had returned to the covenant of our boyhood following the collapse of his second marriage. He was still living in the village where we had grown up together in which it is nigh impossible for an adult resident to be promiscuous without committing multiple adultery or a more serious offence; but in accordance with our old covenant he forced himself to undertake three hours of honest searching before attempting to bed a married lady. So everybody then was living promiscuously.

MacMarshall wrote that he was eager to find a third wife. He thought of himself as a married man at heart, even the ceremony meant something in his eyes.

I wondered if Loyshka was having those nightmares she once told me about. Disembodied sexual organs.

The Countess and I, in desperation more likely than not, started being friendly to each other again. She confided that since separating from Ralph she became frigid if she slept with the same man more than twice.

Myself, I lost the ability to distinguish between one woman and the next. I never confused one name with another but simply forgot the name attached to the face. I ignored the embarrassment I caused and continued to dish out keys to anyone who wanted to have permanent access to my flat. Cosy dinners and breakfasts were often interrupted by unannounced arrivals; the worst happened regularly; but I wanted everybody to be friendly towards my other friends. Slaves in the same galley, did we not owe each other certain considerations?

This life was not always grim. Its advantages included constant variety of a sort, utter irresponsibility, a dashing reputation and a multiple-entry visa for the land of oblivion; but like the simple life to the millionaire, high adventure to the chartered accountant, it was enviable only to those congenitally incapable of tolerating it. Lolling the streets at night I was fair game for anyone with nothing better to do, and in the afternoons I preyed on the wives and lovers of my acquaintances. The world, I could see, was indeed in a pretty state with so many people walking about in the same condition as myself. I maintained my self-esteem by pointing out that what I was doing openly, publicly, was being done in secret by more people than one might guess. Just as my roofing technique had attained trade union standard by this time, so had I developed and refined the techniques of the champion seducer—the ever-attentive ear, the excessive chivalry tempered with outrageous repartee. And of course there were gonorrhoea, thrush, pubis pediculosis, and those *nonspecific* venereal complaints about which the doctors are so wonderfully uninformed and evasive. My green card for the Special Clinic grew worn and grubby and the follow-up lists lengthened, but the young doctors were sympathetic, even lighthearted, knowing that I was not one to sabotage their research into these thought-provoking phenomena of nature.

Intellectually I began to take particular interest in the sort of woman who approaches sex as if it were a craft or discipline, who does all the right things—generally at the wrong times—and asks you later if it was a good orgasm. The Ouspensky-Buggery people in fact. Was it the ghoulish mechanical quality that fascinated and awed me as I stood outside myself watching her outside herself watching us?

Clive Stapleton-Bald was the only man I had much time for during this epoch. Both Cruikshank and Sol Bartok were now living happy and creative conjugal lives in Amsterdam, a state of grace to which they were surely entitled after the pandemonium I had witnessed in their company only a matter of weeks earlier. The *B.I.F.* had taken its last international action—in a court of law on charges of fraud—and The Green Man had ceased to be anything more significant than a traffic light. Cruikshank was writing his "cheerful books" and Sol, again at the height of his powers, was speaking of his "wild run" as being a direct result of "an argument with God." But, as I say, this was all happening nautical miles away in Amsterdam.

My only solace came from the yards of correspondence, typed on telex rolls, which continued to hurry back and forth in accordance with Sol's suggestion that the three of us write to each other on the subject of Love with a view to publishing the results. I supplied the dirt.

Clive Stapleton-Bald, in contradistinction to me, was an exponent of the *new chastity* and a severe advocate of it, notably with regard to my own life; but on the other hand he was a hard drinker with much to forget about at nights since his wife had gone off for a protracted visit to her parents in California. So I saw him often, always in pubs, and we were always the last to leave after the final bell.

"The trouble with you," Stapleton-Bald said to me as we graduated from beer to malt whisky, "is that you are virtually unscrupulous. You don't believe in anything."

"Correct," I said, hoping to raise a laugh.

"But I mean it! It's serious."

"I know you mean it. I know it's serious."

". . . fucking around, picking people up, giving them the slip, married women . . ."

"It was good enough for Baudelaire."

Poetry, after Socialism, is Stapleton-Bald's guiding passion.

"Exactly! See where it got *him*. An adolescent afflicted with rheumatism. Shite and onions and a pox on't." He drank his whisky and wiped his mouth. "Actually, I was reading Apollinaire last night. First time for ages. Now if I could write like that . . ." The call for last orders interrupted him and he leapt to the bar to refill our glasses. And thus would the evenings go by, controversy being deftly channeled by me into the friendly conversations which I found to be so sustaining and which prevented me from making desperate late-night phone calls to people I was better away from and they from me.

"You were saying earlier," he said as he sat down, "that you support the Labour Party. So why don't you join my branch? We need everybody we can get, especially now."

"I can't," I reply to this familiar request from him.

"Why not for Christ's sake? It's high time you . . ."

"Because I am a socialist."

"You're a bloody encyclopaedia," he says exasperated, "of indefensible opinions."

The closing-time bell sounded and I was saved in the time-honoured manner. *"Arise ye discontented lilies!"* he yawned loudly, quoting from his own works.

It was through Clive Stapleton-Bald that I met Mandy Nelson. He had arranged the meeting with reform in mind, for Mandy was my female counterpart except that she was far more promiscuous than I and had more opportunities to maintain that status. Worse still, in Stapleton-Bald's opinion, she was a socialist and had just turned eighteen. Mandy and I were embracing in the Stapleton-Balds' vegetable garden within an hour of being introduced, and our relationship developed apace from there to a modified adaptation of the new chastity.

Mandy wanted to be a model, in fact she was currently working in that capacity although to call it modelling was "a bit of a syllogism, I mean a euphemism." It was soft porn really, nothing too awful, *nice people,* and it was a starting point because she'd already had one offer to go to the Mediterranean and star in a television commercial for soap.

Mandy had long straight hair, which she wore in a variety of styles and colours congruous to her protean character. Sometimes she looked like a model, a schoolgirl, an artist, a whore, a peasant, and she owned hangersful of carefully selected outfits. Her figure was almost negligible, a fact she delighted in emphasising, and her mind was wholly philosophic; from every conversation or chance remark she drew parallels and generalisations, and when she was drunk she wrote short essays in the ingenuous style of Montaigne. Her sexuality struck you at once, in the solar plexus, and even the Yorkshire accent was wise and seductive. *Sidooctiv.* Her eyes had a way of going suddenly utterly blank: I wondered if this threw any light on why such a gifted and intelligent person should want to be a model. She said her parents were poor and she wanted an easy life.

The advent of Mandy Nelson marked the end of my descent into what Stapleton-Bald described as "whoredom and its corollary boredom." The women who possessed keys to my flat, not to say an intimate knowledge of each other's tastes and habits, set aside their mutual hostilities and joined forces against me now that I had taken up with "that tarty little show-off." I was exposed as the villain, a paradigm of immaturity and selfish lust. I lived up to this description fully by getting rid of all of them in one batch of phone calls.

"That's that," I said to Mandy who was beside me on the bed and was playfully smudging her nipples with lipstick.

"My turn," she sang out operatically, taking the receiver. Bareback against the wall, the phone between her spreadeagled legs: clothed or naked she often sat like that. She is unaware of my gaze as she speaks seriously into the phone, eyes closed except when she raises them in exasperation or glances at me when a smile threatens to become laughter. All these people we were rejecting . . .

"Life is beginning to feel less complicated," she said, replacing the receiver for the last time and springing up to assume a favourite ballet pose. "At least I *think* it is."

She had made more than twice as many phone calls as I.

"Stapleton-Bald," I said, "is quite right to prescribe his new chastity." Incongruously, as I spoke, the face of Suzanne Winchester came into my mind. What was she doing there? Ah! Here I was, nearly twenty-eight, with a girl ten years younger than myself. Drive carefully.

"Stapleton-Bald?" she said uncomprehendingly, *"new chastity? Is that what we've been doing all day?"*

We had no delusions about being in love but our lust and friendship were forcefully vivifying. She moved into my flat and I into hers on alternating weekly cycles. People she met through her job would offer me roofing work and we arranged it so as to be professionally engaged on the same days. On other days we normally sat up till dawn, talking, writing letters to each other, making love incessantly, eating fried egg sandwiches with honey, cold chicken with hot wine; then we would sleep until noon.

We went to parties and made each other jealous, often at a prearranged signal, just to enjoy a skirmish on the way home. Mandy always growled when I kissed a hello to the Countess, but what did I not do when I saw the magazine pictures of my sexy girlfriend, Christabel she called herself at work, distressingly exposed in the public interest. Occasionally a well-spoken woman would telephone saying she had a job for Mandy: this was film work, simulated sex, all a bit of a laugh and it paid well. I never saw the films myself but she sometimes reenacted them at home just to show how innocent they were, how hard it was to look passionate and depraved without giggling.

Happy again in this life of uninterrupted lightheartedness I began to scan the horizon for a vocation. I had for a long time been uncertain of things future, but after three months with Mandy it seemed appropriate to do something more exciting with my powers than climb ladders and leap about on roofs. I started to daydream of things that were to come, tomorrow, next autumn, myself as an old old man. It was all quite fruitless. I could see no farther than an extended present when I tried to envisage time unpassed. I saw myself unaltered in essence, only deeper, more replete in contentment, more windswept; and I saw more laughter, yes, I certainly saw myself laughing more, and louder than ever too, louder than anyone had laughed without dying on the spot. . . . *"Exquisite!"* I exclaimed from my reverie, waking Mandy with the sudden noise. She rolled over and sank her teeth into my neck. As for my vocation, well, clearly I had my work cut out for me already.

The Stapleton-Balds invited us to dinner to celebrate the end of their second honeymoon and the beginning of their third. These dinners were generally pleasant enough so long as husband and wife didn't get going on an argument about politics; but this had already happened when Mandy and I turned up.

"But darling, it's downright exploitation! *Oh hello mateys,* sit y'selves down and have a drop of the Blushful Hippocrene."

"Hi people," Anita says before turning again on her husband.

"Listen babe, your attitude shows a fundamental prejudice against anyone not born working class."

"Oh come off it *sweet*heart, these bloody councillors have got their hands in the till up to the bleeding elbow . . ."

"Now now!"

Young Max appeared in the doorway uttering these words in the voice of authority that is well used to dealing with minor uprisings.

"Max my dear fellow!" Stapleton-Bald gushes in upper-class tones. "Where have you been all day?"

"In my room. Evenin' all."

Everyone is pleased to welcome young Max, the house thinker, who makes everything go smoothly even though he seldom speaks sentences of more than three words.

"Let's shelve the polemics, okay honey?"

"Yes darling, come on Max my boy, crack open another bottle of the Blushful."

"Ah! The Bashful Hippodrome."

"Mandy Nelson: Max Holmes."

"Is Arnold at home tonight, Clive?"

"Yes, he'll be down later."

"Not Arnold the *Vegan*?" Mandy asks.

"Yes," Anita says with disdain. "You don't know him, do you?"

The one known as Arnold the Vegan walked in before Mandy could reply. This fourth member of the Stapleton-Bald household, taken off the streets as a much-regretted act of charity, was unorthodox not only in dietary terms. Arnold never stepped out of doors without first donning a pair of stereo headphones as protection against the noise of London, leaving which was almost his sole topic of conversation; that and clean air. But Arnold could never summon the energy to leave London.

"Hello friends," he greets us in his candyfloss voice, standing in the doorway nodding and smiling beatifically, dressed in his walking-out kit of long flannel dressing gown, gumboots, arctic parka and rucksack, the headphones in his hand.

"Aren't you staying to dinner, Arnold?" Stapleton-Bald inquires, glad to see that he is not. "At least sit down and take a drop of the Blushful."

"No thank you," Arnold smiles politely, a notorious teetotaller who gets tempted nightly by Clive and young Max.

"Have a seat," Max slides a chair over.

"Leave him be," Mandy says sharply, nervous about being outspoken against our hosts.

"No thank you," Arnold repeats. "Are you all *well*?" he smiles, looking suspiciously at the lamb casserole.

"Poisoning our bodies as usual Arnold," Anita trots out. "You know what we're like."

"Come on Arnold, old mate," Stapleton-Bald murmurs to himself as he fills and offers a glass, "try some of this, my acker, the old beaded bubbles winking at the brim, eh?, the purple stainèd mouth."

"Oh that's nice," Arnold lights up. "But really I must go. I need some *grains*."

"Bloody bananas!" from Stapleton-Bald as Arnold tramps out. "But let's away to table. For Poesy is on the wane."

"Not Poesy again," Max chokes and puts a record on the turntable.

> *They were not believin'*
> *When you said you were leavin'*
> *They used to think you odd*
> *And now you're getting even . . .*

". . . no, but I've done some artist-modelling in the past."

". . . and I want to turn the whole poem into a palindrome, you know, madam I'm Adam."

"Bugger all really, but I'm enjoying it."

"From Tucson, Arizona. Originally I mean."

". . . yes *sir*, a scholar and a pederast."

". . . but Clive just said, 'Pardon me matey while I micturate from this asphalt promontory.' "

The dinner then was little more than a gathering of people with different things on their minds; but as Mandy and I were getting ready to leave, early, we were handed an envelope by young Max.

"Have a present."

It was a printed card inviting Max and friend to a party.

"Whose party is it—will it be okay for us to go?"

"Mate of mine. BBC bloke."

"Oh let's go," Mandy said grabbing my hand. "We'll take a taxi."

"Should be good," Max said at the door. "Tom Elliot's his name."

The cab stopped outside an impressive block in Knightsbridge. The door was on the latch so we adjusted our dress and walked straight in. A party was indeed under way, loud dancing music, food and bottles, cocaine on the table, ashtrays and tidbits everywhere and so many people that our entry was scarcely acknowledged. The party was a smart affair so I kept the invitation to hand.

We got rid of our coats, mixed some rum and apple juice and found a space in the dancing room. Mandy's scant clothing and pronounced gyrations drew immediate attention from young men in expensive shirts and their dangerous-looking ladies. I closed my eyes to this and let myself be swallowed by the music, danced close with her, moved away and came back. We had been dancing for a quarter of an hour when I turned once more to face her and found that she had vanished. Careful reconnaissance led to the discovery that she was discussing her career with a middle-aged fellow wearing chamois trousers and an earring.

"David I lost you! Here, this is Jeremy Plank."

"Yes. Hello Jeremy. My name is Max actually."

"Oh sorry Max," she kissed my nose, "I keep forgetting. Jeremy's just been telling me he's a film producer."

"Not," I asked, "Gruber & Plank Productions?"

"Oh you've heard about us."

"I read it somewhere. Anyway," I turned to Mandy, "I'll stop interrupting your conversation. I think I'll investigate the other rooms. See you later."

"Yes you will," she spat in mock annoyance, referring to an oath we'd taken about always leaving parties together even when we had eyes for someone else.

"May I suggest," Jeremy Plank whispered discreetly as I left, "that you try the room at the top of the stairs."

The stairway was broad enough to accommodate an average family car. Walking up it I swore that if it was to the lavatory he had directed me I would break Plank's nose and drag Mandy home by the hair. Did Gruber & Plank make porn or was she gunning for a part in a conventional film? Surely she wasn't attracted to him personally. It is impossible for anything to be impossible. I tripped quickly back down the stairs to spy on them. Mandy was talking and smiling animatedly, gripping Plank's arm to get her point across, moving her hips towards and away from him as I'd noticed her do with me when she'd ask, "Do you want to come and have a bath?" Fair enough. I ascended the stairs in threes. I'd kill him if it was the lavatory.

The room at the top of the stairs was comparatively small, the lights dimmed and the music quiet. An orgy appeared to be in progress, unless it was something more structured like a Black Mass or tactile therapy routine. No, it was definitely an orgy: a couple drifted in, stripped off and got down to it with a third man who'd been lying on his own. Not so much as a by your leave. To avoid censure I had begun slowly to follow suit, taking a long time with my shoelaces and shirt buttons.

There were more than a dozen bodies in the room, all resembling inflatable dolls and squelching, panting, coughing, in pairs and threes except for one plump little lady who was squatting on the couch with a man beneath her, another behind her and a third standing up in front. The Isle of Man symbol popped into my head. In a darker corner, bent over one person's knee a second person was having its bottom chastised with a flat object, maybe a book. Did Jeremy Plank intend bringing

Mandy into this? If so I'd have scored a point by being there first. And I'd keep an eye on the door with a view to tumbling her the moment her clothes were off, if they weren't already hanging over the back of a makeshift casting couch. Maybe, I let out an involuntary guffaw as I crawled into the fray with bayonet fixed, maybe this was only a rehearsal for Gruber & Plank's latest opus.

Concurrent with these thoughts was a heavy dose of angst about what I was doing. Under normal circumstances I should probably have left the room at once and gone in search of a more orthodox antidote to jealousy, but this was a special case: Mandy had never been propositioned by a real film producer before and one could hardly blame her for ditching a roofer for the night. Besides, this was a rare opportunity to participate in a real orgy, my first.

This one, however, seemed to be approaching its death throes. No one was talking except in mildly erotic monosyllables and everyone felt rather wet. Erections were at a premium so I quickly became something of an attraction, and with a little encouragement from a Jamaican girl with a chain around her waist I was soon going at it with what is called gusto, moving in for a brief tournament wherever I detected a vacancy. What shocks you can get in the dark! It was hard not to laugh at fleeting thoughts in connection with other sporting events, notably golf, but humour was out of place in the tough atmosphere of seriousness and competition that was perceptible through the easygoing weary mess and bleary musk; except when somebody farted above the music, or the plump lady on the couch got a fit of giggles which crescendoed into an exact transcription of the braying of a mule.

I climbed on top of my second prey who promptly tipped me over and got on top of me. I pulled her close, determined to identify the features of at least one person but I was frustrated in this by a thin man who started smothering her face in slurpy kisses. My nervousness had returned with the realisation that I had been fucking away for aeons, feeling very little, haunted by

Mandy and Plank, trying not to think of Plank . . . I might as well have had a vibrator between my legs. I felt the loneliness welling up, the sadness and self-pity, the detailed vision of Mandy and Jeremy Plank making love together, alone in a room like civilised . . . oh my God, was I going to start *crying*? I fucked like a demon, tearing this lady's buttocks apart. The third person moved away, sensing the anguish no doubt. An orgasm was out of the question—I'd heard but never had experience of this side of impotence—so I manufactured one, just like Mandy in her films. The lady didn't seem to notice me crawling away.

Underpants, trousers, socks, shoes—mine were still by the door where I'd left them. I got dressed and began searching for my shirt. A couple was entwined on the spot where I presumed I should find it, "'Scuse me," sschloopf!, "sorry about that, my shirt." *"Pleasure."* It was damp and creased but it would soon dry out. I was buttoning up by the door when I heard:

"But is David . . . I mean is Max in there?"

"Does it matter?" I heard Plank's incitement of a voice: *"Amanda* lovey! Poor little Mandy's worried about her brute!"

"He's my friend," Mandy said coolly. "And he *might* hit you."

If I'd walked out then . . .

"Listen darling, if your Max is in there . . ."

"Yes you're right," Mandy sighed. "I'll come. But there's one thing," (I made ready to hide behind the couch) "I'm not sure yet Jeremy, I mean about coming home with you."

"Ya, ya, I understand," said father Plank: "Hang on a sec while I pop off to the loo."

I got down behind the couch, unable to face Mandy at the other side of the door. Holy fuck, I *would* end up in tears if I didn't get out of here soon. It'd be easy once they got into the swing. Sitting in my hideout I noticed for the first time a second door in the room: maybe it was an alternate exit; and maybe, I thought as I opened it, it led on to even greater horrors.

I crawled into the dark room, stood up and closed the door behind me, coughing loudly in case this was the West Wing and contained a mad granny. I jumped at a heavy movement in the far corner by the window. My eyes began to make out a shape.

"Please just leave me alone," a female voice sobbed across the darkness.

"It's all right lass," I said in my friendliest Scots. "I'm only a refugee from next door."

"*David?*"

It was Loyshka.

— 3 —

IT all came as a shock to me—not least the revelation that anything falling short of the whole truth is a dressed-up lie. The gilded mendacities must therefore be construed as signposts, compass needles which will sooner or later lead, if I pay attention and follow faithfully, to the truth about things like Loyshka and me and our miraculous life together. I was pledged to tell a story of love—the desire was eating me away. Why should this have been? That and questions like it is what we hear in the wind on any day in any country, as if chanted by battalions of massed choirs tubthumping away in the unison born of applied rehearsal; at any rate, that is what happens where I live: and I ignore it, hold it in contempt or at least pretend that I'm not listening.

I wanted to terrify people out of their minds. That was my wish, and since when, dare I say it, have my wishes not been granted? But I have to admit that I am a changed man.

Somewhere outside my window is a tree with no leaves. Not far from this tree there is a different tree, one with all its leaves. It may not make a great deal of sense, but I now believe firmly in both trees and am happy to look upon them, climb them or lie beneath them.

The very last thing I want is to understand my lover: the same goes for anything real, true, beautiful. I had so much understanding visited on me that I began to limp from the weight of it, and it accumulated so gradually, never decreasing, like lead poisoning, that I didn't notice until it was almost too late. But for meeting Loyshka again I might have lived the rest of my life with a permanent stoop of which I had no awareness, and an understanding which was, perhaps like all understandings of life, essentially spurious. For example, I believed (it makes me laugh now, or shudder) that we parted because we *didn't* see eye to eye.

It isn't anything she says or does, or if it is it's everything she says and does: her effect on me comes solely from her presence, her being. We have little interest in each other's opinions. Something happens, that's all, and I am transformed through her into myself, and I call it love. She doesn't have to talk to me, be kind or unkind. Often I really do not care what she thinks of me or feels for me. With Loyshka I am learning to understand less each day, to see more, to contain and become more. God's vessel, if you like Rilke.

I have even become something of a poet myself and am often pompous, consistently foolish, and sadly deficient in the true manly virtues. But in my defence I may say that I am a poet whose aesthetic aim is to lose interest in poetry, particularly his own.

On a similar subject: it is postulated by more than one high-minded cynic that it is impossible to tell a love story until that love is dead and buried; and it is easy to picture lofty brows looking up from books to mutter, "By Jove that is a true fact of life!" For the difficulties commence as soon as you take a long hard look at your lover (nobody gets away with fiction nowadays) and see, nine times in ten, your relationship dissolve before your eyes, a newborn *poisson soluble*. There is love, and derived love: one lasts forever and the other is a soluble fish that disappears forever the moment you transfer it from imagination into its proper element. The more repugnant things Loyshka and I discover in each other, the deeper our love asserts itself.

"With a bit less faith you'd make a fine preacher," Loyshka applauded me following a conversational rendition of the above.

"Is that all you can say?"

"No," she bent forward and bit my toes, "but it's all I'm saying."

"I think I'll subject you to choice atrocities."

Three weeks had gone by since I found her in the orgy antechamber. She had come to the party with a film director she knew through her job with the Worldscape Anthology, and had entered and escaped the mirthless debauch by much the same route as I.

In the dark we held on tight and cried, then laughed, then opened the ornately leaded window and laughed over Knightsbridge until the tears came back. Hand in hand, Loyshka squeezing mine at every step, we made our way out through the bodies. They had turned the music full blast, someone was being playfully whipped, and Mandy Nelson was on her feet, snuffed full of cocaine no doubt, dancing over heaps of flesh and teasing the absently groping paws. I caught her eye and waved with the hand that wasn't in Loyshka's. Fingers to lips she blew me a kiss, and then she danced away.

"Is that the girl you came with?"

"Yes."

"She's pretty."

"Yes."

At the foot of the stairs we met Loyshka's director, talking to no other than Jeremy Plank who was wearing only a towel.

"I'm sorry," I heard Loyshka say evenly, "but I'm going now."

"I see," the director glanced at me. "Well I wouldn't want you to be going home unescorted."

"Shut your trap," I said involuntarily.

"Take it easy Max," Jeremy Plank put a paternal hand on my shoulder, charming now that everything was looking rosy.

"Max?" Loyshka turned at me as if I'd deceived her personally.

"No, it's a mistake," I explained. "My name is Rudolph," I said to Plank; "be seeing you."

"I'll phone you," Loyshka was telling the director. And to me as we walked out into the free world: "Let's go to my house and have a shower."

In the taxi she began to tremble and lay down across the seat with her head in my lap.

"I'm afraid I stink."

"Yes you do. Do I?" she gave a shaky laugh.

"I don't mind."

"That thing," she began quietly, "that . . . that sex thing, it was so *repul*sive. I wanted to switch off that music and put the lights on and scream at them to stop. Stop and look at each other. It was *hideous*," she said through clenched teeth, head pressing into my stomach.

"There was certainly something missing. But what made you go in exactly?"

"*I* didn't want to go in," she said as if I ought to have known better. "I mean it was Timothy really. I'm glad you didn't hit him by the way."

"When have you seen me hit someone, Loyshka?"

"Anyway, he's a nice bloke really. He didn't want to go into that thing, that orgy, what a silly word, but he got it into his head that *I* did, he was convinced of it. Idiot. He kept insisting, saying how *good* it would be for us, especially for me because I'm so often bored by him. But really he didn't want to do it. I was twice as sick of him by the time I agreed. God . . . and to think that I was next door crying while you were in there doing . . . you must have been in there for almost an hour! Oh God. Ho hum. Seeing you was like coming back to life."

"Yes. And here we are. My lass."

"Yes. Yes. I love you so much," she said barely audibly,

bringing her mouth up to mine, the first kiss for so long, on top of so many kisses.

A kind of future took shape inside me, a boundless silhouette developing, infinite, infinite.

"Did you hate me," she looked up from my lap, "when we stopped seeing each other?"

"On and off for three days. Then I tried to drill myself into forgetting you."

"I hated you," she laughed self-consciously, "in my innocuous way. Until I had to go to sleep without you."

"I didn't sleep for the three days."

"So we're equal."

"Absolutely."

"Are . . . are we together again now?"

"Absolutely."

Her hands closed around my wrist and she lay there for a long time motionless like a child in a deep sleep as the cab raced through the empty morning streets.

"I bet," she said at the door, searching for her key among books and cosmetics, "that you've had millions of lovers."

"I bet you have."

"So we *are* equal. Absulootly," she grimaced in her abridged Scottish accent, and we walked into the log cabin in Kensington.

Under the shower I ran my hands over her skin, those shoulders so fine and narrow for one with such breasts and hips. Loyshka's startling figure, I smiled wistfully within as other bodies passed ghostly through my fingers, nothing like it could belong to anyone else. . . .

"Why did we ever separate?" she shouted above the sound of the shower, streams of water running into and out of her parted mouth. "I never understood properly what happened."

"Nor I. We were mad."

"It didn't make any sense," she yelled, shaking wet curls.

"Does anything?" I bellowed through my teeth as she rubbed shampoo into my hair.

"Everything does, you daft man," she mumbled in my ear, wrapping my arms round her, holding my hands against her bottom. "Everything makes sense!"

"All right then, it started with the baby, didn't it?"

We were wrapped in towels, drinking coffee in the bedroom.

"But we didn't split up over me having an abortion. Did we?"

"No it wasn't that. But when we fought about the abortion stuff it was like, well it was the only bad thing that ever happened to us. I found it so easy with you to think in terms of perfection, you know, nothing ever going wrong, so when . . ."

"*Yes,*" she sat forward in recognition, "I felt exactly the same. Actually," she looked to check for boredom, "shall I tell you what I think about all that?"

"I'll listen all night."

"Well," she took a deep breath, "what I think—you might think I'm stupid—what I think is that we separated *because* everything could be so wonderful between us. It used to scare me. I started worrying that something might go wrong. Not anything I could think of. Just a vague dread that everything was going to collapse and destroy . . . well . . . as you said, destroy the perfection. I couldn't bear it because I was always thinking how easy it would be to lose it. We," she said, sincerely but sententiously, "jumped at the first excuse to avoid perfection."

Were such things possible?

"I know it sounds odd," she said in response to my laughter, "in fact I knew beforehand that you would think it hilarious. But it's what I believe."

"It is hilarious," I said, "but I believe it as well."

"So it doesn't matter now," she explained to ears that would accept anything, "if we fuck it all up again. *Because we know.* We know that everything can be made all right. Maybe it sounds too simple . . ."

"Nothing's too simple for me!" I declared indignantly. "And

to tell you the truth I think that all this is extremely complex. But I told you already: I believe it."

"Do you? Shall I tell you what it means to me? Being in love with somebody I mean: it means that things will only go all wrong when we are stupid."

"Hmm . . ."

"No! I mean that when we're stupid and *ordinary*, you know, wanting to *escape* from horrible things, disagreements, rough times . . ."

"Like throwing knives at people?"

"Yes, if you like. I did wrong, I know it, but so did you . . ."

"I know . . ."

"But it's no longer possible for me to be that way. You don't understand do you?"

"Well . . ."

"I'll tell you. I know you consider yourself unusually brilliant—shut up! I do too—but there's something you don't quite know. Don't interrupt me and I'll tell you. Being in love, see, is like being *trapped* for the rest of your life by all the things you've ever wanted. And the peculiar thing is, *you can't escape!*" She seemed to find this amusing.

"Miraculous," I said ambiguously, feeling some distaste for these ingenuous notions; but I couldn't deny that something was falling into place inside me.

We looked at each other across the room, wondering at the puzzling certitude in the air.

"Do I look funny in this towel?"

"I wasn't thinking that."

"No," she said lowering her eyes, "neither was I."

"It is strange," I pronounced apropos of nothing, "how easy it is."

She was examining her fingers. "I was thinking about that abortion," she said nervously. "Whether I would have done it or not."

"It doesn't matter now," I said. "It's not so terrible is it?"

[214]

"It matters to me," she said, still very nervous. "Do you know—I was horribly disappointed when they said I wasn't pregnant. Even when I didn't want to be . . ."

"Nobody can be expected," I said against my better judgement, "to know about things like that. Don't crucify yourself."

"I'm not," she said. "I don't feel that way." She laughed. "But I don't know how to be the way I really am."

"I like you just the way you are."

I watched her crossing and uncrossing her legs. The towel was too short and she was trying to be demure so as not to interrupt our conversation.

"I met an actress," she said out of the blue. "She had three children."

"Yes?" I said expectantly, not catching on.

"Well," she said as if addressing a man of renowned slow-wittedness, *"actresses have babies."*

"True," I said indulgently.

"Trew!" Her face lit up and she looked at me with one of her huge smiles, as if I ought to be feeling honoured at having my accent mimicked. "And I'm going to be an actress," she said provocatively, "even though you hate them."

"Grand." Her towel fell away as she walked across the room and sat on my knee.

"And I've decided to settle for everything."

"Grand."

I stayed on at Loyshka's house for several days, each one an inauguration, a feast day. Breakfast was a ceremonious banquet, a walk in Hyde Park a voyage of rediscovery. Even the cinema, which I seldom enjoy, could fill me with religious awe as if I were a savage witnessing the first Magic Lantern show. I became remarkably easy to please and hard to disappoint, finding in everyone I met something unique and worthy of special attention. Beggars in the street received fistfuls of cash and a cheerful earful, unpleasant public servants a sympathetic lecture on human relations. When Loyshka and I walked out together, wilfully gullible, demonstrative upholders of public morale, it was hard not to look upon the world as a suitable place for people to live.

We slept chastely, Loyshka and I, on that first night that was already morning, as we had been obliged to do on a different first night a long time ago. Then it had been contraception, of all things, and this time it was . . . we didn't talk about what it was.

And the best part of a week went by during which we found ourselves disciples, albeit reluctant ones, of an aspect of the new chastity that would have perplexed even Stapleton-Bald.

We wandered naked through the house, we slept together every night, we wanted each other with the desire of unqualified love, a desire not only for pleasure and release but for that transformation without which there can be no rest for those who are in love.

Perhaps we were still afraid of something and only gradually might we burn bright enough to dispel the fear. The fear of perfection! Or perhaps it was merely a consequence of the circumstances under which we had rediscovered each other, and the long chains of sexual involvements that lay behind each of us; for in love there seems to be no such thing as sex.

Lying naked with her at night, she asleep in my arms, I was reminded of something I had read about marriages in some remote region of Czarist Russia, country of Loyshka's ancestors. There, so it was said, it was a common thing for husband and wife to spend the first night of their marriage lying quietly side by side, probably in their nightshirts, and not as much as touching each other. And this conduct would prevail day after day, often into months. Until one night.

When you come into your true lover and your faces alter subtly, rapidly, as you live in full the loves half-felt throughout a lifetime, and you discover, again for the very first time, the flash of pure colour in her eyes and you want to say something but you cannot remember it, or how to speak . . . you are breaking and entering the eternal circles, relinquishing all the rights and privileges you ever laid claim to and agreeing to be your own slave and master for life.

And if you are me you hear the sounds of all the rivers you ever slept beside, you swim the scent of your lover's skin and you feel you are striving for and against all the rivers, colours flooded, as they pour through you, breaking on your face, making you catch your breath . . . and you strike into the current, are submerged in it, and you surface, eyes open again, to know that you have been borne away on it, and she is with you, you are both part of it and it is absolutely inexorable . . . her eyes are wide again, her mouth, her body is open. Somewhere between you is the heart of her, the perfect matrix, your own heart, drawing you always closer, more of you, drawing all of you until inner and outer, lover and loved, woman and man, action and thought, singer and song, living and dying are welded, multiplied, reversed, rendered wholly indistinguishable and finally annihilated . . . leaving only the hammering caress of lover against lover and the beginning and end of myth.